Montano

ALSO BY

Enrique Vila-Matas in English translation

Bartleby & Co

Enrique Vila-Matas

Montano

TRANSLATED
FROM THE SPANISH
BY
Jonathan Dunne

Harvill *Secker*
LONDON

First published with the title *El mal de Montano* by
Editorial Anagrama S.A., 2002

2 4 6 8 10 9 7 5 3 1

This edition has been translated with the financial assistance of the Spanish Dirección General del Libro y Bibliotecas, Ministerio de Cultura

First published in Great Britain in 2007 by
HARVILL SECKER
Random House, 20 Vauxhall Bridge Road,
London SW1V 2SA

Random House Australia (Pty) Limited
20 Alfred Street, Milsons Point, Sydney,
New South Wales 2061, Australia

Random House New Zealand Limited
18 Poland Road, Glenfield,
Auckland 10, New Zealand

Random House (Pty) Limited
Isle of Houghton, Corner of Boundary Road & Carse O'Gowrie,
Houghton 2198, South Africa

Random House Publishers India Private Limited
301 World Trade Tower, Hotel Intercontinental Grand Complex
Barakhamba Lane, New Delhi 110 001, India

The Random House Group Limited Reg. No. 954009
www.randomhouse.co.uk

A CIP catalogue record for this book is available from the British Library

ISBN 1843432153

Papers used by Random House are natural, recyclable products made from wood grown in sustainable forests; the manufacturing processes conform to the environmental regulations of the country of origin

Designed and typeset in Quadraat by Palimpsest Book Production Limited,
Grangemouth, Stirlingshire

Printed and bound in Great Britain by
Clays Ltd, St Ives plc

To Paula de Parma

What will we do to disappear?

MAURICE BLANCHOT

I

Montano's Malady

At the end of the twentieth century, the young Montano, who had just published his dangerous novel about the curious case of writers who give up writing, got caught in the net of his own fiction and, despite his compulsive tendency towards writing, suffered a complete block, paralysis, a tragic inability to write.

At the end of the twentieth century – today, 15 November 2000, to be more precise – I visited him at his home in Nantes and, just as I had expected, found him so sad and so dry that some verses by Pushkin could well be used to describe him, saying that Montano 'lives wandering / in the shade of the woods / with the dangerous novel.'

The good thing is that wandering in the shade of the woods has led my son – the fact is that Montano is my son – to recover a certain passion for reading, and I have benefited from this. Not long ago, and on his recommendation, I read *Prosa de la frontera propia*, a novel recently published by Julio Arward, a strange writer whom I had never fully trusted, believing him simply to be playing at being the double of the novelist Justo Navarro.

Today, among other things, I thanked my son for

having recommended this book by Justo Navarro's double, less his double since he wrote this novel. It is a good book and, reading it, I was often reminded of something I heard Julio Arward say on the radio one day: 'A girlfriend once told me that all of us have a double in another place, living their life with a face identical to ours.' Reading this book, I was also reminded of something I heard Justo Navarro say one day, which I have sometimes given to understand was said by me: 'There are coincidences and chances from which you die laughing and there are coincidences and chances from which you die.'

The narrator of *Prosa de la frontera propia* is one of life's strangers and at the same time a hero who appears to have walked straight out of a Chinese tale and who has a shadowy twin brother, or rather first cousin, who looks just like him and, to cap it all, has the same name: they are both called Cosme Badía.

The theme of the double – and of the double's double, and so on ad infinitum in an extensive set of mirrors – is found at the centre of the labyrinth of Julio Arward's novel, a novel which – and now I am writing as the literary critic that I am – is a fictitious autobiography in which the author pretends to be Cosme Badía and, recalling with a memory that is not his own, invents the world of the two first cousins and makes out that he is recalling this world without for a moment forgetting Faulkner's description of the novel as a writer's secret life, a man's shadowy twin brother.

Perhaps this is what literature is, the invention of another life which could well be our own, the invention of a double. Ricardo Piglia says that to recall with a memory that is not our own is a variant of the double, but it is also a perfect metaphor for literary experience. Having quoted Piglia, I observe that I live surrounded by quotations from books and authors. I am literature-sick. If I carry on like this, literature could end up swallowing me, like a doll in a whirlpool, causing me to lose my bearings in its limitless regions. I find literature more and more stifling, at the age of fifty it frightens me to think that my destiny is to turn into a walking dictionary of quotations.

The narrator of *Prosa de la frontera propia* is someone who seems to have just emerged from a painting by Edward Hopper. There is nothing unusual in this, since Arward has felt fascination for this American painter ever since 1982 when he bought my first book – the first of five, all of literary criticism, that I have published – and he only bought it because on the front cover it had *Nighthawks*, Edward Hopper's painting about night drinkers. At the time Arward had never seen a painting by Edward Hopper and he bought the book for the front cover – he did not even know me then – which he cut out with some kitchen scissors and hung on a wall of his home. He told me this himself a few years ago, when we met. I was not in the least offended, since I also remembered having cut out from a newspaper an article of his, 'Life's Strangers', which I had pinned to a wall of my study just to remind myself that I had to call Justo Navarro and tell him that there was a chap by the name of Arward who was copying him, in particular when he wrote, for example, 'The lonely drinker in *Nighthawks* appears to be recalling past adventures in China. His neck, his back, his shoulders, bear the burden of the cold light of memory and of the years.'

Prosa de la frontera propia, which recalls Cosme Badía's past Chinese adventures, led me the other day to remember when I put my name to an interview with Justo Navarro which he had in fact written himself, while on the facing page there was an interview which I had written, but which Justo Navarro had put his name to. Both interviews began with the same question, agreed beforehand: 'Would you swap places with me?' 'Right now,' I replied. 'Not right now,' answered Justo Navarro. 'Another time I'd love to, but not right now. At the moment you're asking the questions and I'm answering them; if I swapped places with you, I would have to start asking them.'

Both Justo Navarro and I have always been obsessed by things which coincide, things which are equal, double. For a long time the police would always ask Justo Navarro for his documents at airports and search his baggage. When it occurred to him one day to ask a civil guard why they only ever stopped him, the guard explained that his appearance coincided with the description of a wanted criminal.

Something similar happened to me in 1974 when I lived in Paris and was arrested in the drugstore of Saint-Germain-des-Prés on being mistaken for the Venezuelan terrorist Carlos. Coincidences and chances. With these in mind, I have suddenly realised that in 1994 Sergio Pitol wrote a story called 'The Shadowy Twin Brother', which he opened with a quotation from Justo Navarro: 'To be a writer is to turn into someone else, into a stranger. You have to begin to translate yourself. Writing is a case of impersonation, of adopting a new personality. Writing is pretending to be another.'

Further coincidences and chances. Without knowing that Justo Navarro and I more than once have pretended to be each other (possibly without even suspecting that we are acquainted), Sergio Pitol has made us coincide in 'The Shadowy Twin Brother', because the story is dedicated to me: 'To my friend from overseas, to the last critic with delirious criteria.'

Today, in Montano's home in Nantes, having confirmed that he is suffering as a result of his literary paralysis, I tried to amuse him by telling him all these stories of doubles and doubles' doubles.

'There are coincidences and chances,' my son remarked, 'from which you die laughing and there are coincidences and chances from which you die.'

'Didn't Justo Navarro say that?'

'And Julio Arward as well, who used it not long ago in an article you may not have seen.'

An expression of deep anguish came over Montano's face. 'Everyone writes,' he said. Next to him his partner, Aline, gave him a terrible look of compassion. Aline is beautiful, silent, intelligent. I do not know her very well – only from two times she has passed through Barcelona – but she inspires confidence in me. In us. Rosa, my wife – and Montano's stepmother – believes that she is the best company that my difficult, unstable son could have.

'No doubt you're thinking,' Montano said to me, 'that I'm worried because I haven't written anything since I published my book. But things are a little different. It's not that I can no longer write, but that I'm constantly being visited by the ideas of others, ideas that arrive unexpectedly, that come to me out of the blue and take possession of my brain.' At this point he made a dramatic gesture. 'To tell the truth, no one can write like this.'

I asked him, with a certain amount of distrust in what he had said to me, what kind of ideas these were that came to him out of the blue. And he explained that, for example, no sooner had I rung at the doorbell than he had received a visit from Julio Arward's personal memories.

'I don't believe you,' I told him.

'Well, you should. It may seem strange, but it's true. Julio Arward's memory infiltrated mine and I saw a corner of the street in Málaga, Garriga Vela, where Arward lives. I saw this before you entered the house and thanked me for recommending that you read his novel. Be in no doubt, I saw it before you said anything about Arward. I saw a corner of the street where he lives, and I also saw the bar, Comodoro Reading, which appears in that terrible novel where he copied Justo Navarro. Not only that, I saw the swimming pools in Granada, Baños de Simeón, which he went to once with his father when he was a boy . . .'

He almost certainly had to be fantasising, perhaps childishly trying to conceal his anguish at his unfortunate inability to write. But in his slightly disturbed look there was a strange hint of truth.

I felt tired as a result of the journey and decided to take my leave, to withdraw to my hotel to rest. Besides, they had not expected me until tomorrow and had planned to have dinner this evening with some customers of the bookshop that they run here in Nantes. Again they insisted that I stay to sleep in their home, something I do not intend to do. I propose to spend these days in Nantes without interfering in their life together. They gave me a lift to the Hôtel La Perouse and we arranged to meet for lunch tomorrow, I shall go around to the bookshop at midday. When we reached the door of the , as I was getting out of the car, I tried to find out if all this about Arward's memory having infiltrated my son's memory was a passing invention, and I made a joke of it by asking him whether at that precise moment he was still receiving Arward's personal memories.

'No, not now,' Montano replied very seriously. 'But when we left home, I received a visit from Justo Navarro's memory. It must be because his memory is infiltrating Julio Arward's.'

Aline gave me a look as if to apologise for Montano's words, which were possibly an attempt to appear clever in front of me and very different from what one might expect of a poor young man who has run out of ideas.

'And may we know what memory of Justo Navarro's you received?' I asked him.

'His memory of the day, I don't know if you remember, when he pretended to be you,' came the answer.

I reacted with British phlegm and took my leave until tomorrow.

A moment ago, pondering Montano's words, I recalled a story by Jorge Luis Borges, 'Shakespeare's Memory', the result of a dream that the Argentinian writer had in a room in Michigan, when he saw a faceless man who offered him Shakespeare's memory; he did not offer him fame or glory – that would have been trivial – but the writer's memory, the memory of the afternoon in which he wrote Act II of *Hamlet*.

I am going to bed, I feel tired after the journey and weary of so much writing in this diary I have kept for years, which right from the start – when I wrote that sentence beginning 'At the end of the twentieth century, the young Montano . . .' – I noticed could be driven by a mysterious impulse and become the beginning of a story that required readers and not to remain hidden among the pages of this private journal.

It is slightly absurd, all I needed now was to turn into a narrator. It is absurd most of all because I came to Nantes for a breath of fresh air, to try to stop literature stifling me, at least for a while. I came to Nantes to see if I could forget a little that I am suffering from literature sickness.

And yet here I am now, in the Hôtel La Perouse, more book-sick than when I left Barcelona. Rosa may have been right when she told me that my choice of Nantes – with Montano suffering from a different strain of the same literary disease – was not exactly the best way for me to rest for a few days from my fearsome reviews and my sickly obsession for books and my habit of seeing everything from a *literary* viewpoint.

Rosa told me that I urgently needed a holiday, to change my excessive dependency on literature for some scenery and songs, to be a non-cultural tourist, to take a break from my demanding work as a critic, to devote myself to the serene contemplation of Mother Nature – 'To sit and watch how tomatoes, for example, grow in fields,' were her actual words – to observe sunsets and to think about her, to think more about her, she could not come with me because of work, but this is what I should do, think a lot more about her. Rosa, however, also told me not to go to Nantes, where my son – similarly wounded by letters, though for other reasons than mine – could aggravate my illness.

And here I am now, worse than when I left Barcelona, suffering more as a result of the stifling encounter between a father and son wounded, albeit with different scars, by the spectre of literature: one (Montano) no doubt wanting to return to it, to literature; the other wishing he could forget it, at least for a while, but unable to do so for the moment and, to make matters worse, bogged down in the opening of something faintly resembling a literary narrative, and furthermore writing it in his diary.

How strange everything is. Father and son suffering from a different strain of the same literary disease. How strange Montano was today, seated in his armchair at home in the rue du Calvaire, anxiously squeezing Aline's hand, his literary horizon blocked by the dangerous novel, trapped in his own fiction or perhaps simply – if he is not making it up – by Arward and Navarro's personal memories, trapped among the trapped, in Nantes, tragically reduced to a state of being unable to write and convinced that he won't ever be able to write again.

Jules Verne was born here.

I cannot sleep, it is horrible, and I have picked up the diary perhaps just to write this, to say that Jules Verne was born here and, when he was young, walking alongside the canals in Nantes' pretty river port, his eyes entranced by the brigantines, the caste of privateers and traffickers was long dead, their riches dispersed, though the ancient splendour still glimmered here and there among the ruins of the private city and a certain colonial fragrance still hung in the air.

I see now the lights of Nantes in the disquiet of this sleepless night and suddenly Aline springs to mind, and it strikes me that this apparently fragile woman is the very image of Jules Verne's mother, whose name resembles a current of air: Sophie Allote de la Fuye. Aline's name also has something of the fresh breeze in it and, even if this were not the case, I need to believe it, I need to trust that she will become my ally and be the current of air which eliminates Montano's literary illness and, if at all possible, mine at the same time.

Jacques Vaché was born here.

And here he committed suicide. Vaché is one of the main characters in Montano's book about writers who gave up writing. Vaché went down in the history of French literature having barely lifted a finger, having written only a handful of letters to André Breton. An opium overdose ended his life in 1916 in Nantes, in the Grand Hôtel de France. The shade of this furtive poet accompanied Breton all his life. Breton used to admire him when he saw him walking along the streets of Nantes, dressed indiscriminately in the uniform of a hussar lieutenant, of an aviator or of a doctor.

Among other things, Vaché wrote to Breton, 'You'll think that I've disappeared, or that I'm dead, and one day you'll find out that there's a certain Vaché living a retired life in Normandy, occupied in the rearing of livestock, who can introduce you to his wife, an innocent, reasonably pretty girl, who won't ever have realised the *danger* she's been in. Only a few books (very few, you understand), carefully stored away upstairs, will testify that something has happened.'

The night now conjures up the memory of when I was tempted to abandon literary criticism for a while and to take a chance with a kind of anthology that would bring together the study of the most interesting cases of youngsters who down through history have stood out by being seriously dangerous: youngsters among whom I planned to include Vaché and among whom today I would include Montano. Montano, by the way, physically – but no longer mentally – increasingly resembles Gérard Depardieu's son, that young man who is an actor like his famous father and who destroys everything in his path and who, when asked about his future, recently declared that he was pleased to have reached the age of twenty-nine and still to be alive.

I have always liked youngsters who pose a serious threat to conservative society, those who find the world stupid and for a time want to leave it soon. I was one of them and my son has managed to be one, something that, until he set up his bookshop in this city, he demonstrated clearly by trashing hotel rooms or risking his life in gratuitous drunken brawls or taking drugs in endless dissolute nights or spitting in the face of the powers he came across. I shouldn't exactly admire him for this, but I behaved in a very similar way and it would be ignoble on my part not to feel an intimate sense of satisfaction at my poor son's wild and suicidal boldness.

To tell the truth, the talent displayed by Montano – by the way, his full name is Miguel de Abriles Montano, but he preferred to call himself just Montano, in honour of his late mother – and his need until very recently to live with danger have always been as great as his sudden mental fragility, which would explain his tragic inability to write following the risky enterprise of a book about writers who give up writing. I remember how much I smiled at his words shortly after he published his book: 'I count on my father, as he counts on me, because I'm not the only one people say terrible things about.'

I smiled because he had copied these words from Depardieu's son, whom he resembled at the time both physically and mentally. I smiled because the terrible things people said about Depardieu senior were not the same things that were said about me, on account of my merciless reviews. And now I smile, thinking how much I would like one day, with Montano, to write that anthology of dangerous youngsters or else, it occurs to me now, the elegant chronicle of how social misfits end up sooner or later becoming more moderate, joining forces and creating art.

When I woke up, despite having slept for barely two hours, I felt well, as if two hours were enough. I was greatly surprised to be feeling in such good form and decided not to sleep any more and to head outside. Since I had plenty of time before my appointment at my son's bookshop, I went for a walk in Procé Park. Literature-sick as I am, I was unable to avoid a private tribute to André Breton, who wrote in *Nadja* that Nantes was perhaps, together with

Paris, 'the only city in France where I have the impression that something worthwhile may happen to me, where certain glances burn with excessive fire, where for me the cadence of life is not the same as elsewhere, where a spirit of adventure beyond all adventures persists in certain souls. Nantes, from where friends may still arrive; Nantes, where I loved a park: Procé Park.'

I did not love Procé Park – it is not my style – but my sense of well-being grew at a time of morning when, given how little I had slept, the most logical reaction would have been to feel irritated, tired or bad-tempered. I felt very well walking in the drizzle, protected by the red umbrella which Rosa gave me for the trip. I paid close attention to the few people I met during my walk in the park and thought that I would have liked to know their full names and even to love them deeply – I preferred this possibility to loving the park – and for each of them to die knowing that their name was on my lips. I paid close attention to their apparently unique faces and saw in their sunken eyes the fear of a senseless slaughter. I derived great enjoyment from this perverse game of loving and killing off strangers and imagined each individual's death, as they commended me, in their passage to the other life, to their nearest and dearest. In short, I played at imagining that I was the absolute king in the land of love and death. In short, I travelled beyond all adventures, I went further than poor Breton.

In the bookshop I found Montano relaxed and pleasant to me. As for Aline, she seemed happier than yesterday, at least she was smiling more. Everything appeared idyllic, but it cannot be said that things went well. Now that I analyse Montano's behaviour in all the time we spent together, I have to say that he was disconcerting, highly volatile, with noticeably pronounced mood swings. As if he were Hamlet. Whether or not he was actually trying to imitate the Prince of Denmark – I shall never know for sure – Montano behaved like a being in surprising and continual transformation. He passed through the following stages at least of Hamlet's character: a) formal and polite, b) sensible, thoughtful, even intellectual, c) emotional and melancholic, d) despotic and mocking, e) pretending to be deranged, vindictive, even stark raving mad.

a) As soon as I entered the bookshop, he displayed extreme courtesy. Let us say he was strange, but agreeable. He bowed to me very low and very affectionately – imitating the greeting he gave me as a boy on the rare occasions that I deigned to go and fetch him from school – and handed me a French translation of *Asparagus and the Immortality of the Soul*, a novel by the Italian Achille Campanile, a master of humoristic literature.

'On presenting you with this book,' he said to me with exquisite, exaggerated but agreeable politeness, very formal, 'I should like to pay tribute to the most incorruptible Spanish critic of all time.'

I smiled and asked him not to joke or flatter me so much, but expressed my gratitude for the detail of giving me the French translation of a novel I had defended so stoutly – as I had defended its author, a writer unjustly ignored today – in my last essay, which showed that he had bothered to read this article of mine. 'I couldn't put it down,' he told me. And then he moved away to greet a customer. At this point Aline, beautiful and fragile as she was last night, came up to me and, after asking me if I was happy to have lunch at La Cigale, in referencc to Montano's current good mood, she whispered:

'He's charming when he wants to be.'

b) In the rain, on the way to La Cigale, it occurred to me to talk to Montano about my *literary illness*, only about mine, needless to say, I did not wish to talk to him so soon about his illness, a delicate matter which I planned to touch on later with great tact. I talked to him about my illness because I thought it might help him to know that his father found literature stifling and desired to abandon it at the first opportunity that presented itself. I thought that talking to him about my disease might perhaps alleviate his own while at the same time my confession would afford me some respite.

'I'm thinking,' he said to me in a sensible and very thoughtful tone, 'that Walter Benjamin speculated about the possible relationship that exists between the art of storytelling and the healing of illnesses.'

I was forced to confess the truth, namely that I had no idea about this curious relationship between narrative and healing. So Montano explained, in a sweet and friendly voice, that the connection between storytelling and curing illnesses had been suggested to Walter Benjamin by a German friend who told him about the healing powers of his wife's hands, saying that their movements were very expressive, but it was impossible to describe their expressiveness, because it was as if those hands were telling a story.

'In such a way,' said my son, 'in such a peculiar way, Walter Benjamin was reminded of an intimate scene: that of the boy who, when he falls ill, is sent to bed by his mother, who then comes and sits by his side and starts telling him stories. As a result of this memory, Walter Benjamin wondered whether narrative might not in fact be the most propitious atmosphere, the most favourable condition, for a large number of cures.'

Montano proceeded to reflect on the propitious atmosphere created by the narrative space, and I felt a little ridiculous for having confided my illness to him and having left myself at the mercy of the expressive movements of his hands as he aired his opinions on the matter. And the thing is I had the impression that, as he held forth, including in his meditation brilliant stories of his own invention, he was seeking to heal me of my illness when this was not exactly what I had come to Nantes to achieve, but, in my role as his father, I had come primarily to cure his illness, his tragic inability to write.

'I have to go back to my childhood,' Montano concluded, 'to the days when I fell miserably ill, and Mum would tell me stories that always made me feel better; I have to go back to my childhood to deduce with absolute certainty something that may seem simple to you, but in fact is not: in the same imperceptible manner in which it began, the illness one day takes its leave.'

c) Once in La Cigale, Montano became emotional and started talking about his mother and how, as soon as I left the house, she would dance for joy. At the top of his voice and on the verge of hysterical sobbing, he introduced the subject of his late mother and did so in that style which is so characteristic of him when he suddenly becomes emotional for some reason, a style which, like the good critic I am, I have analysed as if it were a text.

This emotional style, which finally drifts into the most disturbing melancholy, involves despising the straight line and wandering, adding personal touches, following ellipses and labyrinths, retreating, going round in circles, suddenly touching that inaccessible core which is the subject of his mother – whenever I have seen him emotional, he has been talking about his blessed mother – and again retreating and again further circumlocutions obeying contrary instincts, until he mercilessly bares and ridicules the truth, any truth about anything liable to be certain with the exception – and here he again advances, again obeying contrary instincts – of one immutable truth, the only one he claims to possess with absolute certainty: that he has only ever loved one person in this world. That person is María, his dear late mother, my first wife of sacred memory.

d) After the meal, Aline, understandably saddened, slightly naively told Montano that he could love her as well. My son pierced her with his blue, perpetually cold eyes, the same cold, blue eyes his mother had. Aline was frightened, and I confirmed that Montano dominates her with a certain ease. That said, her fear quickly passed, and shortly afterwards she dared to tell my son that persevering in obstinate grief over the disappearance of his mother was to behave with impious stubbornness. It wasn't the best thing she could have said. Montano adopted a very sombre and strange air. I immediately asked him if anything was wrong, other than his anger towards her. He looked most unusual, with a wild expression in his eyes which I had never seen in him before. I again asked him if anything was the matter and he still did not answer me. His blue eyes were colder than ever.

'You look very sombre,' I said to him.

'Sombre, me?' he answered in a mocking tone. 'Not so, my lord; I am too much i' the sun.'

He answered like Hamlet – 'I am too much i' the sun,' exactly what the prince says – and I began to draw conclusions, one at least. He may have wanted to avenge his mother's death. More than once he had stupidly insinuated that I had killed her. But perhaps this was the wrong conclusion to draw and he was not thinking about Hamlet or anything, his enigmatic and volatile behaviour was due simply to the confusion he felt at his tragic inability to write.

Whatever the reason, Hamlet's unexpected appearance reminded me of an idea that came to me in the hotel during the night, when I could not sleep. The idea was in some way related to Hamlet's ghost and was intended to help Montano overcome the anxiety caused by his writer's block. The idea originated as follows: during the night, unable to sleep, I suddenly switched on the light in my bedroom, when I thought I saw a spider crawling across the carpet. The spider, incautious and overhasty, came limping sluggishly towards me, stopped, suddenly noticed the gigantic shadow in front of it and, not knowing whether to beat a retreat or to keep on going, contemplated its enormous enemy. On seeing that I barely moved, it plucked up courage and continued forwards, with a mixture of rashness, guile and fear. As it passed next to me, I was about to crush it because it disgusted me, but instead I lifted up the carpet and helped it to escape, I spared its life. Why? Because my philosophy went beyond an all too easy impulsive gesture, just as Hamlet – I thought at the time – hesitates between *knowledge* (doing nothing) or rejecting knowledge in favour of an ancient moral custom we call revenge, which basically is an all too easy, animal gesture. Part of the greatness of Shakespeare's *Hamlet* derives from this hesitation, a theory I expounded in my penultimate book.

In this way I moved from the spider to *Hamlet* and from there to my colleague Harold Bloom, who in a recent essay asks, 'Why does Hamlet return from the sea?' Hamlet could have gone to Wittenberg, Paris or London. But the truth is, Bloom goes on to explain, he cannot return to Wittenberg to study, because the prince of Act V has nothing left to learn, *he already knows it all*. It is a ghost who returns, whom I imagined in the middle of last night to have something in common with Jacques Vaché.

This is how things went last night in this hotel room where I continue to write this diary which is turning into a novel. Bloom's question suggested to me a similar one that I could ask Montano today, which might help to put him on the ideal path on which to escape from the tragedy of his blocked literary horizon.

The question was this: 'Why does Marcel Duchamp return from the sea?'

On mentioning that Duchamp returns from the sea, I would be referring to how, after a long stay on the other side of the Atlantic, in the United States of America, one fine day Duchamp returned to Paris, where, with the clear-sighted vision of someone who, in the field of artistic creation, *already knows it all*, he continued in his practice of renouncing the all too easy gesture of 'crushing the spider', by which I mean of creating works of art that merely repeat exhausted formulas.

Wide awake in this room last night, I thought that as soon as I saw Montano today I would tell him that, if his only problem was writer's block, it had an easy solution. À la Duchamp. All he had to do was calmly devote himself to doing nothing, the same as those artists who *already know it all*. Was it so dramatic to go through life like Duchamp, declaring oneself to be at a distance from artists who repeat what has already been done and personifying the wisdom of someone who has seen the sea and seen it all and who, therefore, is a happy ghost, whose daily gestures are no more than the contented succession, for example, of the invisible books one writes not on paper but in the thin air of every day or on life's furtive surface?

A good plan for Montano. To follow Duchamp's example and, like him, without surprise or suffering, to claim to be doing nothing. A good plan for my son, a plan that would enable him to escape from the constricted geometry of his blind alley. A plan as complex – it necessitated connecting a spider and Hamlet with Bloom and Duchamp – as it was basically very simple. In any case, a good plan for Montano. It came to me last night, as I lay wide awake in this hotel, but today, when I woke up, I had already forgotten it. However, the sudden irruption of Hamlet's ghost into La Cigale brought it back to mind.

All I had to do was ask him, innocent as can be, why Marcel Duchamp returns from the sea.

e) La Cigale is a historic restaurant and not just because Jacques Demy shot his famous film *Lola* there in the 1960s. We were talking about all this and arguing about who should pay the bill when suddenly, possibly at the wrong moment, perhaps to stop him arguing about who should pay and also – why not say it? – trying in good faith to lend him a hand and to help him overcome his inability to write, at the wrong moment I decided to ask him the question I had formulated in my hotel room.

'Why does Marcel Duchamp return from the sea?'

I know, I should have put him in the picture and told him first about Bloom and the spider and all the paraphernalia of my literarily sick mind, which had led me to concoct this twisted but basically simple question intended subtly to help him, because I only sought to help him with this question which set in motion, I thought, my very well-intentioned Duchamp plan.

My son went from courting Hamlet's ghost to becoming a monster which seeks revenge, also like Hamlet, I should add. The change in his expression was terrifying, his pupils suddenly dilated in a quite astonishing way and, on answering me, he almost breathed fire:

'To see the sea.'

I remembered when he was a boy and one day, for no reason at all – unless it was to give us a good fright – the expression on his angelic face suddenly changed and turned into an enormous, horrible grimace, at which point he told us, warning us of his future literary calling, that the sea was paved with human faces, the faces of the dead. That day his mother, the ill-fated María, and I knew that our son would be difficult, though of course we had no way of knowing that later in Nantes he would choose to behave like Hamlet's ghost in such an unstable way.

'I don't think you understood me,' I replied today in La Cigale, 'I asked you about Duchamp because it seems to me that living without writing, being a literary Duchamp, isn't such a bad plan.'

I shall never forget his words or his deranged look, which suddenly sought revenge.

'Thanks to you,' he said, 'thanks entirely to you, look what is happening to me at this precise moment: the memory of Gonzalo Rojas is infiltrating Justo Navarro's and I am reliving the night when that poet wrote those verses in which Rimbaud painted the hum of vowels, Lautréamont howled at length, Kafka burned with his writings, Ezra Pound discussed an ideogram with the angels, and my mother, my poor mother . . .'

It was terrible, his pupils dilated even more.

'And my mother,' he continued, 'listened to the piano recital that her charming murderer gave for her.'

At this point all I could think was how right Rosa was when she warned me that Montano, the one person who had inherited all my tastes and neuroses, was the least suitable human being in the world to help me dampen the obsessive presence of literature in my life.

At this point I clearly saw that remaining at Montano's side could only make my illness worse. It was obvious that Montano's malady, just like mine, was due to literature sickness. And I told myself that, since Montano had inherited his father's disease, I should name the illness after my son and call it *Montano's malady*.

I looked at my son and confirmed my opinions. With his Hamletism, his aggressive theatrics and his story about writers' memories infiltrating the memories of others, Montano posed a real threat to his father and could only aggravate the latter's literary illness.

'You killed her!' Montano suddenly exclaimed.

This was the last straw. He evidently believed that he was Hamlet and wanted to entrap the King's conscience, my conscience.

'For crying out loud,' I answered, 'I didn't kill your mother!'

At this point Aline burst into tears.

It is raining outside, the rain is falling on Nantes and this hotel room is really very comfortable. But let's get one thing straight: I did *not* kill his mother. Let there be no doubt. The idea that I murdered her is the classic literary construction of someone suffering from my son's illness. It is raining on Nantes and this reminds me of Barbara's song, where it also rained on the streets of this city. I gulp down two glasses of water in the hope that they will help me to mitigate the harmful effects of the evil, of my Montano's malady. A moment ago I looked out of the window and saw a man with his arms half raised, in different positions, turning towards the mist – fairly thick at that time – as if he intended to enter it.

I did not kill his mother. What I do remember very well is the mad dash towards the balcony, the terrible jump in the air of María, the mother who left poor Montano feeling melancholy, the mother he won't forget.

I remember her deranged dash towards the balcony, which left the wood in our house on Provença Street in splinters, her jump from the sixth floor with the indifference of a housewife who empties a bucket of dirty water out of the window.

At the funeral, making out I was eternally bereaved, I read some verses by Eliot: 'Ash on an old man's sleeve / Is all the ash the burnt roses leave, / Dust in the air suspended / Marks the place where a story ended.'

I did not kill his mother.

Today in La Cigale, in an attempt to still the bloody thread of his runaway imagination, I said to him:

'All you ever do is revive the flies which suck my blood.'

I came out with this improbable sentence in part because I had again evoked the sea that he saw paved with the faces of the dead, and this reminded me of an old friend who always used to say that he wanted to crush two paving stones with the same fly. I came out with this sentence in part because of this and in part because I had the impression that my son, aware that I was suffering from Montano's malady, sought to suck my blood and was trying to give me a final dose, a deadly overdose of literature.

This was not so very unusual, since my son could simply have it in mind to kill his father, a not uncommon desire in the West. The only strange thing was that he sought to do so by literary means. But, given Montano's strangeness, nothing ever seems sufficiently odd. Whatever, the point is that, being in La Cigale, I understood that I could not run any more risks and that the best course of action was to leave Nantes as quickly as possible. I could not carry on hesitating like a vulgar Hamlet, wondering whether Montano was mad or simply pretending, or whether the poor boy was suffering on account of his inability to write (and that was all), or else he really did want to avenge his mother's death, or he intended to aggravate my Montano's malady by giving me his own and so end up eliminating me by an overdose.

'What flies are you talking about?' he said. 'You're always trying to lecture me from your critic's pedestal.'

This was all I needed. All I needed now was for him as a narrator to reproach me for being a critic. I stared at him with the most authoritarian expression I could adopt at that moment. And suddenly, I don't know how it happened – I suppose it was down to the constant presence of Hamlet's ghost – I remembered a gravedigger I once saw in Roses, singing while he dug graves. And immediately I remembered that in performances of *Hamlet* there is always such a character, a singing gravedigger.

I was so annoyed with my son that I was on the verge of telling him that I would sing on the day that I dug his grave. But it didn't seem a good idea to add fuel to the flames. However, I did ask him what on earth the matter was, and told him that I had never seen him acting so strange. I already had it clear in my mind that, according to his response, I should make a swift exit, before he had a chance to administer the overdose.

'You're the one who's acting strange,' he said. 'You come to Nantes and tell me you're literature-sick, which is pretty obvious, and then you start asking me about the sea and

Duchamp.' I immediately regretted having confessed so freely yesterday that I felt saturated with so many books and so many quotations. I'm very glad I didn't, but I was about to elaborate on yesterday's confession by telling him that since arriving in Nantes I have felt trapped in the pages of a novel which I am copying down in my diary and whose enigmatic rhythm is being marked, with noticeable regularity, by Montano's malady.

In the end the tension in La Cigale became so great that I told Aline and my son that I was walking back to the hotel and would come and see them in the bookshop at the end of the day.

I prepared my suitcase an hour ago. I shall finish writing these lines in my diary and then go to the station, where I shall take the first train out of this city, I shall leave on the first train. I know that this is a very literary thing to do, I also know that trains are very literary, but it does not matter, on the first train I find I shall leave Nantes, I shall leave and let my son sing while he digs the grave of whoever he likes, so long as it isn't mine.

The train steals out of Nantes, I am leaving Verne's city behind, the relief is immense. In his diaries Ernst Jünger says that people with dilated pupils soon arouse distrust. I would add to this that sons, especially if they turn so exceedingly dangerous as mine, come into the world just to aggravate their fathers' illnesses, sometimes just to kill them. It is supposed to be a fact of life, that some die so that others can be born. But I do not wish to die of a literary overdose, nor do I have any desire to suffer vengeance by Hamlet's sword. I have no problem with the father being killed, just so long as I'm not the father.

I am leaving Nantes, abandoning the Danish court.

Even if I discovered now that my son is the sanest person in the world and I am simply odd, it would not change anything, I would still leave Nantes, because it is clear that my son, whether he is innocent or a dangerous killer, has not stopped aggravating my literary illness since I arrived in this city. I am sure that, had I stayed a few hours longer in Nantes, I would have ended up – if I'm not already – turning into the most literary being on earth.

The distance swallows up Nantes, elegant provincial city with its river, a city exposed to the four winds, an open city and yet, also, an enclosed city, a literary city: Verne, Vaché and Julien Gracq among others were born here or hereabouts.

Very soon I shall start thinking about tomatoes and asparagus and all sorts of natural products of the earth and I shall forget about so much literature. At least for a time, I need to have a complete break from literature, to rest in whatever way I can. Also, even if it is only for a short period, I am going to shelve this diary which was turning into a novel. I need to concentrate my mind on natural things, to meditate on whatever tittle-tattle comes into my head, which I cannot easily relate to literature. 'It is possible to speak of a writing malady,' I remember now that Marguerite Duras wrote. I wish to escape from such a malady for a good long while.

That's enough literature for now. Fortunately, dangerous Nantes recedes into the distance. I am going to watch the countryside and look out for silly cows grazing in green meadows under the pretty rain. Anything that isn't writing or thinking in literary terms. I feel sorry for Montano, he may have had high hopes for me. But he can find himself another victim, not me. He can sing while he digs another's grave.

At the end of the twentieth century, I went to Valparaíso to think about gunpowder. It isn't that I went to this Chilean port with this express purpose in mind, but circumstances combined in such a way that on New Year's Eve, on the hanging terrace of the Brighton Hôtel, watching the fireworks that saw out the century, I ended up having the impression that fate had secretly planned it so that I would travel to Valparaíso to think about gunpowder. And about death, I should add. Gunpowder and death more than anything occupied my thoughts there on the hanging terrace of the Brighton Hotel, as I contemplated the water of the bay, which at that moment was a smoking black plate, in the pleasant company of Margot and Tongoy.

I had gone to Chile under Rosa's strict orders. She was so tired of me that she had asked me to go as far away as possible for a few days. 'To Chile,' she said, 'Chile, for example.' There was the delightful Margot Valerí, our intrepid aviator friend. She could help me, Rosa said. Among Margot's many attributes was the fact that she did not have a clue about literature and she never spoke about books.

I travelled to Chile one day before the end of the century and I went to this country without this diary which was turning into a novel, I went to Chile with the intention of not reading or writing at all, purely to see the

Pacific Ocean for the first time in my life, to see its famous violent blue colour and to think about anything that I could not relate to literature or to death, which was what I thought about most since forcing myself not to think about literature.

Rosa came with me to the airport and gave me a big kiss goodbye. 'Off you go,' she said to me, 'come back when you're well.' The days prior to my departure had been absolute hell for her. After my brief stay in Nantes, I had returned to Barcelona in a worse state than when I had left. From Nantes I could have gone to Paris, which would have been the most sensible thing to do, but I had been an idiot and taken the first train to appear in Nantes station – that idea of the 'first train' has always been as literary and romantic as it is pernicious – and a few hours later, fool that I am, I was back in Barcelona, where, because I did not allow myself to think about anything referring to literature, the days became empty and devoid of meaning and I ended up thinking about death, which is precisely what literature talks about most.

I thought about death even when I was asleep. One afternoon, in the sitting room at home, I told myself that it would be better to try reading a book again than to switch on the television and watch those programmes about the lives of the rich and famous, which, while they did not refer me to literature, made me so anxious that I always fell to thinking about death. However, my choice of book was not a good one. With my eyes closed, I picked a book out from the shelf and found myself with a biography of the writer Sir Thomas Browne, whom initially, I do not know why, I imagined to be a jovial lover of life.

But in a matter of seconds I was more anxious than ever, having read that on one particular occasion Browne imagined seeing sleeping bodies from on high and suggested that, if one were to pass across the globe, following the setting sun, one would see the whole world as a vast city of the dead.

Anxiety everywhere! I put down the book, threw it on the floor as if it burned, switched on the television again, they were showing a football match and focusing on the pained expression of a player lying sprawled on the turf. Anxiety everywhere, I went back to thinking about death.

Every day in Barcelona became horrible, very morbid. I would cry in my sleep and then wake up and tell Rosa that it was nothing, really, Rosa, just a dream or something like that, nothing, Rosa. But it was not a dream or even a nightmare, it was a mournful voice, I knew this very well, a voice that even at night prowled about me and told me that I was going to die and that I didn't have long to go. I would wake up in the night and tell Rosa that it was nothing, just a dream, but shortly afterwards I would go to the kitchen to have a drink and Rosa would follow me to the kitchen and, as soon as she caught me with a bottle of something, she would tell me that I was in a very bad way, that it would even be better for me to start writing reviews again and to think about literature or else to travel, yes, to travel to a faraway country, I needed it. And I would stand there, open-mouthed and sad, staring silently at the kitchen calendar.

I decided to start reviewing again, and the first book they sent me was *The Rings of Saturn* by W. G. Sebald. It was as if the editors of the newspaper had decided to send me this book so that its style of an extreme glacial beauty would finish me off. I knew this because I had been told, but I confirmed it by reading the book: the narrator viewed the world dominated by a strange quietness, as if all we humans looked through various sheets of glass. At times the narrator did not know whether he was in the 'land of the living or already in another place'. Anxiety everywhere. The narrator set off to walk the county of Suffolk, 'in the hope of dispelling the emptiness that takes hold of me whenever I have completed a long stint of work'. Visiting small villages, landscapes and solitary ruins, he was confronted by traces of a past which referred him to the entire world. His pilgrimage along the coast lacked joy, light and vivacity. For a dead man – the narrator seemed to be saying – the whole world is one long funeral.

The next book I was given to review, which had just been reprinted, was *The Encyclopedia of the Dead* by Danilo Kiš, a collection of nine stories, the strangest of which – its long shadow would accompany me to Chilean lands, as I was soon to discover – was based on real events: the story of a man who on a trip had been forced to spend the night in a miserable hostel 'in the middle of the woods' and suddenly, in his dreams, had witnessed in minute detail the murder that would take place three years later in the same room where he was sleeping at the time; the victim would be a lawyer by the name of Victor Arnaud. It was possible to locate the murderer, because the dream stayed in his memory.

Anxiety everywhere. One afternoon Rosa found me quiet, almost frozen from fear and from glacial beauty in front of the kitchen calendar, only the golden label on the bottle of rum from Martinique giving the scene some colour. It was then that she suggested that I stop thinking about literature and about death and that I travel to Chile to visit Margot Valerí, who was eighty years old, but was life itself and would surely help me.

I didn't hesitate, Rosa was right, I needed to travel. Rosa and I had met the intrepid aviator Margot Valerí in the summer of 1998 in Barcelona and we had become good friends. In case one day we decided to travel to Chile, she had invited us to her house in Tunquén, in the bay of Quintay, facing the Pacific. Margot had a delightful biography, which made her the ideal person to combat Montano's malady. She had been born in Trafún, near Río Bueno, and as a girl had enjoyed horse-riding and rowing on the River Pilmaiquén. When riding or rowing through the scenes of her childhood, she would often notice the aeroplanes constantly flying over the river. At the age of nine, she was given a pair of binoculars by her mother and was able to take a closer look at the Lan Chile mail-planes flying very high over Trafún on the route connecting Santiago with Puerto Montt. Margot, she soon discovered, was destined to be an aviator. In the Second World War, she had been a pilot with the Free French Air Force, something of which she was very proud. At the age of eighty, she continued to pilot aeroplanes, she was a woman who seemed to travel through life without the need to refuel, and she had no ties with death or with literature. In fact, one day in Barcelona, I remembered having asked her what she thought of the writer-aviator Antoine de Saint-Exupéry. She had answered that literature bored her stiff – possibly because her grandfather had tried to drum it into her – but most of all she hated the 'aviator-mystique' surrounding this insufferable French writer whom I had just mentioned and who, to cap it all, was not such a good pilot as he was rumoured to have been.

Isn't it wonderful that literature bored her stiff? Only once had I heard her say something vaguely literary, it was when I asked her if I should believe that at her age she still piloted aeroplanes. 'Yes,' she answered, 'of course I still shake the skies.'

It was this sentence I reminded her of when I called her to find out if I could visit her at the end of the year and century in her house in Tunquén, in the bay of Quintay. First she joked and asked me if I had split up with Rosa. I explained to her what was going on, how Rosa had to stay in Barcelona because of work – she was taken up with preparations to shoot a film in the Azores – and how she, more than anyone, needed a break from my neurotic literary ills.

I slept almost all the hours of the outward journey to Chile. The few moments I spent awake between one sleeping pill and the next were criminal. I could only think to flick through the in-flight magazine, where I came across some verses by Pablo Neruda, perfect for reminding me that death and literature existed: 'There are lonely cemeteries, / graves full of bones without sound, / the heart passing through a tunnel, / dark, dark, dark, / as in a shipwreck we die from within . . .'

Startling verses of a great funereal beauty, but not at all what you want to read between one sleep and another. When after two naps brought on by different sleeping pills and a Nerudian interlude I arrived in Santiago, I was cheered by Margot's lively smile as she stood at the foot of the steps, but saw that she was accompanied by a very ugly man, a kind of ultra-gloomy Nosferatu, and for a moment I couldn't help thinking about Neruda's verses and death.

'Allow me to introduce you,' she said, 'to Felipe Tongoy, the ugliest man in the world. You will become very good friends.'

Short pause for Felipe Tongoy, the ugliest man in the world. I met him on the penultimate day of the twentieth century at Santiago airport, as I just related in this diary which I took up again after my return from Chile. Funnily enough, I am here in Barcelona writing about the time in Santiago when I met the ugly Tongoy and, in ten minutes, I have to leave home and have lunch with him at the restaurant Envalira in the district of Gràcia. My friend Tongoy is currently in Barcelona because he is due to work on the documentary about the world of whalers which Rosa is preparing and which will be shot shortly in the Azores.

Obviously it was I who suggested to Rosa that she offer Tongoy the part of a bogus whaler in the film. His appearances in the documentary may well have a disturbing effect because Tongoy is an authentic Nosferatu and has been in the acting profession for many years; he is a seasoned actor and somewhat famous in France, where he has lived for the last half a century. I think that he will excel in his role as a bogus whaler cum outlandish Nosferatu.

Rosa's documentary aims to record the depressing current state of the world of whales and whalers in the Azores, with *Moby Dick* as a permanent literary backdrop.

But it also aims to invent, to blend fact and fiction, and it is here, in the fiction, that Tongoy can shine, in the lines which, in my collaboration as scriptwriter, I have prepared for him to deliver at the start of the film.

My friend Tongoy is really very ugly, but one grows used to finding him less hideous on account of his good nature, his eccentric but elegant dress sense and his refined manners. When I saw him for the first time at Santiago Airport, I quickly thought of Nosferatu. I kept quiet, however, because it is rude to tell someone you have just met that he looks like Dracula, but above all because I myself have always borne a certain resemblance to the actor Christopher Lee, who played Count Dracula in films of the 1950s. And also because he almost immediately brought up the matter of his remarkable physical oddity.

My friend Tongoy is seventy-four years old, has a shaved head and ears like a bat's. He has lived in Paris for half a century, but he was born into a family of Hungarian Jews who emigrated to Chile and settled in San Felipe. My friend's real name is Felipe Kertész; he recently became quite famous in France when in a film he played the role of a sinister old man who goes about kidnapping children. He is also relatively well known for his roles as dragonfly-man in a film by Fellini and as Bela Lugosi in a biopic of this Hungarian actor.

With Margot's valuable assistance, it took the ugly Tongoy and me very few minutes to establish a feeling of mutual sympathy, which led him to ask me, before we had even left the airport, whether I wanted to know how as a boy he came to realise that he was odd.

'I'd love to know,' I told him.

'Well, listen. I must have been about seven and I went on a trip with my family. We were accompanied by Olga, a friend of my mother. Olga was pregnant and at one point, having stared at me for a good long time, she asked my mother, 'Do you think my baby will suck milk from my blood?' When I heard this, I said to Olga in my childish way, 'How can you be so stupid?' She turned on me in a rage and said, 'My God, how can you be so naughty and so ugly?' When we got back home, I asked my mother if it was true that I was ugly, and she replied, 'Only in Chile.' At that precise moment I swore that one day I would have the world at my feet.'

In fact Tongoy has never felt ugly. Once, when he was young, a certain girl fell in love with him. She frequented a shop which was situated in the same basement where he lived. There was no light. She ended up pursuing him. Tongoy explained to her that her enthusiasm was an effect of the light, that it wasn't good to be so literary in life and that she would die if she found out that he liked men. In this way he nipped her nascent feelings in the bud.

Tongoy is of the opinion that love stories for the most part are not sexual stories, but stories of tenderness. Tongoy maintains that people do not understand this or, even if it is only for ten minutes, they do not wish to understand this.

Talking of ten minutes, I have run out of those I had to write all this down. I'm off in a hurry to make my appointment with Tongoy, monster and friend.

I'm back, having had lunch with Tongoy at the Envalira. He's clearly very excited about the film in the Azores. We spent a large part of the meal talking about this diary which I am currently writing. We also talked about Montano and I thanked Tongoy for the good advice and good ideas he was able to give me in Valparaíso. After that we went on to remember when we first saw each other, our meeting at Santiago Airport. We recalled the journey at nightfall in the Chevrolet driven by Margot, which took us along minor roads to Tunquén, facing the Pacific. I was seeing this ocean for the first time and for ages I stood on the terrace of the house contemplating it in silence and missing this diary, which I had left in Barcelona, wishing I had it with me so that I could record some stimulating impressions of this moment I had waited so many years to enjoy: my eyes before the violent blue of the Pacific, the long, impressive sunset, unforgettable. And the low but brutal murmur of ancient battle reaching me from the sea.

Tunquén consists of a few isolated, beautiful wooden houses supported on tall stilts, a few houses in a wide open space facing the ocean. Margot livened up the evening by singing songs from the mountain and the sea and by telling stories about some of her more risky excursions by aeroplane. One story in particular sticks in my memory, perhaps because of the special emphasis she gave to it; she talked of the day in the middle of the war when she lost control of her plane and realised that the anti-aircraft batteries were firing on the enemy and she was caught up in the crossfire. When she got back to base, she saw that a missile had hit her back wheel.

Tongoy, hearing this story, turned to me and said that he had an almost identical memory to Margot's, all he had to do was substitute back wheel of a fighter plane with Achilles heel, hit not by a missile but by a Chilean train.

I asked Tongoy if he would care to elaborate.

So he spoke of the day when he was seventeen and wanted to die and tried to get run over by a train going so slowly – back then all Chilean trains went slowly – that it had time to brake and he to scramble clear at the last minute, at the last second, although in chilling detail he left half his heel under the wheel and had to give up any plans he had of becoming a dancer, since he had no way of supporting himself for the acrobatics.

As the evening in Tunquén wore on, we laughed a fair amount, listened to many stories, I told some of my own, concentrating on certain memories. I recalled the figure of my father, a 'self-made man' like Kafka's father – obviously I couldn't avoid the literary reference – and I also recalled my poor mother, who bore some resemblance – again the literary reference – to the Argentinian poet Alejandra Pizarnik, who was fragile and strange and, like my mother, was addicted to barbiturates and had clear suicidal tendencies. I remembered the time in the 1970s when I lived between Berlin and Paris and considered myself to be a radical leftist – with the help of my family's money – and was friends with people in the underground movement like Ingrid Caven. I recalled my first wife's suicide, how she jumped from the balcony as if she were a bucket of dirty water – she may have been, I said. I recalled my childhood in Barcelona's Rovira Square during years of monotony and moral misery which I spent disguised in school uniform, a perfect fool holding a ridiculous stick of chalk in front of the blackboard, with the irresistible look of a real bore. I remembered Rosa slaving away to establish herself as a film director. I remembered how my generation wanted to change the world and said that perhaps it was better that our dreams never came true. I recalled how as a teenager I read Cernuda a lot and sometimes cried if it rained. And then I remembered how I used to see myself remembering seeing myself writing and finally I remembered seeing myself remembering how I used to write.

After that I didn't remember any more, because it was late and we went to bed, Margot and Tongoy together, it seemed to me. I stayed awake in the upstairs bedroom and, when I finally got to sleep, I thought I saw in minute detail – just as had happened to that character in Danilo Kiš' story – a dramatic fight that would take place – perhaps I should say 'will take place' – three years later in the same room: an argument between Montano, dressed as a British airman, and poor Margot, defending herself with a sabre.

I woke up in a sweat and confused, and decided to go down to the porch to smoke a cigarette. While I was smoking and contemplating the Pacific, inclined as I am to think about everything in literature, I recalled a very precise moment in the life of someone I admire, Cyril Connolly, a moment reflected in his diary: he is alone in a railway carriage, playing records of slow foxtrots as the English countryside of the 1930s flashes past the window, and he feels that he has succeeded in becoming an interesting person.

The change I experienced was very pleasant. In a short time I had managed to go from my inner nightmare with Montano to a sense of outer happiness standing in front of the Pacific. I also, if I chose to think in this way, was an interesting person. I thought I heard a foxtrot, looked up at the sky and confirmed that there was a full moon. There's nothing like being alone at night, I thought. I decided to search for another stimulating memory from another private journal. Inclined as I am to think about everything in literature, I soon hit upon a new memory. I recalled a scene similar to Connolly's, taken from a page in André Gide's diary, where it says something like, 'Though the silence be too great, I enjoy travelling in this railway carriage in the company of Fabrice [*N.B. Gide is talking about himself*]. Today, travelling first class, wearing a new suit cut in an unusual fashion, under a hat which suits him prodigiously well, he approaches himself in the mirror in amazement and is seduced, finds himself the most interesting person in the world.'

Conceited for no obvious reason and euphoric at the same time, I decided to go for a wander in the vicinity of the house, I took a few steps in the night – two, four, eight. In a couple of minutes, almost without realising, I left the group of wooden houses which comprised Tunquén behind. As I emerged into open ground, a mildly irritating wind arose. Inclined as I am to think in literature, I recalled Goethe: 'Who rides so late through the night and wind?' As was to be expected, nobody answered, and the silence together with the short gusts of wind began to erode both my conceit and my euphoria. With no clear direction in mind, I proceeded to climb a steep slope, thinking that, when I reached the top, I would find no more houses, I would find nothing else, there would be nothing on the other side, in the same way – I told myself, almost stifled – as there is nothing after death. However, there was something.

A hundred yards away, on the ground floor of a house with the lights on, a group of youngsters was engaged in lively conversation. I hid among the trees and, protected by the shadows of the night, gradually approached the house, intending to get close to those youngsters and perhaps be able to overhear what they were saying, I gradually approached a position that I understood to be discreet and above all strategic, where I thought I would be able to see and hear everything, but, on reaching it, I soon realised that I was mistaken and that, if I wanted to spy on the house, I had to draw nearer, with the inherent risk. Also I was frightened to steal along in the shadows, since I could end up being discovered and taken for a thief or at least a strange and possibly dangerous visitor. But curiosity – as Borges said – was stronger than fear. And I drew very close, so much so that I was suddenly surprised to find out that they were not youngsters in the lively group, but old people. Ancient people, I should say, who appeared to have walked straight out of a fantasy tale.

What had started as a happy outing in the light of the full moon, making me feel that I was an interesting person, had drifted into something sombre and ancient. No, I said to myself, so much literature is not possible, so much anxiety, old people and death, heavens above, it is not possible, I went for a simple, happy wander and have ended up coming face to face with death, some old people and fantasy literature, clearly I cannot escape this personal, angst-ridden closed circle, even in Chile.

I spied on the group of old men and women for a few

seconds and heard one of them say that in his time it was customary for all the mirrors and all the paintings showing domestic landscapes in the house of the deceased to be covered over with silk crêpe in sign of mourning. 'Not just paintings with landscapes,' added an old woman, 'any painting showing human beings or fruits of the earth.'

Everything was shamelessly sad and real. Profoundly literary as well. Death seemed to preside over it all. In Tunquén I didn't seem to be able to forget the obsessions that haunted me. Taking the necessary precautions not to be discovered at the last moment, I started back towards Margot's house in great distress, as if it were my first outing after death and my soul should avoid becoming distracted by mirrors or landscapes, hence I walked with my eyes glued to Chilean soil in the bay of Quintay, terrified, to tell the truth more frightened than ever, as if I were walking along the first shore of my life after death.

It is five in the afternoon, I shall stop here for a while; now is a good time to prepare a dry Martini, though, after the excesses of today's lunch with Tongoy, what I really need is an Alka-Seltzer. Or an aspirin, because I have a slight headache; it isn't easy receiving Tongoy, having lunch with him and then coming home to write an account in these pages of my trip to Chile last New Year's Eve and, owing to the needs of the script, having to delve into an episode of disagreeable memory, my angst-ridden nocturnal wander in the vicinity of the house in Tunquén.

I had not one but two dry Martinis. As I was finishing the second, I heard the jangle of keys, Rosa was entering the house. I told myself that the time had come to introduce a topical theme into this diary, so that it might appear a little less like a novel, to carry on recounting my trip to Chile later.

In the hope of having something fresh and homespun to relate in these pages, I decided – it isn't difficult – to pick a fight with Rosa. The simplest tactic was to let her come into the kitchen and catch me with the second dry Martini. But this was too easy. As I concealed all traces of my alcoholic crime, I recalled a biography which I read recently, the biography of a man who had become heavily addicted to alcohol: but, thanks to the strength of his constitution, was able to control his addiction, to ration out the alcohol: he never drank before midday and after lunch he would not drink again until five. This man knew that it was a hard struggle and always would be. At weekends he would paint doors, chop wood, mow the lawn, look at his watch every ten minutes to see if it was time to drink legally. At five to five, with a sweaty face and trembling hands, he would take out the cocktail shaker and prepare himself a dry Martini.

I let Rosa catch me in the kitchen, but drinking a glass of water. 'Things are not going well,' I said to her, thereby causing a mild fight that would introduce a small dose of hot topicality into this diary. 'I don't know what you're referring to,' she replied. 'Do you really think it is normal for a man and a woman to live together like this?' I asked her. 'No,' she answered. 'So let's talk.' Her face was tense and pale, her eyes not swollen but glazed, her eyebrows slightly raised, clearly she was exhausted from work. 'How is Tongoy?' she asked me. 'He sends you his regards and says to remind you that he'll be in your office tomorrow,' I replied. 'You destroy everything you love!' she exclaimed suddenly. I hadn't expected her to warm to the theme quite so soon. 'I love my children and I haven't destroyed them,' I answered jokingly, I really had not intended to pick a serious fight. 'What children? Don't bring Montano into this, you've done him enough damage already, stuffing literature into the poor boy, he speaks in book – do you know what it means to speak in book?' I stopped and thought for a few seconds and, before I explained that I had planned the fight only for this diary and we would do well to continue the idyllic state in which we had been living since my return from Chile, replied (not wanting her to believe that a literary critic of my stature was incapable of answering her question), 'To speak in book means to read the world as if it were the continuation of a never-ending text.'

The following morning – to return to Tunquén – the wonderful Margot had prepared a splendid and very generous breakfast for us. Unable to conceal the bags under my eyes and my air of preoccupation, I ended up telling them about my strange nocturnal jaunt, the youngsters who were in fact old people, my anxiety about the hellish siege to which both literature and death were subjecting me.

'All this would pass if you could unite the two anxieties and channel them into a single preoccupation, a separate concern of deep humanistic import. The death of literature, for example,' Tongoy said as he sipped his third coffee of the morning. 'Has it ever occurred to you that, in this savage age in which we live, poor literature is beset by a thousand dangers and directly threatened with death and needs your help?'

I heard his words, but failed at that moment to capture their full meaning, because Margot, believing – I would later find out – that I was being further tortured by new cultural problems, quickly changed the subject and proceeded to give us a series of instructions for the journey we were to undertake along minor roads to the Brighton Hotel in Valparaíso, on the marvellous hanging terrace of which we were to see in the new century.

At the end of the twentieth century, I went to Valparaíso to think about gunpowder. It isn't that I went with this express purpose, but the truth is that fate arranged everything in such a way that, on the terrace of the Brighton Hotel, watching the fireworks that signalled the end of the year and century, I ended up with the impression that I had travelled to this place to think about gunpowder.

The hanging terrace of the Brighton Hotel afforded a perfect view over the bay. The spectacle at midnight was unforgettable, it will remain as one of the most important memories in my life: from ships anchored in the bay, fireworks were launched to the prolonged hoot of sirens.

During the dictatorship Valparaíso's fireworks had been a kind of secret popular response to Pinochet's gunpowder, which meant some on the eve of a new century were carried away by the inertia of so many years of silence and crime and, from the Brighton's terrace, took up the famous resistance song: 'He's going down, going down . . .'

Tonight I could write the saddest verses, I thought as

I traced the gunpowder's drawings in the air. Margot and Tongoy, seeing that I was not well, tried to cheer me up, but I was very metaphysical, in my mind wandering through spaces of gunpowder and lonely cemeteries and graves full of bones without sound. And when the electric Valparaíso came to an end, it seemed to me that the night turned into a vast hospital and, like Rilke one day, I asked myself, 'So is this where people come to live? I would have said they die here.'

I looked out to sea and saw only a black tear of smoke, and slowly, as if overcome by Montano's malady, I succumbed to absolute melancholy.

I do not search for oddballs, I find them. And these oddballs – it is not easy to elude one's destiny – always have something to do with literature. In the afternoon of the first day of this century, I abandoned the Brighton's Victorian terrace, I left Margot and Tongoy getting drunk, and went for a walk on my own in the streets of Valparaíso. Although I struggled against any melancholic thought, it was impossible for me, in the air of the city, in each particle of its air, not to breathe the existence of fatality, terror, mortality.

At one point during the walk, in an attempt to escape from so much mortal air, my eyes came to rest on the tender image of a young woman who was seated on a bench, rocking a child's pram. I had the unhappy idea of approaching her. As I went to sit beside her on the bench, I saw that the child had a very visible rash on its forehead. I immediately moved away. The child slept with its mouth open, it was alive, and I thought that this was the important thing. It was best to be content with little, I told myself. The fact that it was alive was already a lot. It was best not to ask a great deal more of life.

I ended up at a lively-looking bar next to one of the city's countless funiculars. Very young people stood laughing in the doorway and I thought that, if I went in, it might help me to get over my depression and to forget the horrible rash on the forehead of the sleeping child. I leaned against the long, busy counter and ordered a whisky. Next to me, a man of about eighty, elegantly dressed, looked me up and down and, seeing me look at him, asked me where I came from. 'Barcelona,' I replied. I asked him where he was from. There was a short silence. 'I was French. I am the late Charles Baudelaire,' he answered.

A couple of minutes ago I decided to take an Alka-Seltzer to counteract both the excesses of lunch with Tongoy and the unsettling effects of two dry Martinis drunk on the sly prior to Rosa's return. It may not seem important for the diary that I took an Alka-Seltzer, but it is, since it is directly related to Montano. In the same way as whenever I crack open an egg I recall María's suicide – no doubt because she used to make fun of me when she saw how incompetent I was at breaking the shell – so since my trip to Nantes I have begun to associate Alka-Seltzers with the literary dryness of Montano, who is hooked on this medicine. Such an association is not without malice on my part, since it is a means of fairly constant revenge – I am always taking Alka-Seltzers – revenge for the Hamletish treatment my son meted out to me in Nantes.

But since the day before yesterday – and this is the

interesting part – the association between pills and Montano has ceased to amuse me, because two days ago my son sent me a short story (compressed like a pill) which he recently wrote and with which he has resolved his tragic inability to write. Since the day before yesterday, whenever I go to the kitchen to take an Alka-Seltzer, instead of exacting revenge by silently laughing at his literary paralysis, I remember that he has written this story, which is not exactly a bad or sluggish story, but an amazing story containing the whole of literature's memory, brilliantly compressed into barely seven pages. I remember that he has written this story – which I like so much I'm even planning to *be* this story – and it's not that I can no longer silently exact revenge on my son, but that I'm overcome with admiration and with pleasure (I should say displeasure), such is the way of things.

Edmond Jabès said that, whenever one writes, one runs the risk of never writing again. Paraphrasing Jabès, I have to say that during my stay in Chile, whenever I spoke to Rosa on the phone, I had the impression I was running the risk of never speaking to her again. From the first phone conversation to the last, I was completely baffled. Rosa's attitude could not have been more odd, everything she said seemed designed to keep me in Chile for as long as possible, sometimes she even seemed to want me never to come back. My first phone conversation with Rosa took place in the evening of the first day of the century, two hours after my strange encounter with the late Charles Baudelaire. I called her on the mobile phone which Margot lent me, I called her from the Brighton's terrace and the first thing that struck me about her was a question: 'How is your stress coming along?' She did not normally use such language. The word 'stress' in itself was ugly, nor did I think it could be applied to me, who bear scant resemblance to a stressed executive. I protested, without knowing what I was letting myself in for. I said that I had never suffered from stress and asked her what she meant by this. 'Heavens above! What is wrong with you then? Montano's malady, literature sickness? I can see you're still thinking about everything in literature. You've given yourself away, you're as bad as ever.' Clearly her words were unfair, no doubt she was speaking with premeditated aggressiveness; what was unclear was why she was behaving in this way. With a choice of good, serene words in an effort to be conciliatory, I told her that I was well again, that Margot and a friend of hers who was identical to Nosferatu had talked to me about dogfights in the air and railway accidents and that I no longer thought in literature at all, at least not in the exaggerated fashion in which I had been doing so in Barcelona. 'You're surely not telling me that you're planning to return?' she then asked me. I was both surprised and understandably hurt. 'I don't follow you. Of course I want to come back soon. I'm already much better. And besides, I never said I was going to stay in Chile for the rest of my life,' I answered. 'Come back soon? Have you gone mad? Listen, I want you back in Barcelona when you're fully cured, without a trace of stress,' she said. Her words sounded almost provocative, my surprise grew by the minute. I am not overly jealous, but I would have to be an absolute fool not to suspect that Rosa might have sent me to Chile to make it easier for her to see someone. 'You're acting very strange,' I told her. These words were my downfall. 'What did you just say?' she asked. I told her again that she was acting very strange, and then she hung up on me and I was left staring in bewilderment at the bay and the horizon. I handed Margot the mobile phone. Both she and Tongoy had been listening to the conversation and were as surprised as I was at the outcome. 'Didn't she even want to speak to me?' asked Margot. 'To Nosferatu, I'm sure she didn't,' joked Tongoy. I decided to borrow the phone again and to call Rosa back, I couldn't leave it like this. 'What do you want now?' were her first, unpleasant words to me. I know I shouldn't have, but I hazarded the following reply: 'To know why you don't want me to come back.' She hung up for a second time.

In view of the tragedy, Margot strove to reassure me. 'The poor thing has a colossal hangover because of New Year's Eve,' she said. I was incapable of putting two words together, I was not only confused, I felt I had been humiliated in front of my friends. In an attempt to help me, I suppose, Margot changed the subject, redirected the conversation and proceeded to talk about a friend of hers, Mari Pepi Colomer, the Catalan pioneer of female aviation – I had never heard of this lady – a woman of Margot's generation, a compatriot of mine who for a large number of years had been living in England, on her British husband's country estate, surrounded by lots of horses. 'It's funny,' said Margot, 'as a girl I also lived surrounded by horses, there is obviously a relation between these animals and pioneers of aviation. What do you think?' I couldn't think, I was very disturbed and worried. My disquiet was so apparent that Tongoy, who was wearing a Panama hat, felt obliged to entertain me and began to remove his hat several times and to greet me with excessive theatricality.

Literarily predisposed as I am, I don't know how it happened but, seeing Tongoy act like this, I was reminded of the figure of Hölderlin, shut away in the home of the carpenter Zimmer as a result of madness. The story goes that, when a potential customer visited Zimmer, the mad poet would remove his hat and begin to greet the customer with exaggerated reverential gestures, in a way that was completely over the top. Probably all that Hölderlin intended with these gestures was to manifest the *true* gesture of the poet, for whom the other, whoever it may be, is someone deserving veneration and respect.

It may be said, therefore, that in Tongoy's excessive theatrics I saw a tribute to Hölderlin and a gesture of friendly respect towards me. But I didn't say anything, I continued with my sombre rictus, I couldn't understand what had happened to me with Rosa. I didn't want, however, to arouse pity in my friends and, making a concerted effort, in a humorous tone I proceeded to relate my recent walk around Valparaíso and my strange encounter with the late Charles Baudelaire.

'Well!' Tongoy remarked when I had finished speaking. 'It really is amazing, you can't escape from these two circles, literature and death, it's amazing, even Baudelaire appears to you, uniting both things in his person. But I think, as I told you yesterday, that, instead of constantly returning to literature and death, you should be less self-centred and concern yourself with the death of literature, a demise that is fast approaching if things continue as bad as they are at the moment.'

That I think about the death of literature, this is what Tongoy was recommending. It struck me as a great idea, and I told him so at lunch today.

The death of literature. There on the Brighton's terrace, listening to Tongoy's words, I first looked out over the bay, then at Margot, who was smiling at me – as if to say, 'That's right, the death of literature' – and finally I gazed back at the bay and the horizon and imagined that on the very edge of the horizon I could see some diffuse clouds which announced a severe storm and, with it, the end of books, the triumph of the unliterary, of false writers.

Tongoy, as if reading my thoughts, noticing that I could not take my eyes off the horizon, remarked, 'Like the sun, you can't look the death of literature in the face'. At that moment, more than one of Fellini's actors, Tongoy resembled a doctor specialising in Montano's malady, and I thought – I think – that it really wasn't a bad idea to stop trying to diminish the influence of literature in my life and to pay greater attention to the obvious threat closing in on literature in today's world.

At this precise moment, something happened that was very important for me. I don't know how, but I was reminded of a sentence by Nietzsche which I have always read in a thousand different ways, it depends always on the meaning I wish to give it each time. It is a sentence I apply to a whole range of circumstances: 'One day my name will be associated with the memory of something tremendous – a crisis without equal on earth.'

One cannot go against one's imagination, and at that instant, on the terrace of the Brighton, I imagined my name and surname in a few years' time evoking the brutal memory of a crisis in literature which humanity will have overcome – the imagination, when it's very powerful, is capable of these things – thanks to my heroic conduct, Quixote, spear in hand, against the enemies of the literary.

What is more, I also imagined, or rather I had the strangest thought a madman has ever had in this world and I told myself, that, following Tongoy's instructions, from now on it would be expedient and necessary, both for the increase of my honour and for the good health of the republic of letters, for me to embody literature itself in flesh and blood, to embody this literature that lives with the threat of death at the start of the twenty-first century: to become *literature incarnate* and to try to save it from possible extinction by reviving it, just in case, in my own person, my own sorrowful face.

I said nothing at that moment to Tongoy about the thoughts that had just come to me, but I was silently grateful to him for having been able wisely to redirect the narrow spectrum of my personal obsessions into a much broader theme: that of the death of literature. I was also grateful to him for having helped me to see that literature could suffer, as I did, from its own Montano's malady and it was only logical that the fight against literature's sickness should take absolute priority over the fight against my own illness, which, all things considered, was so small compared with the common illness.

That night, in my hotel room, observing my sorrowful face in the mirror, I told myself that at the start of the twenty-first century – obviously I was already thinking like an open book – literature could not breathe at all well, despite the irresponsible optimism of some. Literature, I told myself, is being harried as never before by Montano's malady, which is a dangerous illness with a fairly complex geographical map, composed of the most diverse and varied provinces or maleficent zones; one of them, the most visible and possibly the most populous, certainly the most mundane and stupid, has been harrying literature since the time writing novels became the favourite sport of an almost infinite number of people. It is not easy for a dilettante to start constructing buildings or, straight away, to make bicycles without having previously acquired a specific skill; it is the case, however, that everyone, precisely everyone in the world, feels able to write a novel without ever having learned even the most rudimentary tools of the trade; it is also the case that the abrupt rise of such copyists has had a seriously prejudicial effect on readers, nowadays plunged into noticeable confusion.

That night, in my hotel room, I turned all these things over in my mind and mentally thanked Tongoy every quarter of an hour for having moved me, albeit only slightly, away from my *literatosis* – how Onetti terms the obsession for the world of books – and for having reminded me how uncertain the future of literature was. That night, in front of the mirror that reflected my sorrowful face, I ended up concentrating my thoughts on the most mundane and stupid province of literary Montano's malady, and I told myself that this geographical zone had existed for many years, in reality Milton, for example, already spoke of it when he claimed to have visited a nebulous grey zone, a province whose inhabitants were in the habit of crushing the elegance of spirit and the literary tradition's most noble currents. Schopenhauer also seemed to have visited this mundane and stupid province when he said that literature was like life: whichever way one turns, one immediately comes face to face with the incorrigible mass of humanity, which multiplies everywhere, filling and staining everything, like flies in summer, and hence the proliferation of bad books, what he termed *parasitic tares.*

Such tares are rife in the most mundane and stupid province on the map of literary Montano's malady, a highly complex map where we find a wide variety of provinces, warrens, nations, bends, woods, islands, shady corners, cities. The truth is that, since that night in the hotel in Valparaíso, I have frequently toured this map; I have often toured this map which I am slowly drawing and which also, by the way, almost on the outskirts – I haven't even drawn it yet – contains a slum called Spain, where a kind of traditional, nineteenth-century realism is encouraged and where it is normal for a majority of critics and readers to despise thought. A pearl of a slum. And as if this were not enough, this slum is connected by an underwater tunnel – which cannot even appear on the map – with a particular territory that recalls the island of Realism discovered by Chesterton, an island whose inhabitants passionately applaud everything they consider to be real art and cry, 'This is Realism! This is things as they really are!' The Spanish are among those who think that, if you repeat something often enough, it will end up being true.

'OK, now I'm boarding the aircraft,' I said tremulously. 'It's a single-engine plane,' Margot pointed out to me.

Single-engine! The phrase inspired me with terror. It made my hairs stand on end. The plane was a Piper Dakota, which Margot occasionally borrowed from the management of Chile Aeronautics, where she had good friends who were prepared to turn a blind eye to her advanced age. I felt an understandable fear, but also, I must confess, a certain attraction towards danger.

'Danger is the axis about which the sublime life rotates,' I observed. 'Stop talking such rubbish and get in!' Margot ordered me. I obeyed. Inside the aeroplane, Tongoy was more panic-stricken than I was. In a few hours I would leave Chile, where I had already spent three fairly happy weeks, although they were overshadowed by the disquiet I felt after each phone conversation with Rosa, who sometimes would suddenly hang up, other times – if I dared to ask what the matter was – would threaten to hang up, and who never seemed to welcome the prospect of my return.

My Chilean happiness overshadowed by Rosa's inexplicable attitude, that day I boarded the intrepid Margot's Piper Dakota. The sky was overcast and the light, shining behind the low clouds, resembled a merciless, steely sword. Our flight would take us to the sun; we were heading from a cloudy Santiago to a San Fernando where the weather was good.

As soon as the single-engine plane took off, I began to have literary thoughts or, to put it another way, in order not to think about death, I began to think about the death of literature. I recalled Saint-Exupéry – so despised by Margot – the writer who for a period conveyed Chilean mail to Patagonia, crossing the Andes at night. And I reflected on Saint-Exupéry's meeting with Julien Gracq in

Nantes and on the pamphlet Gracq would write years later, 'Literature in the Stomach', in which he maintained that literary art was not only the unfortunate victim of massive massification, but was also subject to the perverse, uneducated rules of the unliterary.

Certainly all this was very interesting, I mean my literary thoughts during the flight, and it was very interesting because, since I had moved Montano's malady from a private to a public level, my own highly personal literary illness had taken a discreet back seat, but at the same time, though it may seem paradoxical, it had grown in strength and intensity, which did not worry me, quite the opposite, since my concern for the common Montano's malady allowed me to have my own Montano's malady at my ease and without the slightest remorse. To put it another way, I had begun to enjoy – and continue to enjoy very much – my recently adopted and highly responsible moral stance in relation to the grave situation facing the *truly literary* in the world. And I was, and still am, delighted to find myself at the service of a noble, superior cause which in passing afforded me a perfect excuse to keep having, even to reinforce, my own Montano's malady, now more than fully justified by the common good, and furthermore saved me the bother of having to apologise for being 'so literary'.

At this point I don't think anyone will be surprised if I say that the flight of that single-engine plane began to open itself up to interpretation as a fragmentary text. What is more, I told myself that, as soon as I returned to Barcelona, in this diary which I had left asleep at home, I would write down a series of fragments or notes on the art of being in the air, an art that for me was a question of pure balance. The single-engine plane that Margot piloted, like any other plane, flew thanks to a highly unusual series of balances and forces and was something of a metaphor for literary creation. After all, anyone writing with a sense of risk walks a tightrope and, as well as walking it, has to weave his own rope under his feet. All this came to me up above, and it also occurred to me that, just as every flight contains the possibility of falling, so every book should contain the possibility of failing. This is what I thought and shortly afterwards, carefully watching Margot handle the controls with some virtuosity, I began to wonder what will happen to us when humanism fails, of whose broken and ancient rope we have been reduced to unsteady walkers, and literature disappears.

I was wondering about this when Tongoy interrupted my concern for the other inhabitants of this world – or my navel-gazing, whichever you prefer – and announced that he was preparing in mid-flight to imitate the dragonfly-man he had played in Fellini's film. That way, he said, at the speed of this famously fast-flying insect, we would plunge headlong into the void. I didn't find the joke funny. And, to tell the truth, I didn't get over my fear until we landed and, seeing how the earth welcomed us back, I could regain the marvellous sense of security that gravity affords, though we sometimes forget it.

Back on terra firma, I looked up at the cloudless sky of San Fernando and saw a bird go by. I followed it. And it seemed to me that following it enabled me to go wherever I liked, mentally to make use of all my possible mobility. A few hours later I was flying in the direction of Barcelona, occupied in drawing an initial sketch of the geography of literary Montano's malady, with its abject zones in the shade, its provinces, religions, islands, gullies, volcanoes, lakes, warrens, bends, cities. By the time I reached Barcelona, I had turned into the topographer of Montano's malady.

As I feared, Rosa was not waiting for me at the airport. She had hung up the last time we spoke, she had hung up after telling me that she didn't like the way I kept repeating my estimated time of arrival. The lights at home were all switched off, except for those in the kitchen, where I came across a cold dinner which Rosa had left out for me, a dinner consisting entirely of a grotesque bowl of soup containing letters, a terrible soup, a soup as chilly as the reception being offered to me, a cold soup with a note from Rosa beside it: 'The sky is a very beautiful faded pink colour and the air is cold as I write you this note to tell you that this afternoon I have taken off with John Cassavetes, I have gone with him to Los Angeles. Farewell, dear, farewell. Have fun!'

The only consolation I derived from reading this strange note was that Cassavetes was dead. I suddenly recalled the many films by Cassavetes which Rosa and I had seen together. I stood there, sad and disconcerted, going weak at the knees, not knowing which way to turn, until eventually I decided to go to the bedroom, from where I could call Rosa's mobile phone. On switching on the bedroom light, I discovered Rosa seated on the bed, wearing an impeccable nightdress, smiling, telling me that Cassavetes could wait.

'I don't understand,' I said. 'Has monsieur eaten his daily literature, his blessed alphabet soup?' she asked me.

'What?' 'Has monsieur had his daily Montano's malady, albeit cold?'

She had behaved like this – she would tell me a little later – to try to make me show more interest in her and so to help me come out of myself and of books and be less at the mercy of what she described in typically light-hearted fashion as 'my mental problem in the form of alphabet soup'. 'OK,' I said to her, 'that's enough of your charming show, which is very apt for a film director.' 'What?' she exclaimed. And for a moment I was afraid she would throw the bedroom telephone at my head.

To tell the truth, I feel only admiration for the tactics Rosa decided to adopt in order to alleviate my Montano's malady and enable her to occupy more time in my life. Whereas Tongoy had been able to relieve my personal illness by making it universal, Rosa had come up with the no less brilliant strategy of channelling some of my attention, albeit in a highly rarefied way, in her direction. And without a doubt the manoeuvre has worked a treat, I have spent the last few weeks following Rosa around, helping her like a madman in the preparations to shoot her film in the Azores, collaborating on the script more than was planned, suggesting that she hire an actor of Felipe Tongoy's international stature, assisting her in any way I knew how. I should add, however, that I have not just been working on the film, but with absolute secrecy have continued immersed in compiling the geography of Montano's malady and in planning to combat the death of literature.

It was the day before yesterday, as I said, when Montano's envelope arrived with its manuscript, a short story bearing the title '11 rue Simon-Crubellier', which I take to be in sincere tribute to Georges Perec and the house in Paris where this French writer centred the history of the world.

The story opens with a quotation from Macedonio Fernández with which my son presumably wishes to comment ironically on the lifting of his writer's block: '"Everything has been written, everything has been said, everything has been done," God heard someone telling him when he had yet to create the world, when there still wasn't anything. "Someone already told me that," he rejoined perhaps from the old, cleft Void. And he began.'

The story in admirable fashion condenses into seven short but intense pages the whole of the history of literature, viewed as a succession of writers unexpectedly inhabited by the personal memory of other, earlier writers: the history of literature seen with a reverse chronology, since it starts with the contemporary period – Julio Arward, Justo Navarro, Pessoa, Kafka – and travels back in time – Twain, Flaubert, Verne, Hölderlin, Diderot, Sterne, Shakespeare, Cervantes, Fray Luis de León, among others – until it reaches the Epic of Gilgamesh; the history of literature seen as a strange current of mental air of sudden alien memories which with unexpected visits are meant to have assembled a closed circuit of involuntarily stolen reminiscences.

I liked the story. It has moments of high poetic tension, as for example when Pessoa is visited by the memories of a Prague writer he has never heard of and then sees a Chinese wall being built and a series of endless galleries under threat, but at the same time perfectly articulated as a challenge against the wear and tear of time; he also sees a hunger artist giving a lecture in Budapest and a cat advising a mouse to change direction because a dangerous *odradek* is approaching.

I liked the story. When I finished reading it, my memory was infiltrated by something Wallace Stevens once said: 'The reader became the book; and summer night was like the conscious being of the book.'

When I reached the end of Montano's story, I played at imagining that I felt the temptation to become the story, that I felt the temptation to embody it and become a walking story, to change my name to '11 rue Simon-Crubellier', turning into a story-man who would fight against the disappearance of literature by reviving the abridged history of its memory in his own person.

Today, while having lunch with Tongoy here in Barcelona, I was unable to contain myself and I told him that the day before yesterday I had played at imagining that I felt the temptation to become the story I had just been sent by my son Montano.

Tongoy smiled at me, lit a cigarette, remained sunk in thought for a moment, and finally said, 'Listen, I'd like to know how one should dress to *be* literature's memory.' He then laughed out loud, looking more like Nosferatu than ever. He told me that he likes such games and, as soon as we are filming on the island of Fayal, in the Azores, he plans to behave, without attracting undue attention, as if he were my assistant in my crusade against Montano's malady. 'I will be your secret squire,' he said to me, 'but only if you give me a handsome reward: the governorship of the island of Barataria, for example.'

⋆ ⋆ ⋆

Here I am in Fayal, opposite Pico, more literature-sick than ever, but a little less naive; I make Rosa think that I'm not so ill, I talk to her about everything except literature and sometimes I even appear foolish, but the important thing is that she fail to notice that for some time now not only does literature no longer stifle me, but I consider it outrageous to have to apologise for being so literary; the important thing is that she fail to notice that recently I have taken upon myself the responsibility of combating the death of literature. I don't need any more problems with Rosa, so I dissemble as much as I can. For example, I am careful to hide the map of Montano's malady which I work on every day. But sick, what is literature-sick, I am as never before, and secretly I rejoice.

I am in Fayal and I am, or rather I pretend to be, a manuscript, I play at dreaming that I am literature's errant memory, I am in the Azores, on the island of Fayal, opposite the island of Pico, and this time I have travelled with my diary, I am in the middle of the Atlantic, far from Europe and far from America, with the vague suspicion that distance is these islands' charm. I am in the Hostal de la Santa Cruz, in Fayal, opposite the mysterious island of Pico. Night is falling, the final colours of the afternoon – as Borges would say – are fainting. I am on my room's balcony, with its perfect view of the small harbour and behind it, extinct in the mist and twilight, the imposing volcano on the island which I visited today with Tongoy, the island of Pico, the strangest of the Azores, an island that sometimes, only sometimes, seems the closest thing to paradise, other times – there are no middle terms in this place – to hell. As we approached Pico this morning, Tongoy suddenly asked me:

'Will there not be another death in paradise?'

I understood that he sensed what I was sensing, but it is also true that the question appeared peculiar to me at the time. However that may be, the preparations for tonight's filming are in the final stages in Fayal's harbour. Today is the first day since we arrived on the island that Rosa has not filmed in daylight, because it is Carnival and the old whalers consider this festival to be sacred and have asked to spend it with their families or their solitude. I can see Rosa leaning against a harbour wall, I take the binoculars to observe her more closely and she spots me and makes strange gestures at me, which I am not prepared to decipher in case I misconstrue them and, above all, because I do not want to waste the precious time I have to devote to this diary and to my secret activity of extending my complex drawing of the map of Montano's malady. I move out of Rosa's field of vision, meaning I enter the room and go to where she cannot see me, so I perversely enter the room – as if I were a film-maker suddenly abandoning an outside shot – but a few seconds later I return to the balcony, where I observe that Rosa is no longer making gestures at me, and then – even more perversely than before – I am the one making gestures, I make them at the paradise and hell of Pico's volcano.

Then I take up the binoculars again and focus on the old whalers, some of whom are standing around Rosa, waiting for tonight's filming to start. Among them is Tongoy, wearing a horrible black and white striped T-shirt, smoking and pensively looking out to sea, looking like Nosferatu at dusk and stranger than ever in that grotesque sea dog's outfit he is dressed in. Nearby, a few real whalers stare at him blatantly, circling him slowly, watching the intruder, I imagine, in some surprise, moving as if they were part of the landscape, as if they were mysteriously connected to the evening light. Their old harpoons, no doubt loaded with a thousand stories, are balanced against the fragile boats on which until not long ago they put to sea. In fact everything, absolutely everything at this hour, seems very slow, dilatory, bloodied by the huge dusk, here in Fayal, on this side of paradise. I have hidden the map I am drawing, hidden also my literary illness, and this forces me sometimes to behave like an idiot; I should like to hide everything, but the diary is always in view, I know that Rosa won't dare to look at it.

As I contemplate the drawn-out dusk, I remember something Gonçalves Azevedo, the owner of Café Sport, told me. Yesterday he was talking to me about a certain fish, the *moray*, which they used to catch on this island at night, under the waxing moon. To attract the fish they would sing a song without words: a mournful song that seemed to emerge from the bottom of the sea or from souls lost in the night. 'Nobody knows this song any more,' he told me, 'it has been forgotten, and this may be a good thing, because it contained a curse.'

I cannot help thinking that this curse has relocated to the innards of Pico's volcano. I sensed it being there today, at that house at the foot of the volcano, and the truth is that, after the experience in the home of that horrible man called Teixeira, I have decided to include the volcano on my map of the illness. I drew it a moment ago and on the inside placed underground galleries where moles, devoted to conspiring against literature, are meant to be working away silently and invisibly. Perhaps these galleries are what Tongoy sensed or saw when on the ferry this morning, as we approached the island and the volcano, despite the beauty of the moment and of the landscape, or perhaps because of all this, he asked me whether there wouldn't be another death in paradise.

If I were foolish, I would be proud to know Montano's story off by heart, but I am not going to commit such a stupid act. Besides, I don't know the story off by heart, I simply *remember it*. Although it's only seven pages long, in the end I have resisted memorising it as if I were obliged to be like one of those grotesque book-men in *Fahrenheit 451*, Ray Bradbury's novel.

What I have done is take on the memory of literature's eccentric history in Montano's free version and so at times, when I enter a trance, I am that memory, even though I do not recite my son's short story all the way through. I merely remember the story as best I can, I remember passages. Sometimes I am visited by one of them. Just now, for example, while I was resting on the balcony – watching the filming start as Pico's volcano vanished into the shadows of the night – I was visited by the recollection of that Montanesque scene in which we see Kafka writing in his diary and suddenly being visited by certain itinerant memories of Mark Twain, an author he is not especially drawn to.

It is night-time in Prague on 16 December 1910. At that

precise moment Kafka is writing: 'I shall never abandon my diary, I have to cling to it, I have nowhere else to do this. I should like to describe the feeling of happiness that rises inside me at times, such as now.'

Immediately after writing the words 'such as now', Kafka begins to be visited by Twain's itinerant memories and with some amazement relives the moment in 1897 when Twain, during one of his stops on his trip to Europe, greets the Austro-Hungarian emperor Franz Josef and tells him that a monarch, however good he may be, deserves the same respect as a pirate who on Sundays carries out acts of charity.

Kafka listens to Twain's words as if they had been uttered by a second-rate literary bumblebee and sees how the emperor arches his eyebrows, but Kafka does not consider this relevant to his diary and continues recording his personal impressions, as if nothing untoward had happened: 'It really is a fizzy thing, which fills me to the brim with light and agreeable quaverings . . .'

In a footnote the narrator of Montano's story contends that this 'fizzy thing' is a timid or veiled, perhaps even involuntary, allusion to Twain, who with his regrettable operatics infiltrated Kafka's memory without being invited.

I went out on to the balcony to see how the filming was coming along and, as if I had a veil in front of me, saw nothing of what was happening at that moment because my memory was infiltrated by the recollection of what I witnessed during the filming yesterday morning: Rosa directing the artificial creation at sea of plumes of vapour which the sperm whales expel through their blow-holes and which in the past would have had the look-outs firing warning shots for the whalers to run straight to their fragile boats.

But that was yesterday. Strangely enough, when I light a cigarette, the smoke, instead of veiling my vision of reality even more, unveils it at once and finally I am able to observe what is going on in tonight's filming. Not that much is going on. Tongoy, for example, is leaning against a harbour wall on which there are various messages written by people from the boats which cross the Atlantic, messages from life's castaways. I deduce that Tongoy is bored. I take the binoculars and scrutinise the expression on Rosa's face. She looks tired and on edge, the filming appears not to be going altogether well.

I enter the room, hide my map of Montano's malady, lie on the bed, my memory is infiltrated by the recollection of something César Aira told me in the Café Tortoni, in Buenos Aires, one day when we fell into a bizarre conversation about the essence of literature. We had started discussing the review I had written of his last book and in a few seconds, with barely any transition from one theme to the other, we became engrossed, almost without realising, in the subject of the essence of literature. 'As a teenager, reading Borges,' Aira said to me, 'I saw where the essence of literature was. This was definitive, but later I also discovered that literature does not have one, but many historical and contingent essences. So it was easy to escape from Borges' orbit, as easy as going back, or as never having escaped.'

Here in Fayal the subject of the essence of literature seems even stranger to me than on that day. However, I focus on it. Extreme tension on my balcony in the Hostal de la Santa Cruz. I look in the direction of Pico, although I can't see anything – not even a trace of the volcano, the night appears to have swallowed it up – and start thinking about the moles I saw there today. Then I stop looking at the invisible volcano and suddenly, completely out of the blue, my memory is infiltrated by Maurice Blanchot; I see him on the evening he said he was fed up with always hearing the same two questions from journalists who were interviewing writers. One question was: 'What are the tendencies in today's literature?' The other: 'Where is literature heading?'

'Literature is heading towards itself, towards its essence, which is its disappearance,' said Blanchot many evenings after having said he was fed up with the same two questions.

Out of a pure sense of the game, albeit also guided by a natural survival instinct, I tell myself that I should immediately turn into the essence of literature, *embody* it in my own modest person. But fortunately I realise that I am taking my responsibilities too far and in fact it is not a good idea, it really is not a good idea, for me to be the very essence of literature, for me to be Montano's well-being or, which is more or less the same thing, to be the eternal rest of literature in its tomb. It is not a good idea, really it isn't! The most prudent course of action would be to continue stealthily being the memory and not the disappearance of literature. It's the least I could do.

Will literature never disappear?

I remember Scott Fitzgerald in Montano's story paying

an unexpected visit to Juan Rulfo's memory and dictating to him in Coyoacán this sentence by Pedro Páramo: 'Nothing can last so long.'

Whatever Tongoy may say, that man Teixeira we found hiding away on the island of Pico seems disturbingly to embody the new man, the man to come or perhaps the man who has already arrived; at least in Pico there is a specimen of what awaits us, his name is Teixeira and I would say that his personality is constantly bidding farewell to a secular way of living the world, of living and conceiving it. I shan't easily forget Teixeira. Stunned by his dehumanised, barbarous laugh, I thought about something Bismarck said when he first saw the modern ships in the port of Hamburg: 'Here begins a new era, which I cannot understand.'

I remove the map, my private geography of the illness, from its hiding place and look at it again, but without paying too much attention, when suddenly, absent-mindedly, I discover that in the underground galleries inside the volcano, where the pencil has strayed most freely, an abyss has sprung up which I did not know and which has probably arisen – like the moles – from the corrupt and rough mental and moral subsoil I thought I observed in the cracks of the pathetic laughter of Teixeira, the man of the future, the man to come.

Will there not be another death in paradise?

TONGOY

* * *

In Pico there is the volcano, which takes up virtually the whole island and is the highest mountain in Portugal. There is the volcano and three coastal enclaves: Madalena (where the ferries from Fayal dock), São Roque and Lajes, which is where supposedly – today we hardly saw a soul – most people live. Lajes has a whaling museum and an enormous church, disproportionate to the size of the island.

We hardly saw anybody this morning in the streets of Madalena when we arrived. Four or five passengers got off the ferry, no more; they got off with their bags and baskets, and in no time at all disappeared down the silent, deserted streets of this ghost town. I asked Tongoy if he knew what we were doing visiting Pico.

'One visits Pico for the experience,' he answered me.

There was nobody in the main square, only two taxi-drivers with their vehicles parked opposite the small town hall (no doubt they had been warned from the pier in Fayal of the imminent arrival of two visitors, people from the film); the two taxi-drivers did not address each other, one was young and looked like a criminal, the other was noticeably old. The young one, with a stupid smile, seemed confident that we would hire him.

We scoured every inch of Madalena in search of a bar or some incentive to stay there, but everything was shut, not even a bar open, not even someone other than the two taxi-drivers, so we made our way back to the main square and again examined the two men; it felt as if we were in a brothel and had to choose between one prostitute and another.

The ferry did not return to Fayal for another three

hours, and that was supposing it would, since a fairly spectacular black cloud was approaching. It became very clear that we had little option but to seek refuge in the old man's taxi and to go to Lajes, to see if there were more people and more things there; perhaps the whaling museum was open – the old man told us he didn't know. 'One visits Lajes for the experience,' I remarked as the taxi pulled away. Tongoy gave me a very dirty look, it struck me – I had already noticed it on the ferry – that he was in a foul mood.

'Have you seen the other cloud?' he asked me. 'Because there are two black clouds, although you can't see one of them. In a short while, this will be one of the darkest places on earth. I think one visits Pico for the experience, but I also think we made a mistake in coming here.'

There was only one black cloud, but I preferred to keep quiet. At that point the old taxi-driver began to act as impromptu tour-guide, he began to explain that there are only three towns in Pico and the rest is lava rock with the occasional vineyard and the odd wild pineapple. Then he said that he had only once left the island, to go to Fayal on honeymoon.

As the taxi-driver was speaking, I paid closer attention to him and thought I observed that he looked a lot like Fernando Pessoa – Pessoa past the age of eighty. I had the happy idea of mentioning this to Tongoy, who reacted very badly and told me he would have had no problem laughing if I were joking, but he was sure I was being serious, and he found this awful, clearly I wasn't just literature-sick, I was literature-rotten.

I preferred to keep quiet and watch the countryside

slowly gliding past the taxi window. Pico's road, the only one on the island, is terrifyingly sad in winter, but if you also happen to be travelling with the old taxi-driver and Tongoy in a bad mood, you can fall into a depression lasting the rest of your days. The road runs alongside the breakwater, with many curves and deep potholes, overlooking a rebellious blue sea. The road, gloomy and narrow, crosses a stony and melancholic landscape, with occasional isolated houses on small hills, in winter normally swept by the wind.

'Here,' said the taxi-driver, 'there's nothing left, but in the past, when I was a young man, this was full of vineyards which somehow grew from the difficult volcanic soil, and they made Pico wine. At the time of the grape harvest, there were parties, lots of parties.' On either side of the gloomy road could be seen the ruins of the old lordly mansions belonging to the families in Fayal who had made their fortunes producing wine in the lava soil of the neighbouring island. Of these once great villas, where the grape harvest would have been celebrated, there remained only a few stones and the deep nostalgia of the taxi-driver, who occasionally, with leaden and melancholic insistence, punctuating his cordial monologue, would say, in a Portuguese marked with a heavy Azorian accent:

'*Festas, muitas festas.*'

Leaden nostalgia for ancient days of splendour, in the most repellent cordial tone.

'*Festas, muitas festas.*'

The fifth time he said it, I fell into a trance and my brain began to whirl round. One of many things I remembered was that I had always to be on the alert against literary Montano's malady. In short, I couldn't help it, though I recognise that Tongoy was partially right when later he implied that I had overdone it and had lost the plot. In short, I couldn't help it: the stupid poetic tone of the melancholic taxi-driver reminded me that there is an activity we might call Proustian, which involves recalling facts from the past with sensibility and intelligence. The taxi-driver seemed unaware of this, he seemed incapable of suspecting that there is a magnificent literary background in the art of telling melancholic stories; the taxi-driver seemed entirely entrenched in the memory of some poor, unfortunate girlfriend he had once had at the time of the grape harvest; the taxi-driver ended up getting on my nerves.

'*Festas, muitas festas.*'

I cannot stand cordial people. If it depended on them, literature would have disappeared from the face of the earth. However, 'normal' people are highly regarded wherever you go. All murderers, as shown on television, in the eyes of their neighbours are always normal, cordial people. Normal people are accomplices in literary Montano's malady. This is what I thought today at midday inside a Pico taxi, while recalling what Zelda said to her husband, Scott Fitzgerald, how no one but they had the right to live, and those other bastards were destroying their world.

I hate the vast majority of 'normal' human beings who day by day are destroying my world. I hate people who are very good-natured because no one has given them the opportunity to know what evil is and so to choose good freely; I have always thought that such good-natured people are of an extraordinary malice in the making. I detest them, I often think like Zelda and regard them all as bastards.

I could not stop myself and I gave the taxi-driver a mental blow to the head. I waited for one of those brief pauses in his pseudo-tourist monologue which ended with the inevitable '*festas, muitas festas*' to ask him point-blank, as I stood at the ready against Montano's malady, if he had ever heard of a writer living in Pico.

It was horrible and ludicrous at the same time, because the man understood that I wanted to know if there were typewriters on the island, typewriters for offices, and proceeded to talk about the lack both of offices and of suitable office equipment on the island. This was the last straw. I interrupted him and asked him if he had ever read Proust, who also talked about parties, lots of parties, but didn't talk much about offices. Silence. Then I told him that his cordial and anti-literary discourse simply disgusted me. Clearly he didn't understand a word of what I was saying and Tongoy intervened very angrily. 'I think,' he said to me, 'we've had enough of your obsession, illness, call it what you like. Try to calm down. And treat the taxi-driver with some respect.' I wasn't expecting such an outburst from Tongoy, I thought he was my accomplice or squire, but it was also true that I had taken my game too far.

In a show of repentance, I softened my manners, leaned forwards and whispered directly in the taxi-driver's ear; I repeated my question in a slow and careful voice, I explained to him – using both Spanish and Portuguese – that I only wanted to know if there were writers – people with an interest in literature – on the island. Finally I got the message through. 'Ah,' he said, 'you mean book people, people with books, there's one on the island, he's not a book person, but he was.' The wretch let out a mysterious laugh. 'He lives on the other side of Lajes, at the end of a dirt track, here we all call him Teixeira, we can go and see him if you like.'

The mysterious laugh aroused my curiosity. 'He's not a book person, but he was.' I thought of Montano, of whom something similar could be said when in Nantes he was suffering from writer's block. At this point we passed through the deserted town of São Roque, nobody in the streets. The hope that there might be somebody in Lajes. I asked the taxi-driver if there would be somebody in Lajes. 'Teixeira,' he answered, and the wretch laughed. I asked if there was no one else living there. He shrugged his shoulders and said there might be, might not be, he was from Madalena. 'Where there is nobody,' remarked Tongoy, whom anything this lunchtime seemed to put in a bad mood. 'That's right,' said the taxi-driver a little uneasily, observing Tongoy's Draculean face in the rear-view mirror with a certain amount of mistrust. 'And why is there nobody?' asked Tongoy in an almost frightening tone of voice, as if his life depended on that question. 'Carnival,' answered the frightened taxi-driver.

As was to be expected, the whaling museum in Lajes was firmly closed. What wasn't closed in Pico? In Lajes only the monumental church was open, and a small bar modelled on an Irish pub. While the taxi-driver stayed in his car, waiting for us to have a look at the two places that were open, we entered the church, where there was absolutely nobody and where what was on view can be seen in so many of the world's churches; we continued to look at it for some time, we didn't have much else to do: carpets, chalices, pews, missals, candles, hassocks, dried flowers, an unobtrusive organ, rancid silence. 'What will happen on the day churches cease to make sense?' Tongoy asked me. Had we already visited Teixeira by then, I could have answered him: 'Well, the new man, the Teixeiras of the new world will visit them in the same way we are visiting this island, without understanding a thing.'

In the pub, which was completely empty – there was only a young waiter dozing behind the bar – Tongoy ordered a beer and asked me if I had realised that the two black clouds had disappeared. I replied that I wasn't surprised the weather had changed, every day here it seemed to change more quickly. Tongoy then declared himself happy that I was talking about the atmospheric conditions in the Azores and not seeing Pessoa whichever way I turned. I ordered a Cardhu whisky with water. 'Sacrilege,' Tongoy said. 'I'm sorry,' I was forced to reply, 'it wasn't my intention to offend you.' 'But you don't order a Cardhu with water,' he said with indignation. We drank in silence. The beer must have gone straight to his head, because he suddenly asked me what I was drawing the map of Montano's malady for and why I kept hiding it and didn't show it to Rosa and why I pretended in front of her by making her believe I was enjoying a peaceful, curative rest when in fact I spent the day believing I was the Don Quixote of the Azores, I was more literature-sick than ever and, though I did not realise it, I was unbearable and that was why Rosa had not wanted to accompany us to Pico, because deep down, though she did not wish to accept it, she sensed that I was worse than ever.

I didn't even feel like making a joke of it and telling him, for example, that I thought he was a better squire than that, a better accomplice in a game we had started for fun in Barcelona, fun stupidly wasted in that pub which it would be better if we left. 'No way,' he said, ordering another beer and another whisky. It came straight from the heart, very spontaneously, and I said to him, 'Listen, if you're in love with Rosa, all you have to do is wait for the film to end and you can run off with her.' He looked at me as if he could not believe his ears. For my part, this brief scene of unfounded jealousy suggested to me an idea for a role I wish to incorporate into the lecture I must give in Budapest, I think at the end of June. I took out a pencil and a notebook and jotted down the idea. 'I know what you're writing there, you're mourning the fact I didn't go along with your game, but you should remember that a squire is obliged to keep his master's feet on the ground, especially if his master has ideas above his station,' Tongoy said. With the third beer, he asked me if I had heard of Flutterbudget Center. 'Nope,' I said, pretending to be a boxer who raises his guard as a precaution. 'Well, it's on a hill, in the south of Oz.' 'I don't know where Oz is.' 'The inhabitants of Oz who show signs of becoming a Flutterbudget are sent there to live.' 'I don't know why this is relevant,' I protested. 'It is relevant because Flutterbudgets, like you, are harassed by imaginary dangers and obsessed by the disasters that might overcome them if the things they imagine were to happen.' I simply told him that he couldn't hold his drink, at which point he ordered his fourth beer and my fourth whisky and this landed us in certain chaos, until eventually we began to study the possibility of visiting Teixeira and finding out what kind of writer this man hiding in a house on the outskirts of Lajes had been. We studied the possibility, thought so hard that by mutual agreement – we had never been so much in agreement – we eventually asked the taxi-driver to take us to Teixeira's home. Halfway there, as we were driving along the dirt track, Tongoy leaned on my shoulder and said to me, 'I was talking to you as a friend, it hurts me to see you take so seriously the fight against Montano's malady, an imaginary disease, my darling Flutterbudget.' Instead of being grateful for his vampiric tenderness, I asked him if he had not noticed that for the extremely complex things he had to say he used a language that was very simple, very plebeian and far removed from my brilliant literary style. He looked at me again in disbelief at something he had heard from me, his eyes shone, his pointed Draculean ears had suddenly gone red. He said to me that perhaps complexity was a weakness and that I had not realised, despite being so wise and such a wonderful critic, that the strength of Kafka, for example, resided precisely in his lack of complexity. He said this and laughed, convinced that he had won the round. 'You don't know,' I replied, 'how glad I am to hear you talking about literature and also how glad I am of your strength, friend Sancho, dear squire of this poor Flutterbudget, you don't know how much I admire an ugly man like you.' In case he hadn't heard properly, I repeated the last bit:

'an ugly man like you'. He stared at me with amusement. 'I like it,' he said, 'when you're simple.'

Seasick, we stood staring at Teixeira, lost in amazement at the sight of such a strange human bird as this. He was a thin man, with sunken eyes and hands with extremely long, gnarled fingers, reminiscent of an insect's tentacles. There was Teixeira, suddenly in front of us. The truth is that, when we had him there, we didn't even remember why we wanted to see him. He made a strong impression. There was Teixeira in his large house at the foot of the volcano, on the outskirts of Lajes; there in that remote house was a man who, in his own words, had previously enjoyed writing outdoors, seated on tree stumps and surrounded by trees that were still standing. 'All my work back then,' he explained to us, 'was directed towards the clarity of the woods, I was strong and weak at the same time, now all I do is give seminars on laughter therapy.'

For someone who taught how to laugh, he was very serious. Here was a man, about fifty years of age, who seemed to have withdrawn to the world's end. He was friends with the taxi-driver and did not stop asking him if he had already told us how he was not a book person any more, but a Professor of Laughter.

For a specialist in this laughter therapy, he could not have been more serious. His head was stuck inside the collar of his military-style shirt – his trousers were also army issue – his hair neatly ordered around his scalp, fixed in place with Pico hairspray, his cheek muscles were the tensest I've ever seen. He was so serious it was frightening, and yet he claimed to be on the side of laughter and said that in the summer he earned a living from classes in which tourists discovered the benefits of laughter for their health.

He told us that in the past – it sounded as if he had made this up, perhaps so that we could have a go at laughing – he had been friends with the Duke and Duchess of Windsor, the Aga Khan, Einstein, Cole Porter, Alfonso XIII of Spain and Caruso, most of all with Caruso. He had turned down a decoration from Mussolini and received the Legion of Honour at the hands of General de Gaulle.

He had led a very mundane life, which he had abandoned in order to write seated on tree stumps in the woods, an occupation which did not help him write what he intended. One day, in Africa, he received divine enlightenment. He was lost in life because he was still writing seated on tree stumps, and because what he was trying to put down on paper was very difficult, since he was in the throes of founding a new form of art, a totally immanent form, one without dimension beyond reason. But – and this was the problem – he could not think up this form. His intention was to produce a work that would be devoid at least of the question of the possible existence or non-existence of God. However, he was unable to discover this third way. There he was in Africa in some desperation and helplessly writing seated on tree stumps, searching in vain for the aesthetic form of the future, when suddenly, in the pygmy village where he was staying, he discovered nothing less than the plenitude of laughter. It was like when Saul of Tarsus fell off his horse, but in his case he fell to the ground after having laughed a lot, he never even got on a horse.

The day he discovered that for pygmies, if you don't fall down laughing, your laughter is incomplete, he thought he could glimpse a new path in his life and he immediately gave up searching on tree stumps for the aesthetic form of the future and decided to carry out exhaustive research in the field of human laughter. In a square in New Delhi he saw three hundred people who each month got together to perform exercises that resulted in laughter. They all lay on the ground in a big spiral, resting the back of their neck on another's navel. Laughter, he explained, is contagious and, because it is linked with the diaphragm, you only need one person to start and there is an explosion of joy. He said this in such an infinitely serious way that I was afraid that the one who would explode was Teixeira, whose extreme seriousness could result in a colossal outburst of laughter. He certainly was an unusual bird. Tongoy asked him if he had a family or lived alone. And then Teixeira's head retreated even further into the collar of his military-style shirt (made in Vietnam) which he claimed a famous Portuguese comedian had given to him while staying in Pico. 'Family dead in Mozambique in laughable accident,' Teixeira replied almost telegraphically while offering us a Sinhalese tea. To drink this tea we had to sit on the floor in a corner of that house modelled, in the worst possible taste, on the inside of a tent. The last thing we felt like doing was sitting down and, given how much we had been drinking, trying a Sinhalese tea. 'Laughable accident,' Teixeira repeated with a sadness that made us sit on the floor, even if only for a minute, since it seemed that this was the only way to avoid an unnecessary mishap.

I shan't forget the tea in a hurry, it was vomit-inducing and I'd swear it wasn't Sinhalese. 'The horror, the horror!' Teixeira would occasionally exclaim with a smile. Did he mean the tea? No, he meant his pet cat, which had a broken paw. 'The horror!' he exclaimed whenever the cat drew near, and then he would be silent for a few seconds and finally come out with all kinds of transcendental phrases. 'The dead do not laugh, laughter is linked to life, only laughter has a future.' He would come out with such maxims and then fall silent again. Suddenly, when we were least expecting it, he had a fit of non-contagious, incredibly disagreeable laughter, as hideous as his tea. I have never seen anything like it. His mouth was one huge black nail with a crack down the middle. His laugh was terribly metallic, dehumanised, as if it were the laughter of the future, the laughter that awaits us, canned laughter, laughter neither with God nor without God, neither with books nor without books, something indescribable it was so repellent.

'Illness draws you in on yourself, whereas laughter makes you more open,' he said with evident satisfaction. And he added, 'The more open you are, the healthier you feel.' His maxims reminded me of a period in Spain when it was fashionable for writers who wished to advance to include maxims in their private journals, it was considered intelligent. However, it had the opposite effect. Thinking is not within the reach of everybody and these maxims which made you feel embarrassed for their authors – 'Women can wait longer than men,' for example – only reminded you that it's different for Walter Benjamin or Elias Canetti to record a thought than for the village idiot to do so.

Illness and laughter. Despite being noticeably plastered, I recalled Oscar Wilde, who said that laughter was the original approach to life: a mode of approach that persists only in criminals and artists. Was Teixeira a criminal or an artist? I set him a small trap and asked him if by illness he meant art. 'I don't even remember art,' he said, and again laughed in that horrific manner which allowed you to see or imagine underground galleries inside his atrocious mouth connecting with Pico's volcano behind him; in fact the volcano was nearer Teixeira's home than at first it seemed.

'I don't even remember art, all I have are scattered images of the tree stumps on which I once wasted my time,' he said, opening his mouth wide and revealing with clarity now the moles tirelessly working away day and night against the literary. This enabled me to confirm that Teixeira was certainly not an artist but a modern criminal, or rather the man to come or perhaps the man who has already arrived, the new man with his indifference to art past and present, a man of amoral, dehumanised laughter. A man of plastic laughter, laughter of death.

Tongoy had been right to ask whether there would not be another death in paradise, he had unwittingly acted like a prophet. I recalled a verse by T. S. Eliot: 'I should be glad of another death.' This was not my case, however, I wouldn't say I felt glad to have discovered the new man with his amoral new laugh, lurking in the centre of the mysterious, remote island of Pico. 'I suppose we'll all have to laugh more,' I remarked to Teixeira, while experiencing a strong desire to put my hand in his mouth and do my utmost to squeeze and tear out the moist skin inside his face hosting those blasted sick moles.

Laughter of (literature's) death in the middle of paradise. I mentioned this to Tongoy as we left the house at the foot of the volcano with just enough time for the taxi to take us to catch the return ferry. But Tongoy did not reply. There was a threatening black cloud again over the channel as the ferry began to make its way towards Fayal like someone travelling through the heart or the very soul of darkness. We took some seasickness tablets which didn't help at all, they merely churned up our stomachs even more, and we spent the entire journey throwing up the whisky, beer and, above all, Sinhalese tea. By the time we reached Fayal, we had turned into two new men. We must have looked awful, because Rosa, who had come to the small pier to fetch us, was visibly shocked. 'What did you see over in Pico?' she asked. 'The new man,' I replied, 'it's not every day you see the soulless man of the future, it's not every day you see the glacial, laughable face that humanity will have on the strange tomorrow that awaits us, this man is currently hiding over in Pico and he laughs a lot.'

Rosa looked at me as if to say, 'You've been drinking.' Tongoy, in turn, stood staring at me with real concern because of what I had just said. In the end he asked me who this new man was, because the taxi-driver was very old and Teixeira was a professor of laughter therapy, lost in a large house at the world's end. For him to understand that the new man we had seen, the amoral man of the future, will resemble Teixeira, I mimicked his metallic, canned and amoral laughter. Tongoy immediately realised who I was talking about and burst out laughing in such an odd way that he looked like a real wreck. It occurred to me at that moment that Rosa's film should start like this, with Tongoy pretending to be an old whaler from the Azores, with his pointed ears and vampiric teeth, reciting some strange sentences that I would write for him, reciting these strange sentences and then letting out an odd laugh, like a wreck. This laugh would be followed by the opening credits.

'Teixeira, the new man?' said Tongoy, scratching his shaved head. 'Don't make me laugh. The guy was an idiot!'

Today, seven days after that trip to Pico, Tongoy again laughed like a wreck, but this time he did it in front of the cameras. I wrote the lines with which he opens the documentary about the lost world of whalers in the Azores.

Real close-up of Tongoy, with his big, pointed ears, his shaved head and vampiric gaze directed with a harpooner's ferocity towards the camera; look in silence for a few seconds until he says, 'Everybody used to talk about Freud when I was young. But I never read him. Shakespeare didn't read him either. And I don't think Melville did. Let alone Moby Dick.'

He laughs like a wreck, the opening credits roll.

Today I spent a good while gazing at the fuzzy silhouette of Pico's volcano and pondering a question Canetti put to himself one day: 'Will God return when his creation is destroyed?'

Anxiety everywhere. I felt trapped both by the volcano and by Canetti's aphorism. To avoid growing more anxious with all this, I resorted to thinking about something else; I thought how quick Tongoy has been these last few days to reproach me for having grabbed the first advice he gave me in Chile to help me combat my literary illness. According to Tongoy, it would have been better to wait for more advice, because I had taken his idea of combating the death of literature too literally. According to Tongoy, it is characteristic of disoriented minds to be concerned about something as commonplace and at the same time as elastic as the death of literature.

Recalling Tongoy's reproaches – for example, he is always reproaching me for my ever growing obsession for transforming everything I see, systematically converting it into concepts or literary quotations, which in his opinion makes conversation with me often dull or unbearable – recalling the persecution Tongoy has been subjecting me to recently with his criticism, has, however, helped me to erase Pico's volcano and Canetti's aphorism, which had kept my soul in suspense. But a possibly regrettable thing has happened. I have erased Pico, and I have erased the aphorism, but I have not managed to take my mind off Canetti. I have not been able to forget the figure of Kien, a character in *Auto-da-Fé*, his only novel: a character who one day, at the time he usually got up, dreamed of a large library standing next to the crater of a volcano which in eight minutes would start to erupt.

Needless to say, with Canetti's return, the volcano came back – not Pico's, but as if it had been – that volcano which I thought I had lost sight of. And with it, as if this were not enough – and my mind were not giving serious signs of how literature-sick I am – the memory of Montano's story and, with this memory, that of the mountains there are in the world, all the mountains, volcanoes included, which Josep Pla – as he explained in his exemplary diary – liked so much, mountains similarly adored by André Gide, who precisely in Montano's story infiltrates the memory of a young Samuel Beckett, who is dining with some friends in Dublin and is suddenly surprised by the mental visit of Gide, who says, point-blank, that adoration for any mountain is characteristic of Protestantism.

'So what?' asks Beckett. 'First the bones,' answers Gide, disappearing as quickly as he came into the mind of Beckett at table, who years later, according to Montano, would write with clear reference to Gide and his unexpected visit to Dublin, 'What were skull to go? As good as go.'

Having freed myself of Pla's mountains, Gide's bones, Protestantism, Canetti and Beckett, Kien and everybody else, including the one who might return when his creation is destroyed; having freed myself of everybody, I was nevertheless afraid of falling into the clutches of any other writer or aphorism or passage from Montano's story, and at this point I was overcome with anxiety, I felt so stifled in reality by my literary memory that I even thought Tongoy may have been right when he warned me that I had taken my idea of combating the unliterary too far.

I felt so angst-ridden that I would have given anything – here on the island of Fayal, where I am a manuscript – to return to childhood, to the simple days when I was fascinated by space and those starry night skies, I would have given anything to return to the days of childhood when I journeyed through the space of the infinite universe and never felt the need to interpret it, let alone to transform it into a concept or literary quotation. I would have given anything, yes. Melancholy here in Fayal, as I think about those simple days in space.

At the break of day, the air was so clear that, without the help of my binoculars, I could see the foam created by the waves that were breaking against the bow of a boat sailing in the distance. For the first time in ages, an image simply referred me to that image. As if I were suddenly cured. A moment's joy at dawn. I felt so alive suddenly that I could have swum to the boat and got on board. The early morning sun shone, the surface of the water was a mirror.

This lunchtime Rosa, in a break from filming, came into the room to fetch something she had forgotten and found me sprawled on the sofa, sleeping beside the great map of Montano's malady, which was lying completely unfolded next to me.

'What is that?' she asked.

I immediately came out of the pornographic dream I was having and, still half-asleep, understood that she was asking me about my wet trousers, not about the map.

How many years was it since my last emission? I had just come in my sleep and soiled my underpants, and that is why the last thing that occurred to me was that she might be interested in the map.

'What is that?'

It was twelve o'clock or a quarter past twelve. Half an hour previously, I had fallen into a deep sleep while working on the map. I had fallen asleep while attempting to perfect the palm trees of an oasis in a South American desert, where the wind blew and human footprints and the marks of horses' hooves from remote times had remained completely untainted by the influence of literature: a desert in which all traces of time and culture had been preserved.

'What is that?'

I had fallen asleep while drawing this Latin oasis of Montano's malady. The excesses of last night in Café Sport had suddenly overpowered me on the sofa. It was a very curious labyrinthine path along which I had reached the no less curious ejaculation. There I was, working on those important details in the Latin oasis, when my brain abruptly ceased to function with agility and I felt so sleepy that I thought I was going to lose consciousness. I closed my eyes and soon fell asleep, with the map dangerously and completely unfolded next to me, my pencil on the floor. I dreamed that I was at the bar in Café Sport, drinking an exquisite Sinhalese tea. Suddenly someone gently took my arm from behind and, turning around, I encountered a faceless man, who I thought could be me. And in effect, when I looked closely, I saw that it was me, though I bore a slight resemblance to the writer Ricardo Piglia.

'To recall with a memory that is not our own,' I heard him whisper in my ear, 'is a variant of the theme of the double, but it is also a perfect metaphor for literary expression.'

'Allow me,' I said to him, 'to laugh at this situation and mention that you do not need to remind me that I always converse with the man accompanying me.'

Piglia (meaning me) did not even raise a smile. He gave me a kind of order in a very serious tone:

'What you should be drawing are the sombre classrooms of certain North American universities where they devote themselves to deconstructing literary texts.'

'OK,' I said, 'I'll draw them when I've finished the oasis. By the way, what does "deconstructing" mean?'

'No, you'll draw them right now.'

I looked at him and it was no longer Piglia or me. Now I had a tedious dwarf in front of me who was telling me that I had to draw him, because he was the king of the moles. Suddenly, perhaps because I leaned too hard against the bar in Café Sport, a strange mechanism went off and shortly afterwards I found myself on the other side of the bar, with the sensation that I was no longer in the bar but in a luxurious hotel room.

I was still accompanied by the tedious dwarf, who did not stop talking, he was an awful bore.

'I'm not the king of the moles,' he was saying, 'you don't need to include me in your map, which by the way is so detailed, so well done. If there is anyone who should be out of your map, it's me. I'm an old-style critic, someone who's against the fierce, cabalistic jargon that has pervaded university circles in the United States, where professors and critics talk of the literary with such indifference to the aesthetic, moral or political ingredient of literature properly understood that it could be said to have disappeared under the debris of theory. Do you follow me?'

'Not a lot. I think I only understand that you're an old-style critic.'

'A sad old critic,' said a woman with a voice of velvet, emerging from behind a curtain also of velvet. I recognised her body, though I could not see her face. The woman quickly removed her clothes, except for a black bra, and slowly came towards me and I heard her say in a drawl – which I also recognised – with a dove's serenity:

'I will spit on your grave.'

Only when she knelt down in front of me could I see her face. It was Rosa. She unzipped my trousers, took out my penis and placed it in her mouth, a much bigger mouth than she has in reality. As she moved her tongue, her exquisite blonde hair swung from side to side in a dazzling, frenzied display. I did not want to come. But I couldn't help it. And then I woke up.

'What is that?' Rosa asked.

I was terrified, I didn't know what I could say to her and I decided to blame her, a ruse to try to get out of a tight spot.

'You know better than I do,' I said.

Only then did Rosa take the map and show it to me, and only then did I see that she was asking me about the map.

I breathed a sigh of relief, but could not relax, since it wasn't going to be easy to explain to her why I devoted myself to drawing moles, provinces, slums – one of them called Spain – woods, bends, islands, underwater tunnels, devilish caves, warrens, intelligence services, Latin oases, shady corners. No, it wasn't going to be easy to explain why I devoted myself to such meticulous drawings.

'World map of Montano's malady,' she read aloud. 'What on earth is that? Have you drawn here your mental problem in the form of alphabet soup?'

Anyone would think I had been with another woman. I was terrified, although I told myself that ultimately it was preferable that she should be asking me about the map and not, as yesterday, asking me if I knew how long it was since we had made love. Had she repeated her question today, I would have been forced to tell her something that was fairly close to the truth, I would have been forced to tell her that this map and Montano's malady, being all-consuming, were one of the clearest reasons why we had not made love since the end of the previous century.

I realised that there was only one way to resolve the situation satisfactorily, and that was to make love to her without further ado, to try in this way to make her forget the map. But nor could it be said that this was the ideal solution at this point in time, since the emission had left me in no condition to confront the sexual act with a degree of self-confidence. What's more, it occurred to me that I should be praying for Rosa not even to think about unzipping my trousers, this could result in a catastrophe at least as big as that prepared by Montano's malady, day by day, with the intention of seeing off the literary.

I decided that the only way out left to me was to try to explain – as skilfully as possible, inventing wherever necessary – why I had turned into a raging amateur topographer, which is to say, to try to justify the inexplicable.

'The thing is I'm inventing a setting for a novel I wish to write,' I told her.

She gave me a terribly angry look.

'Well,' she said to me, 'I've just about had enough. Either you explain to me right now what Montano's malady is and why it has a map. Either you tell me right now what your son has to do with all this, with such a childish map, and, while you're at it, why it's so long since we had sex. Either you explain all this to me properly or you can start packing your bags and go and finish your map elsewhere. Do you hear me? What is Montano's malady?'

'A novel,' I whispered.

She can't have heard me.

'Where is it?' she asked.

'Where is what?'

'Montano's malady.'

I went to the night table and produced the diary, this diary. And showed it to her.

'Here it is,' I told her.

She read a few pages of the diary and, horrified, asked me whether I had signed up with the group of idiots who think that literature is ending and the market is to blame, whether I was one of those numbskulls who believe that literature is in crisis, under threat. Then we had sex. We fucked wildly. We fucked as if the world and literature were coming to an end. We fucked with the enthusiasm of the day we first met. When it was all over, I went out on to the balcony and saw the foam of a few waves breaking against the bow of a boat sailing in the distance. The midday sun shone, the surface of the water was no longer a mirror. And I don't know. I'd say I began to lose sight of Montano's malady.

II
Dictionary of Timid Love for Life

On 27 June, I shall go to Budapest to deliver a lecture as part of an international symposium on the diary as narrative form; I shall go to Budapest, I shall return to its Museum of Literature – where I was a few years ago – I shall think a lot about my poor mother, who wrote an essay, 'Theory of Budapest', which she concealed in her secret private journal: an extravagant essay which omits to mention any theory or even Budapest, a city she neither knew nor was interested in. On 27 June, I shall go to Budapest and once again stay at the Kakania Grand Hôtel and think about my mother and be glad to be back in this city where I felt so well on my previous trip, since I had the impression that walking down its streets allowed me, even though he was not from Budapest, to be closer to Robert Musil, someone I have always liked to feel close to.

Rosa will come with me to Budapest, and Tongoy may travel with us; I am trying to convince him to visit the country of the legendary Bela Lugosi, a distant relation of his. During the last month I have more or less lost sight of Montano's malady, my obsessive tendency towards the literary has abated. I would say that I have ceased to behave like Borges, who acted as if people were only interested in literature. I have not lost sight, however, of *Montano's Malady*, the *nouvelle* I finished writing in Fayal after fornicating wildly, the *nouvelle* in which fiction and my real life are intertwined. *Montano's Malady* contains a fair amount that is autobiographical, but also a lot that is invented. For example, it is not true – I hardly need say it – that Rosa is a film director. Rosa, as many of my readers already know, is a literary agent and, most of all, my eternal girlfriend. We have been living together for twenty years, we have not had even a civil wedding, we have not had children, nor have we had them with third parties. Hence Montano does not exist.

Tongoy, however, does exist and really is an actor living in Paris, who is quite well known in France and Italy, not so much in Spain. It is completely true that his physical appearance evokes Nosferatu, as it is also true that I met him on a recent trip to Chile, his country of origin. The aviator Margot Valerí, however, is someone who does not exist, she is invented by me and any likeness to a real person is purely coincidental. I did not make it up when I said that Tongoy, Rosa and I had travelled to the Azores together last month. Needless to say, however, we did not go to film a documentary, only on holiday, since I was curious to see Café Sport, the mythical bar which appears in *The Woman of Porto Pim*, a book by Antonio Tabucchi.

I imagine there is no need for me to say that I am not a literary critic, but a narrator with a long and distinguished career. This is true, as it is that I finished my *nouvelle* in Fayal and, coming back from the islands, had the idea of giving this diary a twist and turning it, for a time, into a short dictionary which would tell nothing but truths about my fragmented life and reveal my more human side and, in short, make me more accessible to my readers: a dictionary with entries listed under the names of the authors of private journals who have held the greatest interest for me over many years spent reading books of this intimate literary genre; some names of authors who, by reinforcing my autobiography with their lives, would help me to build up a wider and curiously more faithful portrait of my real personality, constructed in part from the private journals of others, which is why they're there, to help turn someone, who otherwise would probably be a completely rootless human being, into a complex character with a certain timid love for life.

So I am going to give this diary a certain change of pace. I have just revised *Montano's Malady*, I have read it from top to bottom to see if my *nouvelle* was missing anything, it's not missing anything, I regard it as finished, I even consider its pages now as somewhat past, antiquated. I recall Kafka, who on 27 June 1919, changed diary and wrote, 'New diary. For the simple reason that I was reading the old one.'

'My fragmented life', I said. And I am reminded of Ricardo Piglia, who says that, while a writer writes in order to know what literature is, a critic works inside the texts he reads in order to reconstruct his autobiography. Although I am not a literary critic, I am going to act sometimes in this dictionary as if I were one. I propose to work away discreetly inside the diaries of others and enlist their collaboration in the reconstruction of my precarious autobiography, which naturally, fragmented or not, will be presented as split like my personality, which is plural and ambiguous and hybrid and is basically a combination of experiences (mine and others') and reading matter.

My life! It will do it good to be reduced to a short dictionary, which I shall write thinking about the reader and the right he has to know me better. Saturated with so much mixing invention and autobiography and thus creating fictional texts, I should like now for the reader to know my life and personality much better, I should like not to hide behind my creative texts. I am with W. G. Sebald when he says he has the sensation that it is necessary for whoever writes a fictional text to show his hand, to say something about himself, to allow an image of himself.

On this April afternoon in Barcelona, I make it my solemn intention not to hide behind so much fictional text and to tell the reader something about myself, to offer him some reliable information about my life. I kneel before the altar of real life and lift a bowl in the air and intone:

'Introibo ad altare Dei.'

In short, I commend myself to the God of Truthfulness.

AMIEL, Henry Frédéric (Geneva, 1821–1881). Owes his literary fame almost exclusively to the book *Amiel's Journal*, published posthumously in 1883, in which this Swiss writer displays a rare talent as a highly astute psychological observer. He examines himself very well, although as a reader, on finishing his diary, I was left with the suspicion that to know oneself well is a bore and leads nowhere. I remembered a character of Scott Fitzgerald in *This Side of Paradise*, who says, or rather cries, 'I know myself, but that is all.' That aside, a remark of Amiel in his diary has always made me laugh: 'These pages act as confidant, by which I mean as friend and wife.'

To tell the truth – and let's not forget that I have commended myself to the God of Truthfulness – I would never have been able to say, for example, 'These pages act as confidant, by which I mean as Tongoy and Rosa.'

This diary has never served as my confidant, and I don't think I have ever wanted it to. But the truth is that it has served for other things. Last year, to go no further, it served as a refuge for me when I suffered a tragic case of writer's block after publishing *Nothing Ever Again*, my book about writers who give up writing. I spent several months devoid of ideas for a new book, as if I were being punished for having written about those who stop writing. But the diary helped me to survive, I began to record all kinds of trivialities, which are so common in this genre, and I went so far as, for example, to describe in minute detail the cracks in the ceiling of my study. I would write about anything just to avoid feeling completely blocked. And it worked out, the diary helped me.

Somebody might think that this block which made me take refuge in the diary is very similar to what happened to Amiel, but this is not the case, far from it. Amiel spent his whole life blocked as an artist and taking refuge in his diary, whereas I was tragically unable to write only for a very short period. I soon overcame my problem, I overcame it in November last year, in the city of Nantes, when, driven by a mysterious impulse, I began to turn my diary into a literary work which might easily require a reader. In fact I went to Nantes with the idea that this city – where I had been invited to some *Rencontres littéraires espagnols* – the city of Jacques Vaché, one of the heroes in my *Nothing Ever Again* and a character I have always believed to bring me good luck, could be an ideal place to start having ideas for new books again. So I travelled to Nantes with some hope – not a lot – that this city could be a key factor in my artistic recovery, I went to the city of Vaché with a certain timid hope, but without ever losing sight of a sentence Amiel wrote in his diary, which kept up my spirits, but also my guard, in the face of possible new events: 'Every hope is an egg which may produce a serpent instead of a dove.'

DALÍ, Salvador (Figueres, 1904–1989). Infinitely better writer than painter. When I was very young, I used to have a great time in Cadaqués reading *Diary of a Genius* a few steps away from his house. I knew some of its passages off by heart and would recite them in gatherings with friends, I remembered passages like this one: 'How can I doubt that everything that happens to me is enormously exceptional?' I liked this excerpt very much, because in it he was laughing at the diaries of writers with mediocre experiences. 'Today I received the visit of three perfectly stupid Swedes.' I write this sentence down from memory, because I didn't manage to find it in my copy of *Diary of a Genius*. Might I have invented it? If so, I beg the Swedes' pardon.

From this diary I also recall a reference to an illness of the stomach and bowels which he considered heaven-sent: 'Bravo! This illness is a gift from God! I wasn't ready yet. I wasn't worthy yet to undertake the bowels and thorax of my *Corpus Hypercubicus*.'

This vision of illness as something particularly positive and heaven-sent reminds me a lot of what happened to me in Nantes when I arrived in this city out of sorts, sick in soul, though with my hopes pinned on the Vaché factor, and very soon my evil was turned to good. But I shall deal with this in GIDE, André (Paris, 1869–1951), the next entry in this dictionary.

To tell the truth, I prefer the diary which Dalí wrote as a young man and which was published recently in Catalonia. These adolescent pages are superior to *Diary of a Genius*, they are more spontaneous, and the permanent display of talent is less forced.

An hour ago, I rang the poet Pere Gimferrer to ask him which of Dalí's two diaries he likes more: 'Why do you want to know?' Gimferrer, who always wants to know everything, asked me. 'I don't know if I want to know,' I told him, 'really I rang you so that you would appear in the diary I'm writing, which has turned into a novel and dictionary and looks less and less like a diary, especially since I started talking about things from the past, maybe that's why I rang you, perhaps to have something to relate that occurred today, that happened this Thursday in real life, I need a bit of present.'

Short silence at the other end of the line.

'If you want,' Gimferrer suddenly spoke, 'I'll tell you what for me most defines and distinguishes a writer's diary.' 'Excellent idea,' I replied. 'What defines and distinguishes it,' he told me, 'is the perspective it adopts, the tone or timbre of voice, and therefore the moral existence of the individual writing.'

'I understand you, I understand you very well,' I told

him. Renewed silence. 'Do you want to add something else?' I asked. 'Don't forget,' he told me, 'that a diary's real substance is not external events, but the author's moral evolution.'

'Thanks, Pere,' I replied, 'thank you, now I can include some daily life in the diary, thanks a lot.'

'No problem. *La vie est belle*,' the poet said. And hung up.

GIDE, André (Paris, 1869–1951). In an unintentional way, this writer's diary tells the story of someone who spent his life seeking to write a masterpiece and did not achieve it. Or perhaps he did achieve it, and paradoxically that great book would be the diary, in which he reflected the daily search for that masterpiece.

With the possible exception of *Paludes* – a short work of genius, which could have been written by Queneau – the rest of what Gide wrote is fairly illegible nowadays, the modern reader sees it as something strange, archaic, distant. The diary, on the other hand, though it falls short of the masterpieces of Proust and his contemporaries, is today a literary milestone, one of the great writers' diaries that exist, it is a pleasure to read, most of all because it is connected with a highly intelligent tone or timbre of voice and because it presents, with all its light and shade and going beyond this – 'the excellent and the worst. Too easy, ah! not to see more than the one or the other' – the fascinating complexity which can arise in the soul of a man seeking to find an *end* to the search, to the spirit's agitation.

Unlike so many mediocre diarists who tediously hand

out their notebooks as if they were parish news-sheets, Gide's voice is always a set of essential sheets, he never confuses literature with literary life. It is also possible to read the pages of his diary like a novel – Gide transformed the genre, he was a pioneer in the use of the fictitious diary – which recounts, over a period of no less than sixty-three years, the intimate and spiritual path of a man who throughout his life enquired into the premise that upholds the principle of morality, although he also enquired into that which upholds the principle of immorality.

I have always noted his sympathy for illnesses, I think he saw in them the starting-point for feverish creative activity. 'I believe that illnesses', he writes in his diary, 6 February 1944, 'are keys which can unlock certain doors for us. There is a state of good health which does not allow us to understand it all [. . .]. I have yet to meet someone who boasts that he has never been ill who is not also a bit stupid; the same as someone who takes pride in never having travelled.'

I arrived in the city of Nantes, literature-sick and tragically unable to write, one rainy day in the month of November last year. I arrived out of sorts on account of my literary block and, to make matters worse, I sought even more reasons to feel bad and worried. I told myself, for example, that I had been a thief of other people's words too often, that frequently I acted as a parasite on the writers I most admired. Hence it might be said that three were the essential dramas I was carrying when I arrived in Nantes: I was sick with Montano's malady – still without knowing that this was the name of my complaint – tragically unable to write and a literary parasite.

I was met at Nantes airport by Yves Douet and Patrice Viart, the organisers of the *Rencontres*, and they took me to the Hôtel La Perouse, where in the bar I drank seven vodkas in animated conversation with them – the main topic being Makelele, a footballer who used to play for Nantes. At around five o'clock, I indicated my intention to sleep until the following day, and they politely withdrew. 'See you tomorrow,' they said, fairly impressed, I think, by the number of vodkas I had consumed.

It was my intention to take my leave of the world until the following day, but an hour later I had already changed my mind and felt a huge desire to go for a walk around Nantes. So, taking hold of the red umbrella which Rosa had put in my suitcase at the last minute, I headed towards the Quai de la Fosse, I walked calmly along the streets of the city of Jacques Vaché and Jules Verne, I walked whistling Barbara's song about the rain in Nantes and came to a halt in front of the old bookshop Coiffard's.

I was so literature-sick that, looking in the bookshop window, I saw myself reflected in the glass and thought that I was a poor child out of Dickens in front of the window of a cake-shop. Shortly afterwards, this child turned into *the man without qualities* from Musil's novel, that idealistic mathematician who would contemplate the streets of his city and, watch in hand, time the cars, carriages, trams and silhouettes of pedestrians blurred by the distance. This man would measure the speeds, angles, magnetic forces of the fugitive masses . . .

There at the door of Coiffard's, just like *the man without qualities*, I ended up laughing as he laughed in Musil's novel and recognising that the devotion to that kind of eccentric espionage was of a supreme folly, 'the titanic effort of a modern individual who doesn't do anything'.

Ah! – I lamented – how I should have liked to write about a man without qualities, clearly even in this type of expression or lament I wish to have Musil ever close, and I also show a certain tendency to act as a parasite on what is not mine. Seeing, in Coiffard's, that I had once again succumbed to literary vampirism – to which I must add physical vampirism, a certain resemblance to Christopher Lee when he played Count Dracula – I decided to enter the bookshop and put these thoughts to one side.

I made a supreme effort to concentrate and rudely dismissed the man without attributes, the *available man* – as Gide called him – the modern man who doesn't do anything, the nihilist of our times.

But I was so horribly literature-sick that, having entered Coiffard's, I was powerless to prevent Musil returning to my mind, which he did with a sentence from his book about the man without properties, about the available man: 'A man without qualities can also have a father endowed with qualities.'

Unlikely as it seems, this sentence, not especially important, would be crucial, decisive, important in my life.

How right Gide was when he said that illnesses are keys which can unlock certain doors for us! I say this because this discreet sentence from Musil's book, which on a whim I linked with my illnesses, was the key which unlocked the doors of the solution to my most pressing problems. The thing is that suddenly, instead of behaving like a thief of other people's words, I began to act as a literary parasite on myself when I decided right there in Coiffard's to turn my complaints into the central theme of a narrative marking my return to writing.

Right there in Coiffard's, while flicking absent-mindedly through a French edition of Borges' *The Aleph*, I invented a son who would be called Montano – I had just seen a French translation of a book by Arias Montano, Felipe II of Spain's secret adviser – a son who would live right there in Nantes and suffer an extreme case of writer's block, from which a father endowed with certain qualities – which poor Montano would lack – would try to free him. The son would run a bookshop in Nantes, possibly even Coiffard's. And would receive the visit of his father, who from Barcelona would travel to Nantes to try to help him overcome his tragic inability to write, an inability he had suffered since publishing a book about writers who give up writing.

The father would be a prestigious literary critic and hopelessly literature-sick, but would not be thinking about himself, but about his son, he would go to Nantes to try to free up Montano's creative block.

It struck me as a useful idea to transfer some of my problems on to an invented son.

How curious, I commented to myself. I have begun to act as a literary parasite on myself, in my problems following the publication of *Nothing Ever Again* I have found the inspiration to return to the world of fictional creation. What's more, I went on, perhaps this will help me to get well. And I remembered what Walter Benjamin said about the possible relationship that exists between the art of storytelling and the healing of illnesses.

Somebody might wonder: why turn Montano's father into a literary critic? I declared that I would be sincere in everything and I shall be so even in this: I am a frustrated literary critic. In fact one of the major incentives I discovered when writing *Montano's Malady* was the opportunity fiction afforded me to be able to pretend to be a critic of the stature of Samuel Johnson, Edmund Wilson, Cyril Connolly, Stanislaw Wicinsky or Alfred Kerr.

I return to Coiffard's bookshop and the moment when I slammed shut *The Aleph* and decided to leave. While squeezing past the other customers, I saw that a young man was blocking the exit, which was still some way off. Not only that, I had the fleeting conviction that this man was the spitting image of a young Musil. However, when I reached the door, I discovered that he was not a young man at all, but ancient, with bulging eyes and virtually green skin, slicked-back white hair and a pop tie, a poor devil without qualities (I drew inspiration from this mistake, by the way, for the episode in Tunquén in *Montano's Malady*, where the youngsters turn out to be old people). I almost gave this disgusting, green-skinned creature a shove. However, when I stepped outside, back into the rain, I had the impression that I had rarely felt better in life. This was hardly surprising. During a brief foray lasting only five minutes into a bookshop, in one fell swoop I had freed myself from my most pressing problems. It was even likely that I had gone some way towards freeing myself from my literary illness, since I was not unaware that I could get well if I wrote an exhaustive commentary on the illness in that narrative about my son which I proposed to start writing as soon as possible.

It is well known that there is no better way to overcome an obsession than by writing about it. I know this from personal experience, the point is to talk about the theme obsessing you until you exhaust it, this is something I have done in some of my books and generally I have achieved my objective and in the end almost completely eliminated the obsession that had me trapped.

I remember myself the following morning seated at a desk in the hall of the Julien Gracq Institute, looking very serious and apparently, in sight of everybody, noting down everything the professor Aline Roubaud said. She was delivering in French a brilliant and very lively lecture about the Spanish Golden Age. But, while it cannot be said that I was not listening to her, the truth is that the notes I was taking had little to do with her lecture; they dealt, instead, with the detailed construction of what would turn into *Montano's Malady*.

I still have these notes and find in them isolated phrases, early pointers, simple and tender words, which today represent an engaging document to me, in that they are the written testimony of what was the timid gestation of *Montano's Malady*.

Two of those phrases or early pointers:

Married to Aline Roubaud. A slightly perverse decision, clearly this refers to my intention to marry Montano to a young French woman named after the elderly lady who at that moment was delivering her brilliant lecture.

Behaves like Hamlet. Refers to the fact that the father would try to help the son overcome his literary block, but the latter would react strangely and behave as if he were Hamlet and sought revenge.

I remember that, while I was taking those notes, I felt

happy, but a little tortured by the idea that I would not get round to writing the narrative I had in mind and would end up resembling the main character in *Paludes*, André Gide's novel, which tells the story of a man who wants to write a book but is always putting it off to another day. This book deals with a man who lives in a marsh and doesn't do anything.

This writer who does not write and is the main character in *Paludes* is sometimes asked what he does, how he occupies his time.

'Why, I write *Paludes*,' he replies always irritably. 'The story of a bachelor who lives in a tower surrounded by marshlands.'

'Why a bachelor?'

'Well, it makes it all so much easier.'

'Is that it?'

'That's it. I'll tell you what he does.'

'What does he do?'

'He looks out over the marshes.'

The years go by and nothing changes, the writer who plans to write *Paludes* does not get round to it.

I was frightened that something similar would happen to me and I would end up stuck in the antechamber of this project I had recently conceived in Nantes. That from time to time people would ask me what my new text was about and I would reply:

'It's about someone who's literature-sick.'

'You mean, someone just like you?'

'No. Worse than me, much worse.'

I was afraid that the years would go by and I would never write that book.

‘What exactly does this Montano do?’ they would ask me from time to time.

‘He looks out over the marshes.’

Parasitic note

I would love to have been visited by Alan Pauls’ personal memories, by the memories of the day he wrote ‘Second Hand’, a chapter in his book *The Borges Factor*. There is in what I have just said a clear desire to be in the skin of an admired essayist, a desire which is really not so strange as Kafka’s desire to be a redskin. The fact that I admire ‘Second Hand’ should not surprise anyone, it is a particularly astute reflection on the great Borges’ literary parasitism, on a theme – that of book vampirism – which in the streets of Nantes had made me very uneasy and concerned, and which I suddenly resolved by beginning to act as a literary parasite on myself. This happy discovery came to me before I knew of the existence of *The Borges Factor*, a book I came across last week in Barcelona, in the home of Rodrigo Fresán.

In ‘Second Hand’, Alan Pauls looks at the beneficial effect on the young Borges of an unfavourable review written in 1933 by one Ramón Doll about *Discussion*, the book of essays which Borges had published a year earlier. Ramón Doll was a nationalist critic who, in his book *Intellectual Police*, launched an attack on Borges, accusing him of being a literary parasite: ‘These essays, bibliographical in their intention or content, belong to that genre of parasitic literature which involves repeating badly things others have said well; or in pretending *Don*

Quixote and *Martín Fierro* were never published, and printing entire pages lifted from these works; or in making out that one is interested in elucidating some point and with a candid air incorporating the opinions of others, to be seen not to be one-sided, but to have respect for all ideas (and in that way the essay gets written).'

Shall I repeat badly something Alan Pauls has said well? I hope not, I assume a candid air and write that Pauls says that poor Doll is scandalised, yes, but his outrage should not overshadow the fact that the charges he levels at Borges sound particularly pertinent. Pauls remarks that Borges, contrary to the policeman Doll's expectations, very probably did not disapprove of the critic's words, but quite the opposite: 'With the shrewdness and sense of economy of great misfits, who recycle the enemy's blows to strengthen their own, Borges does not reject Doll's condemnation, rather he converts it – *reverts* it – into his own artistic programme. Borges' work is teeming with such secondary, slightly obscure characters, who like shadows follow the trail of a more luminous work or character. Translators, exegetes, annotators of sacred texts, interpreters, librarians, even lackeys of beautiful people and brawlers: Borges defines the true ethics of subordination in this gallery of anonymous creatures [. . .]. And Pierre Menard culminates a long series of literary submissions by rewriting some chapters from *Don Quixote* – what is Pierre Menard if not the ultimate parasitic writer, the visionary who takes the subordinate vocation to its highest point and to its extinction?'

These secondary characters, ethics of subordination, unite Borges with Robert Walser, the author of *Institute*

Benjamenta, a novel that is also a diary with a memorable beginning: 'One learns very little here, there is a shortage of teachers, and none of us boys of the Benjamenta Institute will come to anything, that is to say, we shall all be something very small and subordinate later in life.'

Walser himself was always a subaltern and could easily have been one of his own characters and also one of Borges' obscure characters. In fact Walser worked as a copyist in Zurich, he would from time to time retire to the 'Chamber of Writing for Unoccupied Persons' – the name appears to be an invention by Borges for a story of copyists or by Walser himself, but it isn't, it isn't an invention – and there, 'seated on an old stool, in the evening, in the pale light of an oil lamp, he would make use of his graceful handwriting to copy addresses and do little jobs of the kind entrusted by businesses, associations or private individuals'.

Walser worked in many things, always as a subaltern, he claimed to feel well 'in the lower regions'. He was, for example, bookshop assistant, lawyer's clerk, bank employee, worker in a factory that made sewing machines, and finally major-domo of a castle in Silesia, all of this with the permanent wish to learn how to serve.

Led also by a certain wish to serve, I should like to tell the reader that, despite the obvious differences, my literary modus operandi can sometimes – though I did not realise it until recently, until I read 'Second Hand' – recall that of Borges. I was a literary parasite in the first poem I wrote, some love verses intended to enamour a girl at school. I constructed the poem by directly copying Cernuda and occasionally, very occasionally, inserting a line of my own: 'I love you in the goodness of your foggy fatherland,' for example.

I failed to enamour the girl at school, but she did tell me that I wrote very well. Instead of remembering that eighty per cent of the poem was Cernuda's, I concluded that it was my own verses – elaborated thanks to the company of a great poet – which the girl had liked. This gave me immense confidence from that day on, it had a decisive influence on my subsequent literary development. Gradually the percentage of copying in my poems decreased and slowly, but with a certain amount of confidence, my own personal style evolved, always constructed – to a greater or lesser extent – with the collaboration of those writers whose blood I sucked for my own benefit. Without haste, I began to acquire a little of my own style, nothing dazzling, but sufficient, something that was unmistakably *mine*, thanks to vampirism and the involuntary collaboration of the rest, those writers I laid hands on to find my personal literature. Without haste, arriving always *after*, in second place, accompanying a writer, all the Cernudas I discovered along the way, who appeared first, original. Without haste, like Walser's secondary or Joseph Roth's discreet characters, who pass through life in endless flight, placing themselves on the margins of the reality which troubles them so much and also on the margins of existence, in the face of the mechanism of sameness – so dominant in the world today – to defend an extreme residue of irreducible individuality, something that is unmistakably *theirs*. I discovered *mine* in the others, arriving *after* them, first accompanying them and later liberating myself.

I think I can now say, for example, that thanks to Cernuda's protective staff I began to walk on my own and to find out what kind of writer I was, and also not to know who I was, or, better put, to know who I was, but just a bit, in the same way as my literary style is just an extreme residue, but that will always be better than nothing. The same can be applied to my existence: I have just a bit of my own life – as can be observed in this timid dictionary – but it is unmistakably mine, which, to be honest, to me already seems a lot. Given the state of the world, it is no small thing to have a bit of autobiography.

I know myself little, but perhaps it's better like this, to have a life that is 'deliberately slender' (as Gil de Biedma would say), but at least to have a life, which not many do. Perhaps it's better like this, for, as Goethe said to Eckermann, 'I do not know myself, and God forbid that I should'.

Never to know oneself. This is what Musil thought happens in private journals. He believed that the diary was the only narrative form of the future, since it contains within itself all possible discursive forms. However, he did not exactly maintain this with enthusiasm, rather he believed that it was a waste of time or a superstition to think that the diary can, for example, help us to know ourselves. The diary he himself kept illustrates his distrust of the private journal, being nothing other than the crushing negative of an autobiography, its most perfect challenge. In Musil's version, the diary was the ultimate genre without qualities, not so strange if we know that he was of the opinion that in private journals the person writing 'has nothing to listen to there' and he wondered what one is meant to be listening to: 'Diaries? A sign of the times. So many diaries get published. It is the most comfortable, the most undisciplined form. And yet it is possible that soon only diaries will get written, and the rest will be considered undrinkable [. . .]. It is pure analysis: nothing more, nothing less. It is not art. Nor should it be. What is the point of listening to oneself there?'

Never to know oneself, or to know oneself just a bit, and to be a parasite on other writers in order to possess a scrap of personal literature. This could be said to be my plan for the future from the day I began copying Cernuda. Perhaps what I have done is to lean on others' quotations in order to get to know my reduced territory, befitting a subaltern with a few vital sparks, and at the same time to discover that I shall never know myself very well – because life is no longer a unity with a centre, 'Life,' according to Nietzsche, 'no longer resides in totality, in an organic and complete Whole' – and yet I shall be able to be many people, a frightful conjunction of the most diverse destinies and a set of echoes from the most varied places: a writer doomed possibly, sooner or later – obliged by the circumstances of the time in which I happen to live – to try his hand at not the autobiographical, but the autofictional genre, although I think perhaps it will be some time before this doom befalls me, I am currently entangled in an engaging tribute to Truthfulness, involved in a desperate effort to tell truths about my fragmented life, before perhaps the time should come for me to pass over to the sphere of autofiction, where no doubt, if no other option is open to me, I shall pretend to know myself better than I really do.

Walter Benjamin said that in our time the only work truly endowed with meaning – critical meaning, as well – would have to be a collage of quotations, excerpts, echoes of other works. In its time, I incorporated into that collage relatively personal ideas and phrases, and slowly created for myself an autonomous world, paradoxically very closely linked to the echoes of other works. All of this to realise that, owing to this manner of working, I would never attain anything or barely attain much, like the trainee major-domos of the Benjamenta Institute. But there is no reason why this should stop me, here in this dictionary, telling truths about my fragmented and slender but sufficient life.

However that may be, I was a parasite and I suffered for it. In Nantes the drama reached its highest point. And I came down, as tends to happen when one scales the peaks of tragedy. I came down and saw that I did not have to worry about my parasitical past, rather to convert it – *revert* it – into my own artistic programme, to turn into a literary parasite on myself, to make the most of the reduced but autonomous part of my anxiety and of my work which I could consider to be *mine*. Then I read 'Second Hand' by Pauls and relaxed even more when I saw, for example, that Borges had been a highly creative and astute case of literary parasitism.

Nothing so comforting as Pauls' idea that an important dimension of Borges' work revolved around the writer arriving always after, in second place, in a subordinate's role – with a minimal biography, but with a biography, which is already saying a lot – this writer always arrives later and does so to read or comment on or translate or introduce a work or writer that appears first, original. It was Gide who said that it calms the nerves to know that original is always the other.

GIRONDO, Rosario (Barcelona, 1948). Let others hide behind pseudonyms or make up heteronyms. Personally I've always gone for the metronymic. Does that word exist, does the word 'metronymic' exist? I would say what is named exists. I have always signed my books Rosario Girondo, Rosario Girondo is my mother's name. I have often had to hear that it was my pseudonym. No, it is my metronymic. How many times do I have to say it? How can the mother's name be a pseudonym?

I remember my mother as a fragile and strange being, at times lost among barbiturates, always depressed and difficult, dreaming of trains that ran her down, my father's silent enemy. She kept a diary in rigorous secret, no one ever knew that she recorded her life in a few squared notebooks, which I found on her death and read. Even her handwriting was unusual in those notebooks, it was an insect's handwriting, microscopic, a special handwriting for her diaries, very different, for example, from the one she used over forty years for the shopping list.

I read those notebooks from start to finish and was affected for the rest of my life. The diary radically changed the vision that I had of her. The diary began on 7 October 1947, some ten months before my birth, it opened like this: 'Today is my name-day, ugly thought. Ugly, everything is very ugly. Life is ugly. Take autumn, nothing but sadness. The trees are without leaves, the sun and the world have lost intensity and at last tell the truth. And one feels fear and cold and notices the little vitality life has and remembers the young woman that two years ago I still was, the poor, naive creature who without realising was heading towards the wrong marriage. I was like one of Jane Austen's characters, one of those decent girls who sought a fiancé and so were fated to change county. But I did not change county, I merely changed life, I married and my life took a turn for the worse, as it had to with such a horrible husband.'

Terrible and somewhat surprising opening to the diary with an insect's handwriting. Her notebooks, as tends to happen in all diaries, revolve around a series of recurrent themes. One of them, in the case of my mother's diary, is the strong conviction that she had made a monumental mistake marrying my father, who was not, by the way, 'a self-made man like Kafka's father' – as it says in *Montano's Malady* – but a simple social climber, a coalman's son, a not very elegant and rather cynical young man, who feigned love where he was only interested in money. Although in honour of the truth it has to be said that he married for money and to improve his social status, after a few months he fell devotedly in love with his intelligent but fragile wife, who, by the time he began to fall in love, had already started to write horrible things about him in her secret squared notebooks, they lived like this for forty years, he blindly in love, she hating him with all her soul, though in rigorous secret: 'An hour ago the great idiot, the hopeless coalman's son, was seated in front of me. I took a good look at this decrepit bore. How wretched I am! I took a good look, he really is extremely ugly, flat-faced, bald with a bit of hair, with a Mongolian's moustache and sweaty, fat hands, how disgusting this life is!'

Another recurrent theme is the compassion she felt for me – I knew nothing of this until I found the diary on her death and read it – a sentiment that repeatedly surfaces in her tragic or painful poems. The fact is that my mother wrote a fair amount of poetry in her secret diary. Although at home we were aware that the art of poetry held great attraction for her – she was a housewife and an almost full-time reader, a reader basically of poetry – none of us could imagine that she devoted herself in rigorous secret to the art of composing verses.

Some of her poems from the 1970s recall those of Alejandra Pizarnik – sheer coincidence, I believe – who was fourteen years her senior and whom she spotted one afternoon in the Taita, a bar in Barcelona, one afternoon in October 1969, an event which my mother wrote up in her diary: 'Today I saw that tiny Argentinian poet, who appears tormented, she was with some posh children from the Calvo Sotelo district . . .'

Some of her poems could have been by Pizarnik herself, as, for example, some verses my mother wrote in the afternoon of 27 July 1977: 'To live free. / In the lamps of night, / in the centre of the void, in the open darkness, / in the shadows the blackness and I. / To live free. / Leaning on the grave, / lost I, / in the sole light of the son.'

What does she mean by 'sole light of the son'? Judging by what it says in the diary, I was the only person in this world who motivated her to live, she felt obliged not to kill herself and to help me as much as she could. She felt real compassion for me and some regret for having given birth to me. This compassion of hers is another of the recurrent themes in her secret notebooks. Compassion drove her to make plans and to decide that, when I was older, were I to show a tendency towards writing, she had to channel it towards a literary activity that was not negative, that was not affected by her negative spirit. This led her to plan for me a kind of writing aimed exclusively as far as I was concerned at the elaboration of a personal myth.

Throughout her diary there is a surprising amount of verbal violence, surprising in someone like her who never raised her voice and was, like many depressed people, a peaceable, very calm person. But in the diary she was terrible, destructive when talking about people. She loathed almost everybody, except Margot Valerí, a supposed friend of hers, an old Chilean aviator, an imaginary woman, perhaps her alter ego, a woman who did not exist and to whom she dedicates this short, strange poem: 'Time 07.15, / direction 243°, / 7,000 feet. / Fog. / You and I are Emily. / Dickinson. / White housecoat and sad dog. / High climate and a goal at the summit. / The spirit's salvation.'

Her verbal violence is surprising, but should not be so surprising. After all, in private journals one is not merely talking to oneself, one is also conversing with others: all the conversations which we can never conclude in real life, because they would descend into outbursts of violence, get deposited in the diary.

When I think about it, I can see that my mother reserved her madness exclusively for her diary. She led a double life: model housewife and at the same time seriously disturbed woman whenever she wrote. Whereas Georges Bataille said that he wrote so as not to go mad, it could be said of my mother that, being a sensible person in real life, she went mad whenever she wrote.

Her writing is linked to the Secret, it is possible that she only understood literature linked to the idea of the Secret. This would explain why, when I began to publish under the name of Rosario Girondo, my mother gave it no importance. Perhaps to her my writing, being neither private nor secret, was not exactly writing, perhaps she considered my writing only as a literature which was a distant relation of what she understood to be real literature (always linked in her mind to the Secret): 'Spanish poets today, / sad, sad, / distant relations / of what one day was real.'

The first Friday of each month, she would imagine a suicide and turn it into a poem, like this one dated Friday, 2 October 1953: 'Today would be perfect / a mad dash towards the balcony, / a terrible jump into the void, / to splinter the wood in this coal-house, / on Provença Street, / the jump into the void, / flinging myself from the sixth floor, / with the indifference of a housewife / who empties a bucket of dirty, / dirty water.'

We lived on Sant Joan Avenue – later in Rovira Square – but my mother speaks in the poem of a house on Provença Street, possibly a deliberate mistake obeying her secret desire for a change of address, to which I would add a change of husband. While the poem is extravagant, even more so is the way in which she brought it to a close, something she explains in the diary three days later, when she says that the Siamese cat – as imaginary as Margot Valerí – interrupted the poem with her paw, at which point she decided it was finished and, what's more, considered that the cat had written it.

When my first novel appeared, a pedantic exercise in style entitled *Errant Necropolis*, my mother simply remarked that she would have given it the title *Theory of Budapest*. And when I asked her why it had to have this title, given that my novel contained no theory whatsoever and made no mention of the city of Budapest, my mother smiled and replied that this was why it had to have that title, precisely because it contained no theories and Budapest was not in it.

Years later, when I read her diary, in the second of her squared notebooks I came across a lengthy essay written in 1956 and entitled 'Theory of Budapest', in which she lucidly disserted on the activity of writing private journals, but made no mention of Budapest, a city that, because of the bloody Hungarian national uprising, was frequently referred to in newspapers in the summer of 1956, when she wrote her 'Theory', which might explain why the Hungarian capital appeared in the title of her essay.

My mother. Ever fragile and living in married hell, at times lost among barbiturates, dreaming of trains that would run her down, silent and long-suffering enemy of my father, whom, however, she needed if she was to write the diary, as becomes clear in 'Theory of Budapest', where she rails mercilessly against my father and against the noisy staircase in the building on Barcelona's Sant Joan Avenue, and against the daily horror, in short, against this, that and everything. And says that she is not happy, but nor does she particularly want to be, since then she would have nothing to write in her precious diary.

The 'Theory' contains some of the best writing in her squared notebooks, but the last line in her diary, the last of all, deserves to be framed, as I have done in my own home. Written three days before her death, when my mother already knew that she had few days of life left, this last line obsessively – as if she were looking at the old school exercise book where she had learned neat handwriting – repeats a verse by Oliverio Girondo, the avant-garde poet whom she considered a distant relation, I do not know if in relation to real literature as well.

This verse by the avant-garde poet – which she had found in a poem by Félix de Azúa – this verse – repeated ad infinitum at the end of her diary, repeated in beautiful handwriting about thirty times, by way of bringing her squared notebooks to an unsettling close – this verse – written obsessively at the end of her diary, as if my mother wished through so much repetition to sum up what had been the repetitive daily hell of her life: a circular, reiterative and unbearable hell – this verse by the avant-garde poet, a verse my mother wished to repeat so many times at the close of the great disaster that had been her life – and it was as if finally by repeating it she were lamenting having reached the dying moments of her life's delirium without the prized, and at times indirectly announced, suicide – in short this once-avant-garde verse said as follows:

What's the use of Pentothal.

'THEORY OF BUDAPEST' (EXTRACT)

Solitude this August afternoon, anxiety controlled by poison, Pentothal for the lukewarm, dead horizon. More than an hour since I started writing this Theory, I feel the time has come for a short rest and I give way to delirium.

Pentothal for the lukewarm, dead horizon. Here I am, quiet and alone, in my white clothes. The afternoon is flat. And there is a cold kiss on the window. I write this August afternoon in a dialect of ice, I write sentences I do not understand, sentences that merit no commentaries. At times I perceive the second life of things, the secret and elusive life that is behind what is on view, behind famous reality. There is nothing worse than fame, and reality definitely has this fame. Whenever I think about this, I recall Seneca, who said that fame is horrible because it relies on the judgment of others. How horrible reality seems to me when it is on everybody's lips, when it is famous and grateful for the judgment of others, and poor reality laughs without realising that it is no more than mere appearance, and I erase its fame, minute by minute, I erase it on the map of the future. Because I perceive what will happen and I also perceive the second life of objects and say things that even I do not understand and that merit no commentary [. . .]. I perceive the secret and elusive life that is behind what is on view, behind reality. At times I see this, what I call the second mask, but I have no one to share this perception with, unless it be Hamlet – I dream in him – or else my poor son, who one day, on some by-road in the night, will bump into Hamlet, who will ask him about me, and by then I shall be only white clothes and blank look of a forgotten back room, the distant echo of a woman who on a day like today, one August afternoon like today, wrote sentences she did not even think, sentences to find rest from an essay that will not merit a single commentary by anyone.

COMMENTARY ON MY MOTHER'S EXTRACT

At the age of fifty, José Cardoso Pires – he himself tells the story in an unforgettable book – decided to smoke in front of the mirror and ask. And now, José.

To smoke in front of the mirror, as everyone knows, is an intelligent exercise, it is also to know how to confront our most ordinary, considered face. I also am now smoking in front of the mirror, it is midnight and I am standing – having been left alone in the city, Rosa has travelled to Madrid during this long weekend on which half of Spain has taken to the road – I am standing and smoking in front of the mirror. And now, Rosario.

I shouldn't have been left so alone at home, on such a long weekend, I am dangerous without Rosa watching over me, I am capable of draining every single bottle in the house during this weekend, I am capable even of ceasing to write this dictionary, I shouldn't have been left so free in such a big house, with so many bottles and the whole weekend ahead. And now, José.

I stand looking at myself in the mirror and I smoke and I think about Rosario Girondo, my mother. And I tell myself that there is evidence of madness in the extract from 'Theory of Budapest' which I have included in this dictionary, but there is madness throughout her diary: conventional housewife, on the one hand; disturbed woman when writing, on the other.

The opening to the extract from 'Theory of Budapest' has an acceptable poetic rhythm – the tendency to say nothing, but in a way that sounds nice. However, my mother soon quotes Seneca and loses the rhythm of the narrative – if there ever was a narrative – and even makes grammatical mistakes, as, for example, 'I dream in him' with reference to Hamlet. One deduces that she meant she dreamed of Hamlet, not in Hamlet. And yet I must be grateful for this possible error of my mother's, since it gave me the idea for a short story, '11 rue Simon-Crubellier', which I attributed to my son in *Montano's Malady*, that story which supposedly condenses into seven squalid pages the history of literature seen as a succession of writers unexpectedly inhabited by the memories of other, earlier writers: the history of literature seen with reversed chronology. This story by Montano contains a series of writers who dream *in*, inside, in the interior of other writers preceding them in time. I believe that thanks to my mother saying 'I dream in him' about Hamlet, thanks to that minute error, I had the whole idea of that spectacular story which enabled Montano to escape from his tragic literary block, from the imposed silence that so tormented him back in the bookshop in Nantes.

I must accept reality. My mother behaved impeccably as a housewife, but as a writer of a secret diary she more than took revenge on her conventional life and filled the diary with the language of dementia. That she was mad when she wrote is perfectly clear in this extract from 'Theory of Budapest', where she herself says that she is going to give way to delirium and where she talks, for example, of Hamlet and says quite naturally that one day he will ask about her, and by then she will be 'only white clothes'. I need not add what she says about my bumping into Hamlet on some by-road. Though this turned out to be somewhat prophetic, since in *Montano's Malady* I talk to my son, who thinks he is Hamlet, I took the idea from her.

Dangerous weekend, which could give way to drink and a tragic trail of traceless days. And now, Rosario.

For the moment, I abstain. I smoke in front of the mirror and tell myself that basically my mother always had Montano's malady, was literature-sick. I inherited the disease from her, this much is obvious. And now, José.

To avoid drinking and writing that I am giving up the dictionary, I decide – it's midnight, a perfect time – to summon the ghosts, to turn into a kind of post-box able, from now on, to receive their messages, their opinions from the other world. I tell myself that I shall listen to their stories willingly and decipher them should they reach me a little distorted by some rare wave. Here I am, waiting for you, ghosts. Waiting for your visits. In the meantime, I smoke, and smoke, and look at myself in the mirror, next to the open window. Time goes by and no one communicates. And now, Rosario.

The time for spirits goes by, it's long past midnight, nobody came, it's a fact. I suppose it was fairly predictable. I shouldn't have been left so alone on this night of the first Friday in May. I keep smoking in front of the mirror, I imagine that I am conversing with Hamlet, I feel strange, and see that I smoke strangely in front of the strange mirror. And now, José.

Tomorrow is another day.

And now, Rosario.

Who said that?

'Now,' says a voice, 'keep smoking.'

Monday

I got up at eight, as normal, just as Rosa with a forceful and very energetic smack turned off the alarm clock. We had breakfast together. A quick instant coffee, cakes from the supermarket and rolled oats. I laughed at one of her clients, one of those narrators she has to put up with daily. As always, she wasn't in the least amused. 'Carry on like this and you can find yourself another literary agent,' she told me angrily.

Around nine, Rosa left for the office and I had another coffee and lit a cigarette and, by way of intellectual warm-up to see if I was in the mood to write – every morning I tend to read a passage from a book I have read previously that I know is not going to disappoint me and generally I end up feeling stimulated by the reading and encouraged to go to my study and to pick up where I left off writing the day before – I immersed myself in some pages by Julian Barnes on childhood memories. In them, Barnes talks of the envy he experienced on a particular occasion on reading an extract from Edmond de Goncourt's diary, where the author said that he had a very clear memory of a morning from his childhood days in which, wanting help to prepare his fishing tackle, he went into his cousin's bedroom and saw her, with her legs open and her bottom on a cushion, as she was about to be penetrated by her husband. There was a flurry of bedclothes and the scene was witnessed as quickly as it vanished. 'But the image stuck,' confesses Goncourt, 'that pink bottom on a cushion with embroidered festoons was the sweet, exciting image that appeared before me every night . . .'

Barnes states that he is amazed by the excellent memory Goncourt has of something that happened fifty years earlier and, most of all, he feels professional envy at how well preserved that memory is, because Goncourt saw and registered in his mind the embroidered festoons on the cushion. Barnes says that this demonstrates Goncourt's capacity as a writer, he reads Goncourt's description and wonders whether he would have noticed those embroidered festoons, had he been the one standing there, staring pop-eyed at the couple.

Around half past nine, I stopped reading Barnes and put on some music by Tom Waits, my favourite song by this musician, 'Downtown Train', the story of someone who is lost and wants to find his way back to the centre of his city, or at least to the centre of something. With music by Tom Waits this morning, I started writing down in the diary my recollections of last Friday, my (not entirely childish) recollections of when I smoked in front of the mirror and called myself either José or Rosario and became drunk as a lord, hearing a booming voice which invited me to keep smoking. It was an interesting and difficult re-creation on paper of a drinking-spree in which I ended up receiving the visit of a ghost.

I wrote until two in the afternoon, this is my most usual timetable. Normally, every day about two, I go down to the lobby to collect my post and from there to the kiosk on the corner to buy the papers. I have a quick lunch in a restaurant nearby, where I read my letters and also the press and come into contact with reality, with the news items which the papers carry and which – perhaps because of my matutinal and fictional enclosure – always surprise and puzzle me. On my return home, I listen to the messages on the answering machine – I reply when I have to reply, meaning only when it is strictly necessary – and then I switch on the computer and inspect my e-mail, and again only answer when it is essential. I do not use the computer to write my literary work, only for e-mail and for newspaper articles.

Letters I received today: two from Buenos Aires (both from Juan Carlos Gómez, *El Goma*, one of Gombrowicz's young friends before Gombrowicz left Argentina in 1963; in his two letters today, *El Goma*, in his aggressive and poorly imitated Gombrowicz style, repeatedly calls me 'sleepyhead' for not writing to him or for being so slow to answer him) and one which has arrived from New York, in which Stanislaw Wicinsky asks me if everything I write in the book I am preparing 'is true word for word'.

Messages on the answering machine: a) From the town hall in Sant Quirze del Vallès, an invitation to deliver a lecture on *Finnegans Wake* by James Joyce, an extravagant proposal, since I have never been regarded as an expert on this book; b) three annoying requests from the press offices of three publishers in Barcelona to present three books by authors who are more or less friends or acquaintances of mine, three books I know to be horrendous and which remind me of something Bioy Casares said, how sometimes there are friends who send you their books seemingly in an effort to make you lose your fascination for literature.

E-mails: only one, but a very special one, coming from the Swiss-German publisher which recently began publishing my books. In it, I am invited at the beginning of

June to catch an aeroplane to Geneva, then a train, after that a coach and finally a cable-car which will leave me at the top of a Swiss mountain: a long trip to the summit of a mountain – which I shall call Matz Peak – to attend a Literature Festival taking place there every year – the participants are all German speakers, I would be the only one from Spain, which means I would not understand a thing of what was said or happened there – and to absorb what in the e-mail is called *the mountain spirit*. It made me think of the hiker Robert Walser, a great walker. And of Mann's *The Magic Mountain*. I imagine the writers on Matz Peak in shorts, with lots of torches and Tyrolese songs . . . I don't think I shall go, I think I shall reply that I have a prior engagement which makes it impossible for me to visit Matz Peak, this would seem to be the most sensible course of action, you never know, I might turn up at the peak, after the long journey, and, while I am absorbing the mountain spirit, be murdered or raped. I shall say I can't go. But what I shall do is keep the e-mail, it really is a very interesting document which, owing to the lack of proficiency in English, veers from the comical to the profound or unsettling: 'I hope all well. Subject: Swiss montains. Precious Rosario Girondo: It would be most kind say to me if you have time to go to the Literature Festival at which we already spoke you. It is a festival in the montains of Swiss, very wonderful, very interesting. A mix of vacations and of intellectual inspiring. My joy if you want to pick up this invitation. (There is people there who speaks Spanglish, at least I . . .) Much greetings from Zurigo, think about it: is the montain spirit.'

At five in the afternoon, many times – today was one

of them – I write one of the four articles I compose each week to ensure a regular monthly salary. Today I wrote on Kafka's relations with his friend Max Brod, I wrote it fairly quickly and sent it, having barely revised it, by e-mail. In the article, I discussed how poor Brod would advise Kafka to choose more elevated themes than the ones he used for his stories of rodents, moles and dogs. I recalled the admirable response by this hero of subordinate aesthetics, namely Kafka: 'You're right, Max, but not entirely, only in one sense. In another, what counts are not proportional numbers, I also should like to be tested in my mouse-hole.'

Around the same time, Kafka also wrote to Brod regarding great themes and other tittle-tattle: 'What am I building? I wish to dig a tunnel. I need to make some progress. My position is too high up there [. . .]. We are digging in the pit of Babel.'

The reader, if he has not already twigged, might be interested to know that the moles which the narrator in *Montano's Malady* saw in Teixeira's home on the island of Pico come straight from Kafka's world, all I did was give the more or less innocent Kafkaesque moles digging in the pit of the Tower of Babel a twist by turning them into hugely pernicious moles, with their head office in Pico, working away inside the volcano against the literary. I think I did well and it is better to know where the enemies of the literary are hiding themselves.

Having written and sent the article, I went down to the street to take a breather. As a writer, clearly, I live like a housewife. So to get out of the house and to go for a walk each day is always beneficial. Otherwise I would end up drowning at home. I went for a wander in the vicinity and unexpectedly bumped into Rosa coming the other way, back from work. We were both overjoyed to recognise each other among the anonymous people in the street. It was preferable to meet there than at home, where there is no surprise and it's always the same, Rosa comes back from work and we give each other a peck on the cheek. But today in the street was something else, we were both overjoyed. It must have been the best moment in a day which is – I hope – already finishing.

Around eight, I took a sedative which relaxes me and calms my desire, at that time in the evening, to start drinking in an attempt to bring the day to an abrupt close and wait for tomorrow to return to my routine life as a housewife who gets up at eight, has an instant coffee, reads for encouragement to write, writes until two, then has lunch in the awful restaurant on the corner, later attends to his post and the telephone and around five writes an article for a living and, with moderate enthusiasm, as the evening draws in, welcomes his wife home, and then watches television and goes mad if he does not take a sedative. If he takes the sedative, he goes mad as well, he just goes mad in a more relaxed way, without, however, ceasing to notice the greyness of his existence as a writer tied for life to his trade and the monotony of his daily tragedy.

OK, not all the days are exactly the same. Today, for example, I took the sedative and, just as it was taking effect, received a call from a friend – whom I envy, I should like to copy him, lead his adventurous life and possess the intelligent vision he, as a literary critic, has of everything he reads, I said before that I was a frustrated critic – who wished to thank me for having recommended that he read César Aira. 'The guy's crazy, but he's good,' he told me. I wanted to know why he thought he was crazy. 'Well, his humour is completely round the bend,' he said. 'Aira's humour is totally unintentional,' I corrected him, on a war footing, a little nervous and uneasy despite the sedative. 'I don't think so,' my friend the critic replied. At this point I felt obliged to explain to him, having to control my temper – at this stage in the day I was fairly irritable and anything could wind me up further, sedative time is never a good time for me, even though it relaxes me or precisely because of this – I felt morally obliged to clarify one or two things about Aira and I told him – as if I were the critic, no doubt motivated by the envy I feel towards him – that Aira never tires of saying that he writes seriously and people find him hilarious and that is why he has turned into a misanthrope. 'It's strange that you should not see that you don't exactly have to believe every word Aira says,' he told me, recovering his position as an intelligent man who defeats me in arguments.

For the first time ever, I took a second sedative. I continued talking to my friend, but every time he said something, I silently exacted revenge thinking about the day in Rome when he told me that he was going to commit suicide and I, already envious of him and also distrustful of his suicidal threats, did not lift a finger to dissuade him – I went so far as to tell him that, if he was planning to kill himself because the critic Stanislaw Wicinsky was miles better than him, he would do very well to take himself out of the picture – I opened a bottle of red Imola wine and sat down in the sitting room of the Roman house and, having taken my seat, waited to see if by chance the explosion went off.

To return to today, at around ten in the evening, suddenly distressed at not being a critic and above all depressed because Rosa was not talking to me – she was absorbed watching a programme on Catalan TV – I started reading Virginia Woolf's diary and wondering whether or not to include it in this dictionary. For a long time I was lost among all those intelligent and angst-ridden pages she wrote over twenty-seven years, always in the half-hour following teatime. 'I will go down with my colours flying,' she wrote in the penultimate entry recorded in her diary, three weeks before her suicide. The sentence contains great pride and is very moving, but it is also true to say that the sentence has an unbearable aura of sadness, which has managed to depress me even more. I decided to forget Virginia Woolf for today and started reading a story by Samuel Beckett, 'From an Abandoned Work', in which an old man, clearly mad, perhaps stultified by age, attempts to remember a day from his past, from the moment he left home in the morning to the time he came back at night. And one has the impression that three days, not one, have gone by.

Even the old man's life seemed more interesting than my own and I told myself that I do well to invent when I devote myself to literary creation and renounce realism, because I would be stuck if I had to talk all the time about my grey existence as a housewife who writes. In short, I read the story of this dumb old man created by Beckett and was on the verge of taking a third sedative. Increasingly anxious and sleepy, I ate a potato omelette that Rosa had prepared and went to bed. I dreamed that I was more dumb than Beckett's old man. Then I woke up and wrote down here what I did today, since I want the reader to have a certain idea of what I am like in my daily life, in which I lead such a monotonous and horrific existence that not infrequently I try to escape from it by writing about realities far removed from my real life. Of course, if I did not write, I wouldn't have to spend so much time at home and perhaps then I would lead a less grey life than at present. But what's the use? 'What's the use of Pentothal,' as my mother would say. I'm not so obsessed about literature sickness as I was when, for example, I arrived in Nantes in November last year. That is why I can now say with an easy conscience that, between life and books, I choose the latter, which help me to make sense of it. Literature has always enabled me to understand life. And for precisely that reason it leaves me outside it. I mean it: I wouldn't have it any other way.

Thursday (extract from Gombrowicz's diary)

I got up, as usual, around ten, and had breakfast: tea with cakes, followed by rolled oats. Letters: one from Litka in New York; another from Jelenski in Paris. At midday I went to the office (on foot, it's not far). I spoke to Marrill Alberes on the phone about the translation and to Russo to discuss the proposed trip to Goya. Ríos rang to tell me they were already back from Miramar, and Drabrowski (regarding the flat).

At three, coffee and bread with ham.

At seven, I left the office and headed in the direction of Costanera Avenue for a breath of fresh air (it's very hot, about 32 degrees). I was thinking about what Aldo told me yesterday. Then I went to Cecilia Benedit's home and we went out for dinner together. I had soup, steak and chips and salad, stewed fruit. I hadn't seen her for some time, so she told me about her adventures in a Mercedes [. . .]. From there, around midnight, I went to the Rex for a coffee [. . .]. Back home, I went into the Tortoni to pick up a package and talk to Pocho. At home, I read Kafka's diary. Went to sleep around three. I tell you all this for you to know what I am like in my daily life.

Friday

'Then,' says Justo Navarro, 'you grab the thing that is closest: you talk about yourself. And, writing about yourself, you begin to see yourself as if you were another, you treat yourself as if you were another: you move away from yourself in proportion as you approach yourself.'

Saturday

In an essay by Alan Pauls on the genre, I have just read that the great theme of the private journal in the twentieth century is sickness. I didn't know, I had never thought about this. And yet – curious coincidence – one of my diary's central ideas, one of its most recurrent themes, is undoubtedly that of sickness, in this case literature sickness, Montano's malady in short.

'The great theme of the private journal in the twentieth century,' writes Alan Pauls, 'is sickness. The annotations which the writer attaches to this illness represent something like a daily, unflagging report, giving an account of its progress, a kind of clinical history which seems only to have ears for the stealthy expressiveness of the ailment.'

As I deduce from what I have read in this essay on the genre, those writing great private journals in the last century did not do so to know who they were, but kept them to know *what they were turning into*, in which unforeseeable direction catastrophe was taking them. 'It is not, therefore, the revelation of a truth that these diaries could or wanted to give us, but the crude, clinical account of a mutation.'

We are, therefore, face to face with writing's clinical dimension. Surely in these pages I have been striving – perhaps without being entirely aware of it until now – to find out where the elimination of my illness, of my Montano's malady, would lead me. To silence, probably. Is this a good thing? I don't think so, because I would be back to where I was in the beginning: seated before the rickety chair of someone who is tragically agraphic. So surely the illness is better than the cure.

But is the illness a good thing? At the moment the best thing would be to keep smoking, to keep writing: to write, for example, that I am smoking. I take a drag from my cigarette and remember that, in Gombrowicz's diary, the writer ends up identifying himself with the evil: 'I myself was the illness, meaning the anomaly, meaning something related to death . . .'

But was Gombrowicz being sincere when he wrote

this? His diary is not exactly a masterpiece of sincerity, that quality so many hope to find in a private journal. In his diary, he accomplished a new invention of the Form and at the same time invented a new form of writing a diary. And he did this perhaps because, as a writer, what Gombrowicz most feared was Sincerity, he knew that Sincerity in literature led nowhere: 'Has there ever been a diary that was sincere? *The sincere diary* is without a doubt the most fallacious, because frankness is not of this world. And also – sincerity, what a bore! It isn't even faintly fascinating.'

Because of all this, he did not allow his diary to become confessional. He understood in time that in his diary he had to present himself *in action*, in his intention to impose himself on the reader in a certain way, in his will to create himself in the sight and with the knowledge of everyone. To tell the reader, 'This is how I want to be for you,' and not, 'This is how I am'. Gombrowicz claimed the right to his own face: 'Surely I do not have to allow every Tom, Dick and Harry to disfigure me as he pleases.'

I am doing something similar here, in this dictionary, resounding *fortissimo* with one of the great themes of existentialism: the creation of one's self.

'But,' the reader might say, 'you've been trying for some time now to be sincere, to give reliable information about your life.'

And it's true, in many pages of this dictionary I have been kneeling before the altar of Truthfulness and offering an amount of reliable information about my life, about how I composed the fictional *Montano's Malady*; it is a parenthesis I have opened here with great pleasure and I have opened it in the form of a timid autobiography, but it's also true that, as soon as I reach Monsieur Teste and Paul Valéry, the final entries planned for this dictionary of writers of private journals, I intend to enter a space bordering fiction and reality, possibly as a way of letting off steam after having been so veracious, after having told truths – for now, I shall carry on doing so – about my fragmented life, very truthful truths, recounted as if I didn't know that the truth is also invented, as Antonio Machado said.

GOMBROWICZ, Witold (Małoszyce, 1904–Vence, 1969). At the end of the twentieth century, Rosa and I went to Valparaíso to think about gunpowder. It isn't that we had agreed beforehand on something so extravagant as travelling to a distant place and, once there, thinking about something so alien to us as gunpowder. No, in reality we went to Valparaíso just to celebrate the end of the century, but what happened was that, once we were on the hanging terrace of the Brighton Hotel, watching the fireworks launched from ships anchored in the bay, neither Rosa nor I could stop thinking about something normally so far from our minds as blessed gunpowder. So much so, that Valparaíso will always be gunpowder and the names of six Chilean friends: Paula and Roberto Brodsky, Andrés, Rodrigo, Carolina and Gonzalo. With all of them we spent the restless night of 30 December in a house facing the Pacific, in Tunquén, and the following day, with the idea of celebrating the end of the century, we made the long car journey to the Brighton in Valparaíso, where we had booked all six rooms in this small hotel equipped with a truly unforgettable terrace, a terrace with a wonderful view over the city and bay, a space that today, with the perspective afforded by memory, strikes me as one of the central places in my life.

In Tunquén, the night before, we had been chatting and drinking until the early hours of the morning, in an ideal atmosphere for me, since our Chilean friends showed – or at least very politely feigned – a certain interest to know episodes and memories from my life: something that does not tend to happen to me in Barcelona, for example, where nobody seems interested in knowing fragments of my life – they behave as if they already knew it – and that may explain why they arrange to meet me in the city's rowdiest bars and restaurants, they deliberately arrange to meet me in a place where they know that conversations will always be disrupted and nervous. In Tunquén, however, I was listened to with respect, laughter and attention. Even Rosa seemed to be amused by my recollections and was especially charming when she laughed in the company of the others.

A long, unforgettable evening, laughter at times punctuating some of my remarks. As, for example, when Carolina – an inspired journalist, a good interviewer in real life – asked me point-blank, almost treacherously, what I should like to be were I not a writer. And, after a brief hesitation, I replied that I should like to be a psychiatrist specialising in dissociative disorders and post-traumatic stress and a member of the International Society for the Study of Dissociation. (Response followed by prolonged laughter.)

I have never recalled so many things out loud as I did

that night in Tunquén. I recalled, for example, the time in the 1970s when I lived between Paris and Berlin and considered myself to be a radical leftist and undergrounder and was friends with people like Ingrid Caven, Paloma Picasso and Ulrike Meinhof (before she became a terrorist). And I recalled how in those days it seemed that my destiny – like that of many of my peers – would be loneliness, drugs, violence and suicide. I remembered my mother, so fragile and strange, a secret poet, resembling Alejandra Pizarnik, permanently halfway between barbiturates and (the as yet unnamed) Montano's malady. I remembered how my generation wanted to change the world and said that perhaps it was far better that our dreams never came true. I recalled the day I discovered that writing is like walking in the library of life. I recalled the day I discovered Cernuda and he made me literature-sick: 'Light is the part of life / that like gods poets rescue.' I remembered how I used to sell apartments with my father on the Costa Brava. I remembered a trip to Warsaw, when I was twenty-five, a trip from Paris made exclusively to have dinner with Sergio Pitol. And finally I recalled how two days previously, on the aeroplane bringing Rosa and me to Chile, I had dreamed that I was married to the Canadian film-maker Julia Rosenberg and how by chance, hours after that dream, I had learned that Rosenberg was married to a writer, the New Yorker Jonathan Lethem, who – and this was the strangest part – looked a lot like me when I was young, as I suddenly discovered in a photograph I came across completely by chance in one of the in-flight magazines; he looked like the young man who had walked in Paris and Berlin in the 1970s, he looked like me before I began to resemble the elegant but vampiric Christopher Lee: a slightly tragic and regrettable destiny, but, when it comes to it, no harder than others.

The evening was a little spoiled at the end, when Gombrowicz's name was mentioned and our Chilean friends, wanting to see how I reacted when I got angry, piqued me by suggesting in a snide and persistent way, using the most varied arguments, that on more than one occasion I had copied the Polish writer.

There the night came to an end.

I slept little and badly. I dreamed that Julia Rosenberg was dancing with an iguana on a beach in the Pacific full of old people talking constantly about funereal themes, about how in their time it was customary for all the mirrors in the house of the deceased to be covered over with silk crêpe in sign of mourning.

The following morning, none of us having rested very much, we began the long and tortuous – owing to the general hangover – journey to the Brighton, where we arrived at about half past one in the afternoon and where the first thing Rosa and I were able to confirm was that the hotel's famous hanging terrace was as spectacular as the Brodskys had told us.

The hotel was occupied by us, but the terrace at that time seemed to belong to the entire city of Valparaíso, there wasn't room for another soul. What I saw as soon as I stepped on to it, I put down to the hangover: beneath a sunshade, an old and very ugly man, with horrible, grandiose ears and shaved head, appeared to be absorbed in reading *Pornografia*, a book by Gombrowicz.

As the Brodskys had told me that we were due to meet

a friend of theirs who had been unable to come to Tunquén, I thought that this horrible, vampiric old man could be the person they planned to introduce to me. Separating from the group and spontaneously taking the initiative as if drawn by the brotherly call of Nosferatu's blood, I approached the old man and jokingly asked him how much the Brodskys were paying him to pretend to be reading Gombrowicz.

The look that man directed towards me I would not wish on anyone.

'The Brodskys?' he said. 'What on earth are you talking about? Those creatures who, with your lordship, have just stepped on to the terrace? Are they the Brodskys? I have to tell you, sir, those kids are very good at playing ball.'

This man was undoubtedly very odd, and not just on account of his vampiric appearance. He was elegant, but very strange. And his elegance was also strange, not to say extravagant. For example, he was wearing a belt strapped around his waist, on top of his white shirt, as if he were tying himself up.

It seemed to me, despite his chilling gaze, that he was joking and I simply had to go along with it.

'They're pretending to be adults,' I said. 'But they're just as much children as you are, who own the ball.'

His next look made me think I was mistaken and this man had nothing to do with the Brodskys, I had been talking to a stranger in the literal sense of the word.

'Mistakes like yours,' he told me, suddenly sounding like Gombrowicz and adopting a very unpleasant tone, 'deserve a flick. And now, mister intruder, clear off if you do not want to discover that my belt is a whip.'

Your head reminds me of a large lily, I thought of telling him. But the sentence was too soft for my liking. Your pale forehead is a confused map. This also seemed too soft, and sweet besides, and even sickeningly poetic. You're the one who's a flick, I thought of telling him. But I found it simplistic. You son of a bitch. This seemed more to the point, but too vulgar and direct. Besides, I had to have respect for my elders. All the same, I felt a sudden dislike for this man, he struck me as rude and detestable, and finally I went for this bold question:

'Did Your Majesty get his Draculean and Dracularsean ears from his lady mother, the Great Arse?'

I thought that he would at least give me a smack or a heavy lash, but he didn't. He looked at me, smiled, and roared with monumental, theatrical laughter, as spectacular as that terrace. Everyone suddenly turned towards us and I almost blushed. His laughter seemed to have no end, but it ended. He then became very serious and reached out his hand to me in a friendly manner.

'Tongoy,' he said. 'Felipe Tongoy.'

He was a friend of the Brodskys, I was not mistaken when I thought this. But the fact he was reading Gombrowicz was in no way related to the previous night's argument in Tunquén. Felipe Tongoy had been a fan of Gombrowicz his whole life, and that was all. Or nothing. Because Tongoy had such an odd appearance, he was seven times Dracula compared to me. And it was difficult to be sure about him, though this much was undoubtedly clear: he was friends with the Brodskys and read Gombrowicz.

'Tongoy,' he said again. 'Felipe Tongoy. I am the

Brodskys' oldest friend. I like dry Martini, Chile, Gombrowicz and vampires. *Garçon*,' he shouted to the waiter, 'ink, please!'

He had ink on his gums or he had just eaten squid in their ink. He aroused in me neither disgust nor fear, I saw him as a friend, but most of all – this calmed me – as a friend of the Brodskys, meaning he did arouse in me a certain amount of fear, or even a great deal, not because of the Brodskys, but because of the strange ink on his gums. My blood was not circulating too well, I could feel it. I had never seen anyone so literature-sick as this monster.

'Girondo,' I replied, trembling. 'Rosario Girondo at your service.'

'Do you like Chile?' he asked me with a devilish look.

I thought hard before answering.

'Chile is OK,' I said finally.

He smiled at me, I suppose so that I could see the ink again. And shortly afterwards, with his left hand, which was the one he had free – because with his right he was again calling the waiter – he touched his monstrous right ear.

I recalled Gombrowicz: 'If you wish to indicate that you liked my work, simply touch your right ear when you see me.'

'Girondo,' I said, also touching my ear. 'Rosario Girondo.'

This tremulous – with Gombrowicz in the background – and extravagant exchange of ears by way of credentials was the start of a great, unexpected friendship.

'My dear Mrs Girondo,' Tongoy said suddenly, with a huge, horrific happy smile, 'welcome to the Brighton.'

Thursday

BUT IT'S RAINING!

The rain is falling on Barcelona, though with less wind and cruelty than yesterday, when I went to the Avenida Palace to meet Rita Gombrowicz. It may seem a very curious coincidence or a very fortuitous chance, but the fact is that, as I was absorbed in the entry under the word Gombrowicz in this dictionary, Rita, his widow, arrived yesterday in Barcelona and I went to see her at her hotel, the Avenida Palace. It may seem a very fortuitous chance, but in truth I had known for a month that Rita Gombrowicz was going to come to Barcelona and that she and I had to present a book by her husband in the bookshop La Central. If I'm honest, knowing this made me linger over the word Gombrowicz, because I did not want to find myself commenting on another author of private journals – Kafka, for example, the next word in this dictionary – with Rita in Barcelona.

Yesterday I went to fetch her from the Avenida Palace. It was a very unpleasant afternoon, rain and a strong wind, a rare winter's day in the middle of spring. I had only seen old photographs of Rita, images from the 1960s, from the time she went to live with Witold Gombrowicz, but I immediately recognised her. Inclined as I am to mythologise writers (Gombrowicz has always been a myth for me, which is not to say that he has influenced my writing, I made this very clear in Tunquén), I was nervous at the beginning of the meeting with Rita, but soon there arose a mutual current of sympathy and intimacy between us, as if we had known each other our whole lives.

It was raining steadily outside, it was raining in an aggressive way which was not at all melancholic, but the conversation in the hotel foyer turned nostalgic and persistent, seemingly enveloped in a strange melancholy invented by a rain that was not the rain outside, and gradually the meeting with Rita inclined towards intimacies: 'He was someone,' she said of her husband, 'who worked a lot on himself, creating his own style. He belonged to a group of writers whose work is the reincarnation of their own personality.'

We proceeded to talk about the close relationship between life and work, and we discussed writers who devote themselves to creating their own style. I didn't wish to say anything about myself, but if there is one point I have in common with Gombrowicz, it is the origin of my literary style, based – as in his case – on a radical departure from the conservative and boring family discourse.

Gombrowicz's style would have been nothing without the participation of his mother, who was naive, gluttonous, comfort-loving, and whose culture was more fashionable than anything else. She was all this by nature, but she believed that she was lucid, intellectual, frugal and heroically ascetic. 'It was she,' wrote her son, 'who pushed me to pure folly, to the absurd, which would later become one of the most important features of my art.' Together with his brother Jerzy, Gombrowicz very quickly hit upon the ideal way to wind her up: it involved systematically affirming the opposite of what she might say. Their mother had only to declare that the sun was shining for the two brothers to reply in unison, 'But what are you saying? It's raining!'

It is no surprise that, years later, Gombrowicz declared that he did not worship poetry and was not overly progressive or modern, or the typical intellectual, or even a nationalist, Catholic, Communist, upright man, nor did he revere science, art or Marx: 'Who was I then? Frequently I was simply the negation of everything the other person said.'

In my case, I learned, every day more skilfully, to interrupt my father's boring discourse on, for example, our country's dreams, bungles and culture. I became the negation of everything he would propose, suggest, programme or declare. But, since my father's discourse hardly ever flagged and was a one-sided discourse – only he could speak at home – I barely had time for my interjections, which took advantage of short pauses in my father's discourse to slip in my small tributes to folly, always in an unbalanced style. 'You're no son of mine,' my father would say. And also: 'I don't know why you always have to be different in front of me.'

To counteract the constant appearance of clichés in my father's discourse, I had to – and this is what I did – concentrate all my energy on snippets of homespun skulduggery, short and avant-garde skirmishes with which I built up a nonconformist and eccentric literary style: an avant-garde style to begin with, which with time has simmered down. A style opposed to family boredom, that of my parents' home, but also to the crushing boredom of the country in which I had chanced to be born. A contradictory style, an attempt always to say something different, with humour if possible, to break with the lack of irony in the head of the family's antiquated and one-sided monologue. A style without too many flesh-and-blood literary characters. A style in revolt against everything, most of all against the sleep-inducing Spanish realism, a style that was always ironic towards the marchionesses and proletarian women, lovers and prostitutes, coming and going at five in the afternoon in today's Spanish novels.

I originate from the avant-garde movement and the skirmishes which family boredom forced me into. And, although I later simmered down, I have devoted my whole life to shunning the established order and trying to create my own style and to say something different. I hate it, for example, when taxi-drivers talk to me about the weather and abruptly initiate a string of set phrases. Just yesterday, when I was heading towards the Avenida Palace, the taxi-driver said something to me about the litres of rain that had fallen. During a pause in his leaden discourse, I hijacked the conversation and said (knowing that this would confuse and silence him), 'Just today I was given the opportunity to kill bad weather. Do you know what I did?' Anxious silence, bewilderment. 'I simply washed the weather's face. That's why it's raining. Though you may not have noticed that in fact it's not raining.'

Thanks to my style, I can survive even in a taxi. With the taxi-driver talking to me about the weather, I must have reached the Avenida Palace yesterday at about seven in the evening. The presentation in La Central was at eight, and *Ferdydurke* the book we were going to speak about. First we discussed other matters in the hotel, and did so with a steady, persistent rain of unexpected melancholy.

The real rain was waiting for us outside, when at about half past seven we started walking along the Rambla de

Catalunya, towards the bookshop. We were protected from that real rain by the red umbrella which had accompanied me in the rain in Nantes and had witnessed the birth of *Montano's Malady*, an umbrella to which I had since attributed creative powers.

A single umbrella for two fans of Gombrowicz. But several rains for them. And even an imaginary sun.

'It's not raining,' I said, 'the sun's coming out.'

Rita understood me, she grasped the tribute to Gombrowicz's anti-maternal style and joked, with a happy and unforgettable wink:

'But it's raining!'

The red umbrella started trying to unbalance me, the wind shook it from side to side and never have two fans of Gombrowicz got so wet. In the face of such an assault, it occurred to me to say to Rita that our umbrella wanted to commit suicide. 'Clearly you're not only concerned about flesh-and-blood characters, you also see a soul in umbrellas,' she said. I would have replied that in my books such characters are conspicuous by their absence, but I preferred not to speak about me and asked her if she was particularly interested in the flesh-and-blood people who appear in novels. She stopped abruptly in the middle of the street, in the rain, and almost took root in the wet tarmac while, among the gusts of wind, she considered her response. 'I'm interested,' she said slowly, 'in the traces of tears and not the tears. I'm interested in what flesh-and-blood characters leave in writing and not so much in them.'

As I was about to say that not everybody leaves something in writing, Rita startled me by referring to an anonymous suicide note. The note simply said, 'So much doing up and undoing.'

At that moment, the red umbrella took flight (its remains rest today in the kitchen at home), drawing a strange parabola and crashing against a tree in the Rambla. To indicate that I had liked the anonymous farewell note, with another wink of Gombrowicz collusion, I touched my ear as a sign of approving of the phrase 'so much doing up and undoing'. But Rita was no longer there, she had sensibly sought refuge in a doorway. While the umbrella left the tree and again took to its wings and started forging its own style on discovering revolt and freedom, I stood there absurdly still in the middle of the Rambla, a flesh-and-blood character soaked to the skin, representing for whoever wished to see the grotesque figure of a madman who has lost his umbrella and touches an ear. There I stood, a victim of my own style, there I stood for a short while, very still, as if I believed that really it was not raining, but a perfect midday sun was shining.

KAFKA, Franz (Prague, 1883–Kierling, 1924). 'My outer ear felt fresh, rough, cold and juicy to the touch, like the leaf of a tree,' writes Kafka in his 1910 diary. His remark refers me to another, refers me to the memory of something I heard Claudio Magris say one evening in Barcelona: 'Literature may also be part of the world in the same way as leaves are, for example.'

Magris' remark not only consoles me, but returns me to the world. Literature and world enter into harmony. I no longer consider it so serious to be literature-sick. It is pleasant to feel, as I feel this morning, in harmony with the world. But I remember a day in the summer of 1965, I remember that day very well, because I think I have never been so far removed from that harmony with the world.

Since, on that August afternoon, the notion of literature barely existed for me – I read little, spy novels, and I still hadn't discovered Cernuda, I still didn't know that I could find a warm but sickly refuge in literature, a refuge from the roughness of life – I could not find a place in the world, I felt deeply lost and disconsolate.

I could not find a place in the world, and not for lack of trying. I was anxious to find a place, however humble, in whatever Order; in the infinite universe, in the greyness of the world of work, in a spy ring, in a lunatic asylum, in a family with parents more sensible than my own, in the mediocrity of a peaceful married life seen as a lesser evil next to loneliness . . .

I had a lot of the sad hero of our time. But since I hardly read anything at all – I was almost completely detached from the literature that would later ensnare me – I could not draw on the happy and imaginative resources that reading offers us, allowing us to escape from the anxiety which sometimes pins us down. And, as for being ignorant, I didn't even know – how it would have helped me that day! – that this is what I was, that at the age of fifteen I was the classic hero of our time. Knowing it would undoubtedly have benefited me, would even have made me feel – in my sadness – like an important young man, would even have given my life a certain meaning, would have helped me not to fall into the absolute disconsolation I fell into completely at around seven in the evening of that summer's day, when, in my father's absence, it was my turn to lock up the office on the Costa Brava where I helped him to sell apartments. On other days when I had been the one to lock up the office, I had felt a special satisfaction at the capacity I now had to take responsibility. But on that summer's day I was deeply disconsolate. I closed the office and looked at the world, I looked at the sea and then at the mountain. Sea and mountain, mountain and sea, sleeping and waking, studying and working, waking and sleeping, so much doing up and undoing . . .

I locked up and sat on the ground, in front of the closed office. I sat on the ground because I didn't know where to go. After a short while, a respectable couple came by, who were friends with my parents. By way of greeting and a little surprised, they asked me, with no intention of interfering in my life or rebuking me for something, what I was doing there on the ground. 'Business is going well,' I told them, 'but I cannot talk to the employees, I cannot talk to the customers.' They were a little perplexed. My father had no employees, or rather I was his only employee. 'Is something the matter?' they asked me. From the ground, I replied with another question: 'Where am I going to go?' A slight panic took hold of them, I noticed that they were disturbed. And shortly afterwards I discovered that the same thing was happening to these two poor creatures, they didn't know where to go either. It seemed odd to me that this should happen to them as well, given that they were responsible and respectable adults. But, however odd it may have seemed to me, this was the case. I felt almost panic-stricken seeing them like this, so disoriented, inhibited and directionless, viewing the world with the same surprise with which I viewed it that afternoon. I should have liked to lend them a hand, but I was not the most adequate person to do this, I was not exactly in a fit state to help these adults, these respectable friends of my parents.

Another Kafkaesque episode, an incident that still haunts me now: the memory of the day I turn eighteen and insult my mother when I discover that she has lent my copy of Camus' *The Outsider* to the daughter of a friend. 'Leave my books alone! They're all I have.' I say this to her, and also other, more aggressive things, charged with real fury. Without realising, I am beginning to suffer from Montano's malady. And then, at night, my parents whispering in bed, in the room next to mine. The enigmatic whisper of their voices. The almost complete certainty that they're talking about me and about my angry outburst on account of Camus' book. My ear pressed against the door of their bedroom and my inability to hear a single word, only the terrible, indecipherable murmurings. I think of suddenly opening the door of their room and telling my father, 'Hold on to her, grab the flesh that's next to you, your wife's flesh is bound to calm you down, stop talking about your son who's an outsider.' But no, I don't open the door of my parents' bedroom. No, I don't open it.

I should have liked to have three sisters and to talk to them in Yiddish, to talk in a language my parents could not understand. It was not good to be an only child and to confront alone the terror which the manly resonance of my father's voice and my mother's weak voice – like the whisper of fallen leaves – caused me. I should have liked to have three sisters and for the eldest to spend the day lounging on the sofa in my parents' sitting room and to have shapely, bare, rounded, strong, dark shoulders that I would spy on at every moment, always proud that these shoulders belonged to the family estate. I should have liked my middle sister to walk about the house in an ash-coloured corset, the lower part of which would be so far from her body that one could straddle it. I should have liked my youngest sister to be my favourite and to have a tender regard for her madness, I should have liked very much for my youngest sister to remind me of that young descendant of Lord Byron whom I saw one evening in Caffè Florian in Venice, that beautiful, deranged young woman who kept on asking for her ancestor. 'Where is my George? What have you done to him?' she would shout out. I don't know, I should have liked to have three sisters and to talk to them in Yiddish and not to have been the only child I was, a clumsy outsider in my parents' home.

Sunday

Incredible, sunny spring day on which Rosa is in Turin and I am home alone and decide to lower the blinds and do without the happy, festive day, purely because I have an impression of absolute freedom, that I can do whatever I feel like, and the only thing I really feel like doing is not being too free and shutting myself up in darkness, thinking about Kafka and this dictionary where I try to comment on the world with my favourite diarists and which, if I am not careful, could turn into one of those texts commenting unendingly on the world.

I don't think anyone is more literature-sick than Kafka. His diary is terrifying. At eight in the morning, he would arrive punctually at his office. He would write documents and reports, make inspections. His superiors did not know that he worked there, in that crowd of miserable workers and employees, only because he knew that he should not devote all his time to literature. He was afraid that literature would suck him in, like a whirlpool, causing him to lose his bearings in its limitless expanse. He could not be free, he needed a limitation, to have all the time to write struck him as dangerous, terrible. He would return to his parents' home at about quarter past two in the afternoon. He said that he felt like an outsider, although he had great love for his family, parents and sisters. From time to time it occurred to him that he should move away from his friends and do so without the slightest consideration, become enemies with everyone, talk to no one. Other times, the opposite: he sought out his friends or favourite writers to establish a dialogue and to begin to comment unendingly on the world, as if what he wanted was to reach the source of all writing.

Incredible spring Sunday on which I close the windows and reread *The Castle*, a novel that cannot end, among other reasons because in it the Surveyor does not travel from one place to another, but from one interpretation to another, from one commentary to another. The Surveyor pauses at every bend in the imaginary road and comments on everything. One has the impression that he writes in order to reach the source of all writing, and in the meantime – in a series of commentaries that become endless – he comments on the world. He seems always to be searching for the first to name something, for the original source. He strives to find the first to write something, the man who wrote the first word or phrase. But, for this, he must take on three thousand years of writing. Unlike *Don Quixote*, Kafka's novel is not explicitly about books – K. is a surveyor, not a reader or writer – and so does not suffer from Montano's malady or pose problems relating to writing, but carries those problems in its own structure as a novel, given that the essential element of K.'s pilgrimage does not involve changing places, but going from one exegesis to another, from one commentator to another, listening to each one of them with avid interest and then participating and arguing with everybody, following a method of thorough examination.

As Justo Navarro told me one day, *The Castle* is the torment of an unending commentary. I think of this statement and tell myself that no doubt it is also the journey of someone searching for the first word, the original word, the source of all writing.

'I know, there need to be two of us.'

'But why two? Why two words to say the same thing?'

'Because it's always the other who says it.'

I wish to free myself from Montano's malady, but hopefully the gods and Kafka won't let me. I wish to free myself from the malady, and that is why I write obsessively about it. However, I know that, were I to achieve this, I could not comment on my achievement, I could not write about it, because, if I did, this would show – since, directly or indirectly, I would have to name the malady to say that I had forgotten it – that I was still thinking about it in some way. This would obviously be as bad as the malady itself and would end up giving me the impression that my progress towards death and my progress towards the word were one and the same. I wish to free myself from Montano's malady, but, should this diary ever reach its final hour and I overcome the illness and my salvation be a possibility, I'm not at all sure that it really will be, I think it will be something I need to comment on. This confirms my suspicion that these pages could go on for ever, and I don't know if it is desirable either that they do so or that they come to an end. This is how things stand and, living as much with dread of this diary's infinite movement as with fear of its death, one calms down on this spring night and even rejoices to see that, although one is writing obsessively about it, one is fortunately still Montano-stricken.

MANSFIELD, Katherine (Wellington, 1888–Fontainebleau, 1923). We had left the vampiric Tongoy in Valparaíso welcoming me to the Brighton's terrace; we had left him there after that strange exchange of greetings by ear, which was the start of our friendship. Hours later, night of the end of the year and the century, endless drinking bout, joyful discharges of gunpowder. At midday on 1 January, I again saw Tongoy on the Brighton's terrace. 'How odd he is,' said Rosa, as we went towards where he was seated in a corner of the terrace, looking like he had an almighty hangover. It wouldn't be long now before our man seriously martyred a fly.

We were making friendly remarks about the awful hangover face or mask he was wearing when he suddenly noticed that a fly had fallen into his dry Martini and was trying weakly, but desperately to climb out again. He gave us a frightful look and smiled, baring his fangs in all their splendour. After that he took a teaspoon and elegantly removed the fly from the glass and plopped it on to a paper napkin. A delicate gesture from the monster. The fly soon began to shake its front legs and, raising its tiny, soaked body, it undertook the heroic and moving task of cleaning the dry Martini from its wings. Little by little, the fly began to recover and return to life. Tongoy did not stop looking at it. 'It's your good deed for the day,' Rosa said to him. Then Tongoy saw that the fly was about to take off again and he seemed not to like this. Using the teaspoon, he soaked it again in dry Martini. Three times he did this, until he killed it. 'It was brave,' he said to us, 'but I'm hung-over and I'm not in the mood to spare anyone's life.'

If he wanted to impress us, he had managed to do so, not a lot, but to a degree he had managed it. We remained in silence for a while. I don't know what Rosa was thinking, I was thinking about Marguerite Duras. I was telling myself that, should Tongoy happen to remark that the fly had died at twenty minutes past twelve, he would be repeating some inspired words by Marguerite Duras, who in a passage from her book *Écrire* explains how she was moved by a fly's death throes in her garden at Neauphle-le-Château and how the exact time at which the fly had left this world had engraved itself upon her memory.

But Tongoy was not Marguerite Duras. If I had to compare him to a female writer, I would say he had something in common with Katherine Mansfield, Chekhovian storyteller and angst-ridden diarist, author of a story, 'The Fly', in which, with her customary poetic attention to detail and what is fleeting – with the same inspired melancholy that enabled Proust, for example, to describe the glimmer of twilight above the trees in the Bois de Boulogne – she recounted the forays into the dominions of death and return to life again and again of a fly trapped – a kind of literary illness – in a blot of ink.

I don't think I shall be far off the mark if I say that the fly was Katherine Mansfield herself, who spent half her life fighting against consumption, fighting against death: 'The clocks are striking ten [. . .]. I have consumption. There is still a great deal of moisture (*and* pain) in my BAD lung. But I do not care. I do not want anything I could not have. Peace, solitude, time to write my books . . .'

'In Mansfield,' Alan Pauls has written, 'sickness is much more than a theme of the journal, it is its only subject matter, its obsession, its favourite prey, and at the same time what gives her writing a rhythm, a cadence, a regularity.'

Sickness was the axis of her tormented life and she spoke obsessively about her illness in the journal, just as the fly murdered by Tongoy – had it possessed the power of speech – could have spoken at great length about its own form of consumption: the moisture of dry Martini.

MAUGHAM, William Somerset (Paris, 1874–Saint-Jean-Cap-Ferrat, Nice, 1965). This English writer, who was born and died in France, published in 1949 a summary of the fifteen volumes of notes he had taken over more than half a century, a diary – entitled *A Writer's Notebook* – which invariably took as its inspiration Jules Renard's diary, one he regarded as a lesser masterpiece of French literature.

Maugham's diary has always accompanied me over the years. 'I am on the wing' is how it ends, and I have always considered this sentence and applied it to my life.

I share Maugham's belief that 'there is in the heroic courage with which man confronts the irrationality of the world a beauty greater than the beauty of art [. . .]. I find it,' he goes on, 'in the cool determination of Captain Oates when he went out to his death in the arctic night rather than be a burden to his comrades. I find it in the loyalty of Helen Vagliano, a woman not very young, not very pretty, not very intelligent, who suffered hellish torture and accepted death, for a country not her own, rather than betray her friends.'

Maugham always reminds me that nobility of spirit exists and this nobility does not come from thought or depend on culture and education. It has its roots in the human being's most primitive instincts. The refuge against despair is perhaps to be found in the consciousness that the spirit's salvation is a possibility.

MICHAUX, Henri (Namur, 1899–Paris, 1984). It's the end of the year, but it's not the end of the century, nor are we in Valparaíso with Tongoy, we are with Henri Michaux at sea aboard the *Boskoop*, which takes him – 'severe and reserved the boat,' he tells us in his travel journal – in the direction of Ecuador, final or penultimate day of 1927, I cannot be sure about the date. If private journals have one limitation, it is the calendar. As Blanchot has observed, the journal, so susceptible to the movements of life and capable of every freedom – since dreams, fictions, thoughts, commentaries about oneself, important or insignificant events, everything suits the journal, whatever order or disorder they go in – is, however, subject to a seemingly trivial, but fearful clause: it must respect the calendar. It's strange, but this respect for dates – I don't know if Blanchot thought about it – vanishes at sea, as is evident in Michaux's travel journal, which right from the beginning is tossed about by the waves: 'Let me see, are there thirty or thirty-one days in December? And is it two or three days that we have been at sea? In the non-calendar of the sea? Poor diary!'

This morning, shortly after Rosa left for work, I went looking for *Ecuador*, I searched for the book in the library in order to reread it before tackling this author's entry in my timid dictionary. While I was searching for it, perhaps providentially, I came across a short essay by Proust on Flaubert, an essay I had forgotten about, which, after I reread it, has ended up influencing the construction of the word Michaux, as will now become clear.

Let us start anew.

MICHAUX, Henri. All his life, Michaux thought of man as a 'broken animal' with an unsatisfied hunger for the infinite. His style is always very dry. His style, did I say? All his writing is in fact a hard struggle against it: 'Style, the ability to install himself and to install the world, is that what man is? That suspicious acquisition for which the jolly writer is praised? [. . .] Try to get out. See far enough inside yourself for your style not to be able to follow you.'

Michaux's travels were always really inner, almost armchair, travels, though we see him at sea or in the thick of the Ecuadorean forest. They were really journeys of self-study. In *Ecuador* we see him board the *Boskoop* and, although we shall pass through varied scenery, we shall soon notice that what most interests us is the traveller himself and that unique way of relating to the environment that leads him to revolutionise the typical travel journal or description of what is seen en route and to turn it into a distressing private journal of anxiety. His language travels inwards and is quick as a whip. Sometimes a sentence consists of two bare and solitary words. He writes, for example: 'radical introspection' or 'intravenous connections with the landscape'.

This morning, while searching for *Ecuador*, I came across the essay by Proust I had forgotten about. I started flicking through it – only to find out what it was about – and in the end I couldn't put it down. In his essay Proust speaks of that confusion – still in force today, by the way – regarding the episode of the madeleine. He bemoans the fact that certain people, some of them extremely learned, ignorant of the rigorous, but veiled composition of *Swann's Way*, believed that the novel was a kind of book of memories, linked according to the accidental laws of the association of ideas. 'In support of this lie,' says Proust, 'they quoted pages in which some crumbs of madeleine dunked in herbal tea remind me of a whole period from my life. Well [. . .], to switch from one scene to another, I simply used not a fact, but the purest and most useful join I could find, a phenomenon of memory.'

Proust then suggests we read Chateaubriand's *Memoirs*, in which he says it is perfectly clear that the author was also familiar with this method of abrupt transition, this *phenomenon of memory*. While in Montboissier, Chateaubriand suddenly hears a thrush sing. And this song he had listened to so much when he was young immediately takes him back to Combourg, urges him, together with the reader, to switch time and place. Immediately the narrative is situated somewhere else.

This technical device, this *phenomenon of memory*, this method of abrupt transition reminded me this morning of the overwhelming simplicity of a method I learned about from Jean Echenoz, the French novelist, who one evening, in the Aviador – a bar in Barcelona, decorated with propellers and shields, remains of airports and air disasters – talked to me about abrupt, but effective transitions in his stories. 'A bird goes by,' he said. 'I follow it. This enables me to go wherever I like in the narrative.' It struck me as a very interesting lesson, one to bear in mind, and I remember that I thought that, viewed in this way, any line in a story could become a migratory bird, for example. I took note of all this because it struck me as a very good means by which, in the moment that a written sentence lasts, simply to start listening to other voices, other rooms. In fact Echenoz applies his theory in *Double Jeopardy*, where the duke, Pons, handles some binoculars in the south of Asia and, on focusing them, sees the flight of some migratory birds – in a way that recalls those minute signs that in *Cosmos* reveal to Gombrowicz the direction of the flight of the narrative

– which in arrowhead formation – apparently pointing to the next chapter – head straight for Paris. As a result, confronted by such an instantaneous change of scene, the reader is likewise obliged to get hold of some good binoculars.

Years later, in *Montano's Malady*, I made use of Echenoz's lesson in the Aviador bar to move the action quickly from a Chilean landscape to Barcelona: 'Back on terra firma, I looked up at the cloudless sky of San Fernando and saw a bird go by. I followed it. And it seemed to me that following it enabled me to go wherever I liked, mentally to make use of all my possible mobility. A few hours later I was flying in the direction of Barcelona . . .'

The technical solution of the migratory bird is surprising both for its effectiveness and for its great simplicity. But this is how certain technical problems that place writers in double jeopardy are often resolved. After all, the instantaneous switch to other voices, other rooms, is one of the secret advantages that literature has over life, because in life this switch is never so simple, whereas in books everything is possible, and often amazingly easy.

To return to this morning, having read Proust's essay, I renewed the search for my copy of *Ecuador*, which I eventually found and began to reread, suddenly experiencing a Proustian *phenomenon of memory* when, seated in my favourite armchair, I embarked on a peaceful journey to Ecuador, which very soon ceased to be comfortable. On various occasions an icy headwind pushed me violently backwards, transferring me to Atlantic scenes that everything indicated were behind me: unmistakable scenes from the Azores and, more specifically, from the islands of Fayal and Pico.

The first time that this *phenomenon of memory* took place was when I read that Michaux, on his way to Ecuador, on the island of Guadeloupe, had a room overlooking a volcano ('My room overlooks a volcano. / In short a volcano. / I'm two steps away from a volcano. / [. . .] Volcano, volcano, volcano. / This is my music for tonight.'), which caused the appearance of the icy, Proustian headwind. I lifted my eyes from the book and travelled back in time to the memory of the voices of that pleasant Atlantic scene in the hotel room Rosa and I shared in February this year in Fayal, with its balcony overlooking the volcano on the enigmatic island of Pico, the hotel room next to Tongoy, who accompanied us on our four-day trip to the Azores. I couldn't help recalling Tongoy as he rested in a hammock in the hotel in Fayal when I read in Michaux's diary, 'Drops of blood fall from the hammock placed over me. This is the danger with vampires, they suck your blood without your realising. Once you have been a victim, the vampires recognise you among the others and are drawn towards you.'

When shortly afterwards I left the image of Tongoy in the hammock in the Azores and managed to start reading Michaux again, another icy headwind blew when I read the description of the climate of Ecuador, so similar to that of the Azores: 'It is difficult to establish the climate of this country. In the altiplanos people tend to say – and it's fairly accurate – four seasons in one day.'

This happened again and again. I would read Michaux, and the Proustian wind would take me back to the Azores.

As, for example, when he describes how he disembarked on the island of Curaçao. The charm he notices there strikes me as identical to that which Tongoy, Rosa and I felt this February when, arriving from Fayal, we disembarked on the enigmatic island of Pico. Michaux writes, 'Nothing so seductive as an island. There is nothing on the planet, I assure you, that looks so like a cloud as an island. Each time we are captivated by it.'

So it is that *Ecuador* at various points contains clear and somewhat mysterious similarities to our trip to the Azores. I would read *Ecuador* and a migratory bird or an icy wind would carry me back, leave me in my memories of the Azores: a nearly constant *phenomenon of memory*. As if this were not enough, I would sometimes come across lines in Michaux which reinforced – in tribute to Michaux, let us call them *intravenous* – relations between Tongoy, Rosa and me: 'On this last day in the month of February, a sudden wind carried me mentally to my house in Paris, where I spent a few imaginary hours in the company of my wife and a friend, before returning intact to this steep, straight Ecuador.'

Although we went to the Azores on holiday, each of us had another reason to add to the idea of travelling for the sake of it. I was prompted also by my curiosity to see Café Sport, which Tabucchi talks about in *The Woman of Porto Pim*, Tongoy went because he had always been curious to experience a whaler's life at first hand, and Rosa – who initially was the only one without a special reason apart from being a tourist – also found an additional reason when at Lisbon airport she bought a book by one António Caiado – 'a secret, hidden writer, like Julien Gracq, who lurks on the island of Pico, in the Azores,' it says on the back cover – and she was so fascinated by the story told in this book that she even planned to locate this 'hidden writer' and suggest being his literary agent.

The story of *The Rest Home for the Beauty-Sick* – the title of Caiado's novel has always sounded almost Japanese to me – was the following: an Italian from Verona who considers himself a 'beauty hunter' arrives in Pico intending to find the perfect home in which to live out the rest of his days, but ends up being admitted to a kind of rest home or spa where a series of unusual travellers live, 'all of whom are beauty-sick'.

It goes without saying that this story unsettled me, since I suspected that beauty-sick might simply mean literature-sick and I found the idea of a spa to treat the literature-sick repulsive. I did not wish to run the risk and continue reading this novel. Tongoy sided with me for different reasons and likewise refused to read the book and also refused to visit the aforesaid Caiado on the island of Pico. Tongoy is not without a sense of humour, and his fears were directly contrary to mine, he was simply afraid of not finding himself in the pages of this book.

The day the three of us travelled on the ferry from Fayal to Pico, there was a stiff breeze, which did not take us back in Proustian fashion to any strange country, but did threaten to land us on our backs on the deck of the boat. Rosa was in a happy mood, perhaps because she was convinced that it was a great adventure to go in search of the 'hidden writer' of the island of Pico. The sea spray dashed against her face and Rosa was prettier than ever, I've never seen her looking so good, though I was silently conspiring against her, planning the way to avoid having to visit Caiado's house or refuge. With her stunning appearance, Rosa looked wonderful, standing quietly, with the sea spray in her face. 'Ocean,' writes Michaux, 'what a beautiful toy they would make of you, if only your surface were able to support a man, as is often indicated by your stunning appearance, your solid plate. They would walk on you. On stormy days, in amazement they would descend your dizzy slopes.'

Rosa looked happy in the middle of the ocean, the wind stirred her hair at high speed and then left just as quickly. I looked at her in delight. But all of a sudden I had a strange sensation and I still do not know if it was due to the stark contrast between beauty and the beast, between her appearance and Tongoy's sombre, vampiric face. The fact is that suddenly, despite the wind and the ocean's extreme mobility, it seemed as if Rosa and the seascape had turned into a dead photograph, a painfully frozen scene, on pause, lacking in nature and life. Weird and dreadful sensation. The sensation that everything was dead, including Rosa, Tongoy and me. Today I tell myself, on remembering that sensation and the appallingly bad weather in the channel connecting Fayal and Pico, that some words by Michaux would have gone down very well and even helped me at that odd moment: 'By dint of pains, of vain ascents, by dint of being rejected from the outside, from the outsides I had promised myself I would attain, by dint of rolling down from almost everywhere, I have carved out a deep channel in my life.'

Hence it might be said that the deathly vision and the ocean, the sudden absence of life and nature in the channel that day, carved out a deep channel, without life or a way out, in my insides. Add to this the realisation that Tongoy was also aware of the deathly panorama and mysteriously asked me, 'Will there not be another death in paradise?' And add on top of this the sense of unease caused by the island of Pico as the ferry approached. There was barely a soul in sight when we disembarked in Madalena's ghostly harbour. The town was deserted and a vast silence hung over it, broken only by the gusts of wind and by the birds. I felt uneasy and anxious; it was as if I had travelled to Comala, the town in *Pedro Páramo* by Juan Rulfo, that town where everyone is dead.

Sad and solitary Madalena. To escape my anxiety, I asked Tongoy what we were doing there. 'Visiting António Caiado,' Rosa interposed. All it needed was for her to say, 'I came to Pico because I was told a mysterious writer lived here.' We watched the four passengers travelling with us disembark from the ferry, they got off the boat with their bags and baskets, in grave silence. In a few seconds they disappeared like ghosts down the streets of Madalena, and that was the last we saw of them. 'One visits Pico for the experience,' Tongoy remarked. We went for a wander in the town, but didn't find or see anybody and, on returning to the pier, we found an old taxi-driver in a clapped-out car, parked opposite the small town hall. He was clearly waiting for us, no doubt he had been warned from Fayal of the arrival of three tourists. 'Where is everybody?' we asked him. 'It's Carnival, a holiday,' he answered. We hired him for a tour of the island, to drive down the road connecting Madalena and Lajes, the only road in Pico. Rosa asked about Caiado and the taxi-driver, after a few moments' hesitation, told us that he lived in a house on a small hill on the road to Lajes, but was never there; it was said on the island that he really lived in New York. 'We won't lose anything if we look to see if he's there,' said Tongoy and, although I protested – perhaps because I felt jealous of the mysterious writer – it was a waste of time, it was decided – two against one – to visit Caiado. I didn't forgive Tongoy his vote, I recall that I stared at him in anger and thought that he looked awful, more frightful than ever. But I later realised – while we were driving down the gloomy Lajes road – that by his presence Tongoy gave me a strange sense of security. Perhaps the kind of serenity he passed on to me was one of the reasons I had instinctively sought his friendship back on the terrace in Valparaíso. Tongoy possessed a monster's warmth. 'Very quickly,' writes Michaux, 'it became obvious (from my teenage years) that I had been born to live among monsters.'

The only road on the island of Pico is – as I already described it in *Montano's Malady* without adding a single drop of fiction – a narrow road that runs alongside the breakwater, with many curves and deep potholes, over against a rebellious and very blue Atlantic Ocean. The road, which was once covered in vineyards and luxurious villas crosses a stony and melancholic landscape with occasional, isolated houses on small hills swept by the wind. In one of these houses on the hills, the taxi-driver had fallen in love, and he told us about it. In another of these houses lived Caiado. When we parked a few yards from the mysterious writer's house, because of the strong wind buffeting even the taxi, Tongoy refused to get out. 'You go,' said Tongoy, 'but I can tell you now that there's no one in that house.' No doubt he was absolutely right. The house on the hill battered by the wind seemed firmly closed. In an act almost of courage, defying the strong wind in that region, Rosa and I abandoned the taxi and climbed the short slope, in constant danger of losing our balance, until we reached the front door.

I knocked at the door and it was like knocking at the door of lost time. We knocked three times, and the only answer we got was the fierce noise of the wind raging at the two pitiful trees that stood on top of the hill. On returning to the taxi, I thought that lost time doesn't really exist, but what does exist – I told myself – is an empty, doomed house.

That night, back in Fayal, we went to Café Sport and drank gin with the old whalers and people from the yachts, all that bizarre set who cross the Atlantic in winter and turn up at Café Sport and chat to the whalers in a fascinating exchange of adventures. With the aid of alcohol, I began to imagine that a character by the name of Teixeira lived in that empty, doomed house on Pico's small hill and taught laughter therapy, a copy of the new man, the man to come, that inhuman man who is about to arrive in the world, if he hasn't already. I imagined him living in the house on the hill, facing the sea, his house secretly connected, by underground galleries, with a world of moles and enemies of the literary inhabiting the inside of the volcano.

Rosa saw me engrossed in thought and suddenly asked me if anything was the matter. 'No,' I said, 'I was thinking about Caiado and how it's a shame not to have seen him.

Do you think he exists?' Rosa looked at me and downed her gin. 'Maybe he's dead,' she replied. I then recalled that death, another death, might also inhabit that famous paradise. And I proposed a toast to all the dead of Pico, to all those Pico souls who, according to the locals, take refuge in the furthest reaches of the wells and courtyards and whose voice is the song of crickets. Various sailors from the yachts anchored in Fayal and one or two of the old whalers joined the toast, all of them drunk and suddenly singing at the top of their voices a song of the Swiss Guard I had never heard before, the words of which fascinated me and I jotted down on a Café Sport napkin:

Notre vie est un voyage
Dans l'hiver et dans la Nuit,
Nous chercherons notre passage
Dans le ciel où rien ne luit.

We then piled out on to the street, gin-soaked. Waning moon, rough sea, persistent moan of the wind. A bird went by. I followed it. Life is an inner journey, like Michaux's travels. Life is a winter's journey and goes from life to death. It is an entirely imaginary journey, as Louis-Ferdinand Céline said. This is where it derives its strength. Now I am in Barcelona, thinking that my problem is not suffering from Montano's malady. This far into the winter's journey, my problem is rather how to disappear – 'What will we do to disappear?' as Blanchot said – how to manage to be a twin brother of MUSIL, Robert (Klagenfurt, 1880–Geneva, 1942), who dissolved in the fabric of his own unending work. Not long ago I remarked that it was not desirable for this diary to go on for ever or to be mortal and have a single outcome. Now I see that what is really desirable may be to disappear inside it.

PAVESE, Cesare (Santo Stefano Belbo, 1908–Turin, 1950). Late into the night I was reading *This Business of Living*, Pavese's private journal, I read to its well-known end ('Suicides are timid murderers [. . .]. All this is sickening. Not words. An act. I won't write any more.'). On closing the book, I told myself that literature cannot teach us practical methods, results to obtain, but only the positions. The rest is a lesson that should not be drawn from literature; it is life that should teach it. The private journal, literature in short, did not help Pavese to live very much, which was what most interested him. Could the diary have helped him in any way?

I closed the book and went to bed. I told myself that Pavese's diary belonged to a period in world culture that tended to integrate existential experience with historical ethics. A period to which Pavese's suicide seems to set a chronological boundary. I also told myself that, whereas Pavese's diary was tragically anchored in life, that of Gide or Gombrowicz – closer to my sensibility – was anchored in literature, which is an autonomous world, an independent reality, it has no contact with reality because it is a reality in itself, a personal opinion of mine that no doubt Pavese would not agree with.

I closed the book and went to bed, thinking about all these things, admiring Pavese, but without being in tune with him, and I soon fell asleep. On a foggy road,

I saw Robert Walser in conversation with Musil. 'Out of here, that is my goal,' Walser was saying. 'However much you cry, you won't manage to be real as I am,' replied Musil. 'If I weren't real, I couldn't cry,' replied Walser. 'I hope you don't think those tears are real,' replied Musil.

They then left, or rather – making me feel incredibly jealous – they disappeared. I came to and wondered whether other ghosts from the dream would dare to speak. 'Are you asleep?' Rosa asked from the sitting room, like a ghost. I pretended to be asleep and did not reply. Shortly afterwards Cesare Pavese deceased entered my room. He had walked a great distance, he told me, he had walked down Pico's mysterious road and carried an empty, abandoned house – the world itself? – in his hand. 'The dead do not laugh,' he told me. 'Laughter is linked to life,' he told me. 'Death will come and will have your eyes,' I told him. He was serious and quiet for a few moments. In effect he carried an empty house in his hand and walked along Pico's road. 'What's the use of Pentothal' he finally said to me. I got up from bed and embraced him. Then Pavese deceased asked me if I was Robert Walser. 'I am,' I answered. 'I've been waiting for you all my death and I'll go on waiting,' he said. He possessed the voice I had imagined for Teixeira's character, a nasal, somewhat sensual, but vaguely stupid voice. 'Anything else?' I enquired. Pavese deceased did not speak. Pavese deceased was still there, but did not speak. 'Not words,' I said. I then fell asleep and dreamed nothing.

Saturday

THE DESPERATE FRIEND

Such is my regret for the lack of respect with which I undertook Pavese's entry in this dictionary yesterday that I have spent the whole day today trying to add a few more constructive lines to this entry. I couldn't, I cannot, correct what I wrote about the 'nasal, somewhat sensual, but vaguely stupid voice' I imagined for Teixeira's character and discovered was the voice of Pavese deceased. I cannot correct this, because it is true that I had this impression yesterday. And, if I had this impression, I am not now going to pretend and deny it; I do not forget that I swore at the start of this dictionary to kneel before the altar of Truthfulness. Nor can I deny that I saw him walking along Pico's road, carrying an empty, abandoned house in his hand. I really did see him like this. What can I do if I saw him like this? By way of compensation, and above all because I was unfair yesterday, I believe I am in a position today to revise my opinion about Pavese's diary and to recall here, without further ado, that, when he died, his friends had to force themselves to approach the bulging folder containing his diary (partly typed and partly written by hand); his friends had to overcome the sense of fearful reserve triggered by those pages, that secret itinerary of a life they had always supposed to be bitter and discontented, the pages of their friend whom they generally understood to be desperate.

Italo Calvino was one of the first friends to open Tutankhamun's tomb, by which I mean Pavese's diary, a dangerous diary because it might infect whoever read it with despair. His friends' initial inspection of those pages was painstaking and restrained. They knew that they would not find there the reason for Pavese's suicide, something sought by columnists in weekly and daily newspapers at that time; they knew that the reason for an act can never be reduced to a formula or an episode, but must be sought over a whole life, the set of constants that Pavese, though not a fatalist, called his own *destiny*. But his friends felt that they were going to find there all the painful tension, the secret vibrations of his soul, which even they, his friends, had not always discerned; the traces of the ill he carried inside, under the guise of his stoicism.

Calvino relates how, on opening the diary at the first page, they realised that they were confronted with an impressive document, convulsed pages, desperate cries that overflowed loudly from time to time. 'But, most of all, we also found something else, the antonym of despair and defeat: a patient, tenacious *labour of self-construction*, of inner clarity, of moral betterment, which is to be reached by means of work and reflection on the ultimate reasons behind art and one's own and others' lives.'

Yesterday I wrote that I admired Pavese's diary, but without being in tune with it. Today I am ashamed to have written this. Because if there's something the pages of my diary darkly pursue, it is *the creation of myself* and a moral improvement, which I seek by means of work and reflection on the precarious state of my life, of the life of others and of the life of literature, which I need so much if I am to survive and which, at this century's beginning, is exposed to the furious assaults of the enemies of the literary as never before.

I'm going to go to the kitchen to have a yoghurt; I shall be accompanied by the desperate friend who always goes with me, that friend who is myself and who, so as not to fall into the clutches of cursed despair, writes this diary, this story of a soul trying to save itself by the survival of literature, this story of a soul no sooner strong and steady than it succumbs to depression, in order then, laboriously, to get back on its feet, to readjust through work and intelligence, constantly battling with Pico's moles. I wonder now why I said yesterday that I was not in tune with Pavese if he is my shadow, I, my reader, the desperate friend who always goes with us literature-sick, who are constantly fighting against despair and defeat.

PESSOA, Fernando (Lisbon, 1888–1935). Invented a character by the name of Bernardo Soares, to whom he delegated the mission of writing a diary. As Antonio Tabucchi writes, 'Soares is a fictional character who adopts the subtle literary fiction of autobiography. In this autobiography without facts, of a non-existent person, is the only great narrative work left to us by Pessoa: his novel.'

Pessoa gave this diary, signed by Soares, the title *The Book of Disquiet*. He simply called the overall project of his work – mysterious and unrealisable, as if he had sought to dissolve in the fabric of his own unending autofiction – The Book (of disquiet), perhaps thinking of that mythical text Mallarmé longed for all his life, *Le Livre*, an impossible volume, whose completion – others may try, but the same thing will happen to them – is probably only ever to be found in the project itself, a project containing the seed of the decomposition of literary genres. *The Book of Disquiet*, like the project it was and could only be, was discovered one day in the trunk that, for almost fifty years, had guarded it in secret: the famous trunk containing 23,000 Pessoan documents. There rested The Book, the insomniac Soares' book. A first version appeared in 1982 and later the publishing house of my friend Manuel Hermínio Monteiro – who went in search of the lost trunk and found it – published a greatly enlarged and definitive edition of the clerk Soares' diary.

What is meant by disquiet? Judging by what the assistant bookkeeper Soares reveals, we are to understand by disquiet a certain unease and, above all, a certain incompetence regarding life. This incompetence is like an illness that, at one point, he himself makes explicit and defines, calling it *mal-de-viver* (life-sickness). Disquiet is very possibly a manifestation of this illness. In his discreet office where he works as assistant bookkeeper, Soares daily discusses death, beauty, loneliness and identity – and the barber on the corner. Soares the clerk writes about all this far from the ballrooms of Vienna or from the luxurious mountain health farms, he writes from the greyness of the window in his office, he writes from the standpoint of the daily and ordinary, of the simple and normal. In short, Soares the clerk and his diary *seem real*.

Soares' look, which from a window surveys all the disquiet of his days and of The Book, is articulated by a strange association between what he perceives and the alteration of these experiential data. The outside world *becomes his I*, meaning that his I takes possession of what is outside it.

It can be said that Soares lives and does not live, his existence is placed between life and an awareness of life. Pessoa became one big Look thanks to Mr Soares looking through him. Pessoa lived and Soares was *life-sick*, Soares had a window and wrote the diary and his disquiet was the manifestation of his *life-sickness*. Perhaps Montano's is just another variation on Soares' illness. However that may be, the most attractive aspect of the Lisbon assistant bookkeeper's bizarre world is perhaps, more than anything, this surprising way of being outside himself and looking. Right now it seems to me that someone who can look in this way is not very attached to life's substance and is a walking ghost. Rosario Girondo, for example – me, not my mother – is also a walking ghost, wanders across these pages trying to learn to know how to read others, trying to be outside himself and to look, because he hopes one day to look as Soares looked, or to read as Pessoa read, always at a slight distance – unless the book were by Soares – because at each step – as happened to me the day before yesterday, when I was reading Michaux – memory would disrupt the narrative sequence: 'After a few minutes, I was the one writing, and what was written was nowhere.' An elegant way of saying that his I took possession of what was outside it. This is what my I has been trying to mimic for some time. And I am not without a window.

Wednesday

I recommend that the traveller wishing to fall in love with Portugal calmly follow the course of the Tagus, see it first gravely flowing through the austere lands of Castile – bare fields and solemnity – and then see it entering Portuguese territory, where the tragic Castilian Tagus undergoes, as Julio Camba wrote, 'a lyrical tendency and is lined by trees, covered in boats shaped like a half-moon, accompanied by songs'. Another world.

Portugal *seems real*, seems like another world. When I go to Lisbon, I walk down the streets of this city as if I had always been there. This was not the case when I first visited it in 1968, when I went to work as a supporting actor in a James Bond film, the first not starring Sean Connery. On that occasion, my excessive and brazen youth made me wander through Lisbon like a 'walking ghost in halls of memories', as Pessoa wrote. I hardly observed anything, I didn't see Lisbon, I didn't see anything. But when I returned in 1989, I had the impression I had always been in this city, at each corner I sensed the diffuse memory of having already turned it. When? I didn't know. But I had already been there before never having been there.

When I go to Lisbon, I spend hours in Terreiro do Paço, on the river-bank, mimicking Soares, contemplating in vain: 'I spend hours, sometimes, in Terreiro do Paço, on the banks of the Tagus, contemplating in vain [. . .]. The quay, the evening, the smell of the sea, all combine to make up my anxiety.'

Excessive anxiety of the spirit for nothing. I go to Terreiro do Paço and then ritually head for Café Martinho da Arcada, where in earlier times the conversant Pessoa's arrival was sad and sacred, punctual and methodical. The poet went every afternoon, according to immemorial usage, from his mournful office to Café Martinho, where he stretched out in thick silences of observation and agile thrusts of irony, and from there back home, slipping through the shadows.

When I go to Lisbon, I go to the Martinho in the early evening – I am Soares in my own way – and listen to what is said in conversations yesteryear and today, because time is annulled, I listen to what is said in conversation, all the 'metaphysics mislaid in the corners of cafés everywhere, the chance ideas of so many chancers, the intuitions of so many little people'.

When I go to Lisbon and walk in the Baixa, I drift like a melancholic child down the rua da Prata, down the rua dos Douradores, down the rua dos Franqueiros, and I feel that tomorrow I shall also disappear and be the one who, like my friend Hermínio, stopped walking down these streets, one pedestrian less in the street life of this city where I have always been: 'Lisbon with its houses / of divers colours, / Lisbon with its houses / of divers colours, / Lisbon with its houses / of divers colours . . .'

In Lisbon I feel at home. 'We meet again, Lisbon and Tagus and everything.' But it's also true that, when I'm in this city, I want to be in Boca do Inferno and, when I'm in Boca do Inferno, I want to be in Lisbon. Excessive anxiety of the spirit for nothing. Often, when I'm in Barcelona, I should like to be in Boca do Inferno so that I could want to be in Lisbon. But today is another day, because I'm in Lisbon, wanting to be here as never before.

I travelled to this city to be in Terreiro do Paço and contemplate in vain. And now I'm here, thinking about Hermínio, on the river-bank, watching the seagulls furiously spread their wings between the Tagus and me, until the animal curtain disperses and I again see the city, the Tagus and everything, I again see everything, including my friend who disappeared in this suddenly moderate climate, perhaps a dream. I am in Terreiro do Paço; I stopped writing this dictionary in the middle of Pessoa's entry, I stopped it in order to travel to Lisbon and so live, on my own boundary, inside this diary. I couldn't write about Lisbon and Pessoa while still in my study, while still in my dictionary.

I am in Terreiro do Paço, thinking about my friend who disappeared. I have spent the day smoking. Slight, very slight, a slight breeze goes by. I am in a café next to the quay where the ferries berth, next to a large window that separates me from the river. For José Cardoso Pires, there was no better place than the one I'm seated in: boats arriving, boats leaving, people coming and going, getting drinks at the bar, and me seated higher up the Tagus.

In this place, in this Café Atinel, Lisbon the city ends, and so does a book called *Lisbon* and subtitled *Logbook*, written by CARDOSO PIRES, José (Peso, Ria Baixa, 1925–Lisbon, 1998), another writer of diaries – in this case, a logbook – who helps me construct my identity in this dictionary.

While *Lisbon* is a guide to this city – according to Melville, almost all literature, in a sense, is based on guidebooks – it is also a logbook, an urban one, since its author journeys through a Lisbon that he sees literally perched on the Tagus, that he sees as a vessel, as a sailing city.

In this Café Atinel is the world's end, *finis terrae*, here ends Lisbon and so does the book, the diary by Cardoso Pires, who had an unerring eye according to his good friend Antonio Tabucchi: 'One look and it had absorbed everything.' Since I am now at the same table where Cardoso – Zé to his friends – finishes his book, the city is at my back. The Baixa, the Chiado, the crowds, Europe, everything has been left behind. 'And don't tell me,' writes Zé, 'that it isn't wonderful to be like this, next to a table, by the water.' Tomorrow I shall go back to Barcelona and to the dictionary written in my study and not at the table of a port café. I shall go back and again wonder how to disappear, how to dissolve in this diary. Tomorrow I shall go back to the dictionary and a cold hand, I'm sure, will continue to squeeze Pessoa's throat, preventing him from breathing life. Tomorrow I shall go back, but I'm here now and I let myself be carried along by Zé's look and Soares' window. I feel anchored, with my unerring eye on loan, in this Lisbon that will see me off tomorrow. I am a look that absorbs everything, I am that look that seems real.

SOMETHING SPARKLES THROUGH THE WORN FABRIC

A sudden silence descended on a place as rowdy as this and I felt that even the invisible beings were hiding. Mystery at dusk. Then the din of people from the ferries returned. Nightfall, which seemed to have abruptly frozen, has now gathered strength. I am still in Lisbon's Café Atinel, thinking about Hermínio, my disappeared friend. I am still here by the Tagus, at my table by the river, at my waterside table. The Baixa, the Chiado, the crowds, Europe, everything has been left behind, at my back. I am at the world's end, free of time like a dead man. A seagull goes by and I follow it, and I am reminded of certain remarks made by W. G. Sebald on mystery and the impact of the fantasy genre on eccentricity, certain remarks also about supposed coincidences and chances that might not be so, were we to possess better means of perception, were it not because, centuries ago, we became mentally very limited after shots were heard in paradise: 'I prefer to write about fairly eccentric people, and eccentricity is somewhat fantastical. These things happen to us as well. For example, recently I visited a museum in London to see two paintings. There was a couple behind me who I think were speaking Polish. A very strange-looking man and woman, they seemed from another age. Later, in the afternoon, I had to go to the tube station furthest from the centre of London, a city of fifteen million inhabitants. There was nobody. Except these two from the museum. There they were.'

Sebald is a great reader of Borges, whom he always praises for understanding early on what a mistake it was to expel metaphysics from philosophy. Because in fact, Sebald claims, there are things we cannot easily explain away, and because it is part of our human condition, before more than now, to maintain a certain relation, not just social, with those who came before us. The commemoration of the dead is something that distinguishes us from the animals.

I am a covert and assiduous reader of Sebald, of his long walks à la Robert Walser, of his exploration of the world of the dead, of his fantastical forays into the space of eccentrics. Referring to the strange case of the Poles in the faraway station, Sebald said, 'These are not coincidences, somewhere there is a relation that from time to time sparkles through a worn fabric'.

Here I am in Café Atinel, at dusk, next to the ferry passengers, working away on this dictionary of writers of private journals in an attempt to relate it to *Montano's Malady*, to mend the worn fabric of relations between the two different texts, for something to sparkle again and remind us that there was once a young and perfect fabric, with a serene thread and logical language in which coincidences had no meaning because everything was cleanly coincidental.

Another seagull goes by and this time I do not follow it, I stay inside Sebald's world, which reminds me of another coincidence, also possibly not at all coincidental, which stopped me in my tracks in February this year on the island of Fayal, the night we ended up leaving Café Sport and piling out on to the street, having toasted the dead of the islands, that legend that says the souls take refuge in the furthest reaches of the wells and courtyards and their voice is the song of crickets. Sebald would have enjoyed this legend from the Azores. I continue his walks in the world of ruins, of what is dead. I continue his contact with a stimulating tendency of the contemporary novel, a tendency that opens new ground in between essay, fiction and autobiography: the road travelled by works such as Claudio Magris' *Danube* or Sergio Pitol's *El arte de la fuga*.

That night in Fayal, as we staggered drunkenly beside the sea, back to the Hostal de la Santa Cruz, it suddenly occurred to me – slave that I was, in part, to the plot I was devising for *Montano's Malady* – to turn into the complete memory of the history of literature, for me to be literature, to embody it in my own modest person, so that I could try to save it from extinction, to defend it against Pico's moles. It meant embodying it only in the fictional *Montano's Malady* that I was writing and needed to move forward. At no point – I don't have so much of Quixote's soul – did I think to turn into this complete memory of literature in real life, it was only an idea for the fiction I was writing, which evolved alongside my life and travels, my private journal. But the truth is neither Tongoy nor Rosa understood me when I expounded my idea to them. They failed to comprehend what I had just told them and, what's more, however drunk they may have been, they reacted terribly. They revealed their complete lack of interest in the subjects that concerned me.

When I told them that I was going to embody literature, that this was my idea to move the story I was writing forward, Tongoy abruptly brought his zigzag steps to a halt. Rosa proceeded to do the same. I don't think the fact they were very drunk is an excuse. The truth of the matter is that they didn't care what happened to literature. They also bore me a grudge and seemed to have been waiting for the right moment to rebuke me. Tongoy stared at me the way you stare at someone you cannot bear for another second. 'Go fuck yourself,' he told me. I was very taken aback, although to be fair I have to say that his comment proved useful to me, it handed me the ending of *Montano's Malady* on a plate. But at the time I was taken aback, astonished, unable to comprehend why he looked at me with such hatred. 'You see everything in literature,' Rosa upbraided me, 'I'm not surprised you actually want to merge with it.' Then Tongoy, laughing at me: 'Our Quixote in the Azores, cor you're a bore.' Tongoy said this with an atrocious look of rage. I returned the look with hatred and contempt. There he was, Fellini's great actor, completely drunk, in his ridiculous sea dog's outfit, nocturnal Nosferatu with a touch of dragonfly. 'You look like a whaler,' I told him, 'all you need now is a harpoon.' 'I don't care what you say,' replied Tongoy, sharing another conspiratorial look with Rosa, the two seemed increasingly in cahoots, clearly they had just been talking about me, criticising me. 'It doesn't matter, the fact is you don't stop seeing everything in literature, it's impossible to talk to you about anything else,' said Rosa. 'All we needed,' added Tongoy, 'was for you to want to turn into the history of literature, that really is the final straw.' 'You've become a book,' appended Rosa.

It was no use – drunk in the night they were soulless – trying to make them see and understand that the plot of *Montano's Malady* required the narrator – not to be confused with me – to embody literature. I felt extremely downhearted when I considered that, if even Rosa, my wife, and my good friend the vampire were unable to comprehend and celebrate with me certain ideas of mine for the fiction I was writing, if neither one was able to share certain concerns about the future of literature with me, then clearly I was very alone in the world, obviously, though I had a wife and vampire friend, I could not be more alone in that paradise of the Azores.

I told myself that the Azores were a paradise because I needed to cling on to a comforting idea in that general air of anxiety. It was then that something happened that has always struck me as unusual, to say the least. It was then something must have sparkled through a worn fabric. Tongoy, as if his intoxication or perhaps an invisible glimmer allowed him to read my thoughts, said in an abruptly conciliatory voice:

'You're very alone in paradise, aren't you?'

Time has gone by and I still don't quite believe it, I consider it now and tell myself that there are more mental connections than we think, but we do not get any further because the original fabric seems to have become very worn and only occasionally does something sparkle in it. We see strange coincidences that no doubt have an explanation, which we do not manage to find. We go through life without correctly understanding many things. 'There's a misunderstanding, and this misunderstanding will be our downfall,' said Kafka.

The worn fabric is perhaps in some paradise where formerly, on a day with light from another world, the logical thread of a verbal fabric that gave life meaning died. They were better times. But someone in that paradise upset the inventor of language and the fabric wore away and our lives became absurd, without the old order and the old meaning. This fabric, unrecognisable today, could be the same one the existence of which, though worn, is sensed by Sebald; although we only receive, when we receive them, fleeting but startling sparkles that perhaps are telling us that we do not know what exactly can have happened and what the misunderstanding was, but there were definitely shots in some paradise or, in any case – as Sergio Pitol said to me when I showed him documents revealing a curious coincidence that had passed through our lives and betraying another sparkle in the worn fabric – 'something must have happened, that's for sure'.

PITOL, Sergio (Puebla, Mexico, 1933). Of all the diarists gathered in this dictionary, he is the one who has collaborated longest in the construction of my timid identity. A key figure in my life. He turns up punctually and mysteriously, like a strange ambassador of the most reasonable thread in the worn fabric, and does so at those moments in my life most closely linked to the fantasy genre. I met him in Warsaw in 1973, when I travelled expressly to this city, hoping to share with him my impressions as a reader of his stories and, in passing, to get to know him. I ended up staying in his home for a whole month and Pitol becoming my teacher. I aspired then to be a writer and was still unclear whether or not I would be, I wasn't even using the name Rosario Girondo. He was already the author of various books of stories and of a novel and worked as cultural attaché in the Embassy of Mexico in Poland. No writer before then had bothered to talk to me about literature as he did over unforgettable dinners during those days I stayed in his home that ended up being key in my decision to write; those days marked my destiny and sowed the seed of my *Montanism*.

On 23 August 1973, the day I left Warsaw, Pitol presented me with a copy of his novel *El tañido de una flauta* and dedicated it to me with some words in English that alluded to Provence. It was the first book to have been dedicated to me and for years I would visualise that dedication, I would often see it and finally knew it by heart.

During those years, we never spoke by phone nor wrote each other a letter, but we would meet, often by chance, in the most diverse places. We saw each other, for example, in Bukhara, Trieste, Mérida in Venezuela, Beijing, Veracruz, Paris, Prague and Mojácar. One day, 23 August 1993, he decided to send me a letter from Brasilia, the first he had ever sent me. On receiving it, I soon realised that exactly twenty years separated the Varsovian dedication and the Brazilian letter. I photocopied the documents, hoping eventually to show them to Sergio and to witness his reaction to this curious, surprising coincidence. The opportunity finally arrived, in the Provence of the dedication no less. Sergio and I met at a tribute to a writer and mutual friend in Aix-en-Provence. One night, in this city, I suddenly showed him the two documents and waited to see his reaction. Sergio pored over the photocopies, then took off his glasses, smiled imperceptibly, allowed the silence to take hold of the situation, put his glasses back on, smiled a little nervously, re-examined the photocopies, raised his head and arched his eyebrows, lowered his head again and finally said, 'Something must have happened, that's for sure.'

I understand that there was little more he could say and what he said was already a lot; he preferred to be prudent and not to speculate in vain, but in any case obviously 'something must have happened' in some place with light from another world, where something occasionally sparkles through a worn fabric.

This morning I read an interview with Sebald, in which he admits to having paid tribute on occasion, albeit without naming him, to the hiker Robert Walser. Forerunner of

Kafka, interned for many years in a Swiss sanatorium, Walser only ever left his enclosure to go for long walks in the snow. After lunch on 25 December 1956, he went out dressed in warm clothes, he emerged into the bright light of the snowy landscape surrounding the sanatorium. The solitary hiker, in search of the mountain spirit, filled his lungs with the clear winter air. He walked for a long time until he fainted and dropped dead in the snow. He was found by two children skating down on a wooden sledge.

Asked about his tributes to Walser the hiker, Sebald says that there is in fact an autobiographical reason for such tributes: 'I was always puzzled that Walser should have died on the same day as my grandfather, whom I grew up with. What's more, the two looked very alike and were both long-distance walkers and met similar ends, since my grandfather also died while out in the snow alone. The places Walser walked in were only sixty miles from my grandfather's house in Wertach.'

Something's happening here now in Café Atinel, that's for sure. I think about Hermínio, my friend who disappeared prematurely. And I hear beside me some voices, voices from other tables, Portuguese and other discussions and conversations, everyman's concerns, the concerns of the quick and the dead. And I am reminded of Pessoa and the metaphysics mislaid in the corners of cafés everywhere, the chance ideas of so many chancers, the intuitions of so many little people. Perhaps one day, with abstract fluid and impossible substance, they will form a God or a new fabric and with the light of another life occupy the world.

RENARD, Jules (Chalons, Mayenne, 1864–Paris, 1910). In his well-known diary, Renard reveals himself to be a man permanently installed on the hardest bunk in the carriage of the hardest drug of literature. Take, for example, this sentence: 'Writing is a way of speaking without being interrupted.' At present I am looking at one of his family photographs and in it he appears with a terrifying expression of bad temper: the classic chronic sufferer of literature sickness. The photograph is taken outside, the day extremely pleasant. The children, his son and daughter, look marvellous. His wife, in good health. But he is in a foul mood, as if someone had interrupted him while he was speaking. He clearly has withdrawal symptoms and thinks that he should be in his study by now.

'Writing,' says Lobo Antunes, 'is like taking drugs, you start purely for pleasure and you end up organising your life around your vice like a drug addict. This is my life. Even when I suffer, I live it like a split personality: the man is suffering and the writer is considering how to use the suffering in his work.'

Such a great and scandalously literature-sick diarist as Renard could not be absent from these pages. He died without knowing that he would go down in the history of literature precisely for the diary he kept without ever wishing to publish it, he died without knowing he would be betrayed and his diary would be published posthumously, astounding, among others, a Catalan countryman called Josep Pla – who would write an exceptional private journal, *El quadern gris* – and most especially André Gide, who would turn this genre in which Renard had proved a virtuoso – that of the *autopsychographical* diary, to use an adjective invented by Pessoa – into a work of literary creation consciously addressed to a reader.

Renard was so scandalously literature-sick that, in the foreword to the Spanish edition of his diary, he is openly treated as such by Josep Massot: 'Fascinating pages of a diary that, as well as being a cruel testimony, [. . .] reflect the insatiable disquiet of a writer who is sick with literature.'

You have to be very sick, you have to be very *seriously sick* – to quote Jaime Gil de Biedma, another great Catalan diarist – very literature-sick to think what Renard thought when, at the end of his days, he fell physically ill and told himself that he could only get better if he wrote: 'I am again off balance. Rock bottom. Immediate cure if I worked.' And a little further on, in the diary's dying pages, he defines himself in this way: 'Man without a heart, who has only had literary emotions.'

The last thing he records in his diary: 'I want to get up tonight. Heaviness. One leg hanging out. Then a moist trickle flows down my leg. It has to reach my heel for me to make up my mind. It will dry on the sheets, as when I was Poil de Carotte.'

Poil de Carotte was a character of his, probably himself when he was a child. Renard died of literature, of his own, he died having turned into one of his characters, having turned into the rustic child he always was. This would explain why, above all in the final years of his life, he pretended to be writing in Paris when in fact he spent his life – like Josep Pla – in the countryside, in his home town, in the world of Poil de Carotte, with his innocent skin, carrot top even, writing literature-sick sentences and, as Musil would later, questioning the usefulness of diaries: 'Why these notebooks? Nobody tells the truth, not even their authors.'

Possibly because I have just arrived from Lisbon, I am reminded of something about 'the truth' written by Pessoa, or rather by his heteronym Álvaro de Campos: 'I am defeated today, as if I knew the truth.'

The truth is that Renard's 'nobody tells the truth' would quickly become fertile ground for fictional diaries, for André Gide's 'life of the mind' and, a little later, for Gombrowicz's 'construction of self' and even for the project of fragmented identity that I am, who have spent days immersed in this dictionary, trying to be as truthful as possible and giving all sorts of reliable information about myself, not always successfully, since I often remark that all I'm really looking for now, defeated by the impossible truth, is to dissolve like a man without qualities in mid-diary.

The afternoon is ambiguously flat in Barcelona today. A bird goes by and I do not follow it. After my fleeting tour of Lisbon, I am once more in my study, every day more devoted – without will, but with an exaggerated regularity, with a monstrous perseverance – to my Montano's malady. I am writing, alone and almost still, with my shoulders draped in a shawl, in my office. Rosa put flowers in it this morning, the whole house is little by little turning into an imaginary hospital. Another bird goes by, which I don't follow either. My mind was trapped, a few moments ago, in the memory of Paul Valéry, another noticeable and extreme sufferer of literature sickness, absorbed in the elaboration of a strange, something more than odd dictionary. 'This man, my father,' his son wrote of him, 'up before dawn, in his pyjamas, his shoulders draped in a shawl, a cigarette between his fingers, his eyes fixed on the vane of a chimney, watching the birth of the day, would devote himself, with a monstrous perseverance, to a solitary rite: creating his own language, redoing a dictionary for his personal use: 250 notebooks blackened with observations, schemes, maxims, calculations, drawings, 30,000 typed pages.'

I have just received a call from Juan Villoro, a friend who in August is going to settle in Barcelona with his family and who is now in the city making preparations for the move. Rosa spoke to him first and then handed me the phone. Long and as always warm conversation with Villoro, in the middle of which, with regard to whatever topic we were discussing at that moment, he quoted an aphorism by Lichtenberg, another great diarist: 'Once you have an ailment, you have a personal opinion.' I didn't tell him this, but I jotted the sentence down, since it seemed to me to bear some relation to the theme of the literature-sick.

After speaking on the phone, I felt full of personal opinions. And that same ambiguously flat afternoon then took me to Lady Macbeth's literary illness and reminded me, as if the afternoon were a prompt, that Shakespeare tells us that in his majesty's absence Lady Macbeth was seen to 'rise from her bed, throw her nightgown upon her, unlock her closet, take forth paper, fold it, write upon it, read it, afterwards seal it, and again return to bed; yet all this while in a most fast sleep.'

Lady Macbeth has an unusual way of sleeping. When the court doctor is informed, he describes the activity of his patient and writer, impatient writer, he describes literary activity in general, literature sickness, in the following terms: 'A great perturbation in nature, – to receive at once the benefit of sleep, and do the effects of watching.'

Clearly the doctor is also Shakespeare and he is also sick.

TESTE, Monsieur (Sète, 1871–Paris, 1945). Paul Valéry's alter ego and paradigm of the coldest and most incisive intelligence, Teste took 'the spirit's most fearful discipline' to the limit. For all their differences – Tongoy does not think so much – this Monsieur Teste was Valéry's *tongoy* and was often almost identical to him, a good friend then, at other times, a monster.

Valéry wrote the life of his mind in a kind of engagement book in which from 1894 until his death, at the birth of the day, he would record impressions and thoughts in what was not exactly a diary but some notebooks without confessions or anecdotes and related, therefore, to Musil's diary, lacking as they did any reference to external or private affairs. Valéry's intention was to capture and record thought as it awoke, to examine his dreams and their relationship with the movements of consciousness.

These notes – like a mental drawing that comes to life – gave birth to Teste, a being who lives only as a result of the activity of his mind. Teste is Valéry in action, the action of writing, of writing the kind of intellectual diary that reflected the life of a mind not made for novels, whose great scenes – he said – their outbursts, passions, tragic moments, far from exalting him, struck him as miserable glimmers, rudimentary states where every form of stupidity is allowed to run free, where a being is simplified to the point of idiocy and drowns instead of swimming in the circumstances of the water.

He shared this anti-novelism with Robert Musil, who was speaking at that time of the *loathsome narrative* and coming out with statements that suit this personal dictionary, constructed in part from the madness of others, extremely well: 'Our whole being is just a delirium of many.' Or else: 'Man's deepest association with his peers is dissociation.' Musil, in *The Man Without Qualities*, ignores procreation, fills his whole novel with childless children, ignores continuity and Oedipal repetition, leaves everything behind, has no offspring and, therefore, eliminates all narrative possibilities from his novel, since – as Magris says in this regard – 'the possibility of narrative presupposes life and the meaning of life, the epic based on the unity of the world and of the individual, on a multiplicity enlightened and ordered by a meaning and a value.'

Musil's story dissolves into a game of symbols and variations that reflect one another without reference to a meaning. After the different variants are combined, there is no story left; after the rays of sun that tremble on the water, there is nothing left. I often think that, as Góngora wrote, everything ends 'in earth, in smoke, in dust, in shade, in nothing'. I often feel close to Musil and to Ulrich, the character in *The Man Without Qualities*, who reveals himself to me now – on this flat afternoon in Barcelona today – to be a fanatic of Montano's malady; you see I have just remembered something he says at one point: 'Our life should be purely and only literature.' Applause for Ulrich.

I wonder how I can have been so stupid, believing for so long that I must eradicate my Montano's malady, when it is the only worthwhile and truly comfortable possession I have. I also wonder why I should apologise for being so literary if, in the final outcome, only literature could save the spirit in an age as deplorable as ours. My life should be, once and for all, purely and only literature.

Monsieur Teste, Ulrich's close relation, wanted to write the life of a theory in the same way – he said – as that of a passion (going to bed) has already been overwritten. Had Teste travelled to Budapest, perhaps he would have written a theory of Budapest – as my dear mother did – where we could have 'finally *seen* with wide open eyes to the limits of things or of sight'.

Teste's adventure always took place within the limits of the self. The kind of horizon on which he wrote his diary about the life of his mind could only be intellectual, it could not be anything else. Teste, like Musil, was not made for novels, and much less for the kind of private journals being written in his time, which continue to proliferate today in rancid fashion, with all their painful introspection – why do they do it if they cannot hear anything there? – with all their sluggish descriptions of the behaviour of others, which they wish to pass off as diaries and sometimes even as novels.

In the era of the autobiographical pact, in an age when the novel of the self has the upper hand, a man named Teste, up before dawn, in his pyjamas, his shoulders draped in a shawl, notes: 'I am the unknown I carry in me.'

I return to the *loathsome narrative* and observe that I am incapable of taking a firm stand against the possibility of narrative, rather I sympathise with Borges when he says there is something of the story that will always last and he does not believe that men will ever tire of hearing and telling stories. I evoke these comments by Borges and yet see that they imply a certain lack of trust in the future of the novel, perhaps because in the future a narrative art will most probably be born under other guises, though the story will continue to survive. Very new forms will flourish, immanent forms perhaps, with no dimension beyond reason. I still cannot imagine these forms. Fortunately, I think. The new man, i.e. Teixeira, in his empty home on the island of Pico, may be imagining them now. Fortunately, I think, I cannot imagine them and it is better like this; I trust that I shall not have to know them, that I can continue a little as before, attempting to transform the art of the novel, which is no mean feat. I realise that there are a thousand ways of doing this and I have to find mine, which in fact is what I'm doing.

VALÉRY, Paul (Sète, 1871–Paris, 1945). Writer who was the youthful passion of Rosario Girondo, who aspired one day, as he says in his secret diary, to be as intelligent as him. 'Stupidity is not my strong point,' Valéry tells us in the opening line of *Monsieur Teste*. I read the sentence a couple of times and ask myself how this afternoon, this false light, this false today, these papers, everything I perceive right now, yes, how this afternoon is different from yesterday's.

I know perfectly well that today is not the same day, but I am only capable of knowing it. Is that to be intelligent?

Was Valéry really intelligent? Has anyone ever been intelligent? Alberto Savinio said that complete, balanced, fertile intelligence has always been a special case. And he added: 'The effort made by man to climb the steps of intelligence is so painful, so desperate . . . The damages resulting from an incomplete intelligence are so much greater than those arising from a frank and submissive stupidity.'

We should doubt the usefulness and real value of such prized intelligence, prized perhaps because it doesn't actually exist. The very fact that some of us – not all of us – search after intelligence simply goes to show that it isn't natural, it isn't human, it isn't of this world. Given this state of affairs, and given that his monstrous perseverance produced some very relative results, Valéry – like the rest of humanity – wasn't so intelligent. 'Intelligence,' says Savinio, 'is the holy Grail, but stupidity, that Cinderella, poor, modest, despised, vilified stupidity, is what the true, spontaneous, lasting love of man in the end returns to.' Savinio thinks that man, even in metaphysics, divides his affection between intelligence (the lover, the holy Grail) and stupidity (the wife or consort). After all the deceptions of intelligence, it is she, good, magnanimous stupidity, who consoles us deeply.

Stupidity is loyal and constant, we have known her from time immemorial, she awaits us in the sweet home to share with us, with imposing resignation, the colossal misfortune not to be intelligent.

O Valéry!

III
Theory of Budapest

FASTING IN BUDA

Ladies and gentlemen, distinguished Hungarian public, I have been in the melancholy and beautiful city of Budapest for several days now, I arrived here with ample time to devote *in situ* to the preparation of my lecture as part of this International Symposium on the Private Journal as Narrative Form.

Until a few hours ago, when the organisers discovered that I was in the city and transferred me to the Kakania Grand Hotel (where, by the way, I have refused to shower and eat), I lived like a beggar, barely touching any food, in a disreputable boarding-house in Buda. There, when I had the time – sometimes you will see me improvise as well, I am fascinated by exposing myself to danger, by risking my life in front of an audience – I began to prepare my words for this evening.

First of all I should like to celebrate the presence among us, in this historic room in Budapest's Literature Museum, of someone I admire, Imre Kertész. It is a great honour for me and a huge responsibility to have him in the audience. I should like also to greet Monsieur Tongoy, seated in the front row, arching his eyebrows at this moment. Monsieur Tongoy is a vagrant of Hungarian origin, a distant relation of Monsieur Teste and of the Hungarian Bela Lugosi. Some of you must already have noticed him, his miserable clothing and the vampiric features of his frightful face, he is the very image of Count Dracula, a strange cross between his relation Lugosi and Murnau's Nosferatu. He is a vagrant, but he is also an actor, he works when he can, when producers forget that he is fascinated by a miserable life. He starred as dragonfly-man in a film by Fellini. And has played Bela Lugosi on the screen. From here I send Monsieur Tongoy, my alter ego, my very best wishes. Greetings also to the mendicant beside him, Rosa, my partner in begging difficulties. I must warn you, before we begin, that I am hungry, very hungry.

Hungry.

I have been fasting hard in Buda for several days, only two sandwiches in one week, seven fruit juices and water. But I want to make it clear from the start that I am hungry because I choose to be, having declined to eat at the Kakania, for example.

Fasting in Buda, I have very deliberately sought to appear before you today in a weak state, having apparently lost control of my thoughts, but not all control, just enough to enable you, live and in real time, to witness the public construction of the private journal of a writer who is hungry and who is pleased to deliver his lecture on the edge of the abyss, to risk his life for all to see, to pronounce some nocturnal words involving a certain risk on the diary as narrative form, always placing himself on the edge of the abyss, but clinging to it in precarious balance.

SO I'M NOT RELAXED

With the sensation that I could drop down dead at any moment – the truth is I have given my best lectures in a state of tension, far from being relaxed – dying of hunger before you all today, I consider it helpful to inform you that my visit to Budapest's Literature Museum has forced me to interrupt the novel I am writing in Barcelona on the subject of writers' private journals, no less. This novel is also a diary, my diary as a literature-sick writer, in Budapest today doubly sick, because of hunger, my hunger as a fasting artist.

I interrupted the novel to be with you today, I interrupted it in a passage referring to Valéry's notebooks, the notebooks or form of private journal which gave rise to the intellectual figure of Monsieur Teste, whose extended shadow – embodied here today by the repellent Monsieur Tongoy – is projected over this historic room. I interrupted it in this passage, but I plan to continue it, using whatever may happen here today, using whatever may take place during this lecture. You are, therefore, characters in my fictionalised diary and must keep alert and wide awake before events and actions that can affect your lives at any stage. So I'm not relaxed, but my distinguished public would do well not to be either and to remember that, as John Donne would say, nobody falls asleep in the cart taking him to the gallows.

EVERYONE ELSE IS DEAD

Not everybody knows that the mendicant Rosa in the front row, the beautiful beggar seated next to the monster, is a femme fatale. What's more, with her presence in this room today, I'm not joking, she could embody the diary's sensationalist fatality as a literary genre.

Yes, ladies and gentlemen, I do not forget that this symposium requires me to speak of the private journal as narrative form, I do not forget this, and that is why I refer to the theme for the first time – my beggarly and professional duty is to stick to the symposium's theme – and I tackle the question of fatality encapsulated in every private journal and also in Rosa and in *Detour*, a film I had the misfortune to see here in Budapest.

I said the diary's sensationalist fatality. Well, sensationalist is the adjective that Alan Pauls uses to describe the recurring fact that, whenever you find a diary ('because a diary never appears: you find it, come across it or stumble on it, even when you've been looking for it with desperation'), next to its pages, often staining them, there is a corpse.

We are faced, therefore, by a dramatic convention that is fatal. We find this convention, disguised as an anecdote, in the preface to the first volume of *Strahlungen*, Ernst Jünger's Second World War diaries, where the author tells us about the seven sailors who in 1633 spent the winter on the island of St Mauritius, in the Arctic Ocean: 'The Dutch Society of Greenland had left them there, with their consent, to carry out research into the Arctic winter and polar astronomy. In the summer of 1634, when the whaling fleet returned, they found the diary and seven corpses.' For Pauls, the scene could be the beginning of another version of *The Thing*, Christian Nyby's classic horror B-movie: 'A remote, frozen landscape, the corpses that turn up, one by one, showing no signs of violence, dotted about the camp, seemingly turned to stone in the middle of a final, casual gesture, the diary kept under lock and key, the forced box, a trembling hand that opens the worn covers and avidly seeks out the last observations.'

The last observation by the last sailor to die was this: 'I don't know if I'll be able to write here what has happened, but I'm the only one who can. Everyone else is dead.'

The corpse of the author is almost always guaranteed in conventional diaries, perhaps less so in diaries that transform the genre – fictitious diaries or diaries construed as literary creation, where, however, the corpse of the author turns up eventually, as a fact of life. This is what sooner or later must also happen – especially if I stay this hungry – to the diary I am currently composing, live and out loud, for all of you. But let's keep going, for the moment let's go on. As long as there's life, there'll always be the hope of reaching the end of this lecture and receiving the fee and being able to give Monsieur Tongoy back the foul cents I owe him.

We have already broached the subject, we have already tackled the theme of the private journal as narrative form, we have already begun to demonstrate live how a lecture can be solemn or simply – as in the case of this one – solemnly free, combining as it does a certain narrative form, the essay's reflective flight and an autobiographical voice among other registers. The last of these, the autobiographical voice, I now reintroduce to say that among other things I owe Monsieur Tongoy the cost of two cinema tickets, since he insisted – on the same day we arrived in Budapest and visited what he terms his 'cabin' – that Rosa and I went with him to see a film by Edgar G. Ulmer.

I had never heard of Ulmer, a Viennese director who settled in the Hollywood of the 1940s. The film, shot in 1945, was called *Detour*. A very strange film, extremely strange and fatalistic, it brings everybody bad luck; you only need to see the way Monsieur Tongoy looks today.

To begin with, I refused to go and see this film because I couldn't spend the few cents I had to pay for our boarding-house in Buda at the cinema. We were visiting what Monsieur Tongoy, who had arrived in Budapest before the mendicant Rosa and myself, termed his 'cabin' and we started arguing because he said I could pay for all of us; if I had enough for the boarding-house in Buda, I also had enough for the cinema. Deep down I am horrified by stupid, drunken arguments between tramps, and even more by the places where they live. Monsieur's cabin was in fact a wooden shack whose door he had ripped off to build a fire. A shack in very poor condition, the window was missing its pane and the roof had caved in at various points. It was all disgusting. In a cow-pat, for example, Monsieur Tongoy had drawn a heart transfixed by an arrow. On the ground, among wine bottles that were his only possessions, was the Kemnitzer Cinema's programme. He became very tedious with the programme and his grotesque praise of Ulmer – just because this Viennese director had shot a film with Lugosi called *The Black Cat*, another ill-omened title – and in the end, tired from the journey and from so much arguing, tired also of seeing the repulsive cow-pat, we agreed to go and see the film, especially when monsieur revealed that he could make an effort and pay for us, after all, he said, I could give him back the money with interest when I received the fee for this lecture.

I shouldn't have accepted this, I should never have gone to see this film, since fatality went hand in hand with it, the same fatality that can reach us one day through some miscarriage, some wrong turning on a road somewhere.

FROM JOHN CHEEVER'S JOURNALS

'In the middle age there is mystery, there is mystification. The most I can make out of this hour is a kind of loneliness. Even the beauty of the visible world seems to crumble, yes even love. I feel that there has been *some miscarriage, some wrong turning*, but I do not know when it took place and I have no hope of finding it.'

IDENTITY

The diary that I abandoned in Barcelona and that I go on writing here is a little like a clinical report that seems only to pay attention to the stealthy expressiveness of an illness: my suffering from literature sickness. My diary is full of detailed observations on the evolution of this illness. In the same way as other diarists, I do not write to know who I am, but to know what I am turning into, what is the unforeseeable direction – to disappear would be the ideal, though perhaps not – in which catastrophe is taking me. It is not, therefore, the revelation of some truth that my diary pursues, but the crude, clinical account of a mutation. I began my diary as a narrator who longed to be a literary critic, I then went about building up a diarist's personality thanks to some of my favourite diarists – I kept others back, like

Cheever and Barnabooth, for this lecture, as I also kept fragments of autobiography – and now I see that I am starving myself of my own volition: I have turned into a proper vagrant, whom I see moving away, governed by his uneasiness, or rather by an uneasiness that isn't necessarily his, but in which he partakes in some way. Who knows, ladies and gentlemen, distinguished Hungarian public, it may be my own uneasiness that is invading him.

STRANGE HELPLESSNESS

In *Detour*, a grey man called Al is content every night to play the piano for his girlfriend, a singer in a bar in New York. When she decides to be more ambitious and to head for Los Angeles, poor Al, the man without qualities, is left sad and defeated and, without knowing it, at the mercy of destiny's darkest forces. One day he rings his girlfriend in Los Angeles and, when she tells him to come and visit her, our pianist decides to hitch all the way to the West Coast. He is picked up by a guy named Haskell, a fake with money, who drives a convertible and promises to take him as far as Los Angeles. It seems like a stroke of luck for Al, but when they make a detour on the road to fill up at a petrol station, this turning – almost imperceptibly at first – will be the beginning of a series of endless fatalities, of continuous nightmarish setbacks that will change the life of Al the nondescript. When they stop again, Haskell dies of a heart attack and Al is forced to usurp his personality to keep going and falls into the clutches of a hitch-hiker, an evil, disturbed femme fatale who knows the convertible's previous owner and blackmails poor Al. When she dies also accidentally – although the police will always believe that she has been murdered, killed by Al – she will leave our grey man with his nondescript character with two unexplained deaths on his shoulders, a fugitive from the law, a man without a credible identity, who has lost his way on some by-road.

On leaving the cinema, I did not fail to notice that the humbug Haskell was a little like Monsieur Tongoy, who sometimes, without having anything, boasts of having something: 'cabins', wine, interest in cinema and a bit of money. Nor did I fail to notice certain similarities between the disturbed femme fatale and Rosa. And I could not help noticing that I resembled the nondescript without an identity, the man without qualities, who in the end wanders along the by-road.

Strange film, probably the oddest and best film that I have ever seen, but that I soon realised brought with it fatality and strange helplessness, which I feel this evening, lacking shelter and food, on life's by-road.

Final fatality: destiny turned its back on Tom Neal, the actor who plays Al, as soon as he finished shooting the film. He fell into perpetual disgrace in Hollywood when he fought with Franchot Tone for the love of a woman, for the love of Barbara Payton. Expelled from Los Angeles and from life, pariah on sombre destiny's road, Tom Neal in 1965 murdered his third wife. He spent years in prison and, when he came out, he led the life of a vagrant in the family of the defeated and one day he was found dead on a by-road south of Boston.

There is Rosa, ladies and gentlemen, distinguished Hungarian public, there is Rosa, impassive in the front row, calm as anything when I call her a femme fatale. I'm not planning to do away with her as poor Tom Neal did. After all, in her capacity as vamp – this alone qualifies her to sit next to her partner in the front row, the vampire – it is some time since my wife gave up her corrosive activity at the end of the 1960s, when she would induce the young poets who crossed her path to commit suicide or else, if she saw that they were not up to it, she would annihilate them from a creative point of view. I never saw anyone with such a hatred of poetry. Today Rosa is a peaceful mendicant, calmly seated in the front row of this room, but when I met her she destroyed poets. She was worse than Calamity Jane, that legendary and disastrous woman of the Far West. Rosa chased poetry and poets to death, she believed that poetry should be written in prose and that verse had lost its *raison d'être* with the invention of writing, a few years after Homer. She was always quoting Leopardi: 'Everything has been brought to perfection since Homer, except poetry.' For Rosa only prose existed and poetry deceived only fools, since it was really prose with a high opinion of itself. As soon as she spotted a poet, especially if he was young, she would do everything in her power to humiliate him and, if possible, to eliminate him. At best she would send him back fit and well to the world of prose. She saw off more than one, more than one fragile poet, singer of the moon and cemeteries. She would wrap them all in the intimacy of her dark love-nest and then ask them if it was true that they hailed from the land of sweet poets and, if the poor, innocent souls fell into the trap and admitted being sweet and being poets, Rosa would lash them with a whip-like sentence: 'You're all poets, and yet I'm on the side of death.'

Rosa for a long time morally assassinated poets. She wanted to go beyond poetry, beyond the prestige of this discipline that got on her nerves and that struck her as fundamentally prosaic and above all opportunistic, a refuge for the mediocre. Rosa attracted young poets, seduced them thoroughly and then threatened to leave them if they continued to believe in poetry or if they did not take it to its limits and place themselves on the side of death. She undermined lyrical morale with all kinds of devilish tricks. And more than one despaired, was annihilated, even committed suicide.

'Are you a poet?' she asked me the night we met. I was a novelist by then, although I had yet to publish anything, but I was also a poet, albeit a secret poet out of respect for and in honour of my mother, who had written poetry all her life without confessing to it. Around that time I was writing secret verses about the moon and the stars. But I didn't tell Rosa anything. Fortunately. I felt good being a secret poet. I didn't tell her anything and at that stage I had no idea that she hated poetry in this way. I simply told her that I was a novelist and this probably saved my life. A few months later, we moved in together and, though no paperwork was involved, we felt that we had married. My poems remained hidden and have done until now, until today when I reveal my secret to Rosa. Shortly after moving in together, we went on a trip to Venice, which we always considered our honeymoon. There was a lot of talk around that time, in Spain's literary circles, about a poetic style termed Venetian, the poetry of the *novísimos*, who were the poets of my generation. Fortunately, however, I made no mention of it during our trip, nor did it occur to me – also fortunately – to say anything about my secret attraction towards poetry; I have guarded the secret very closely until this evening. I don't know what Rosa would have thought if I had shown signs of interest in the poets of my generation, for example, or if she had suddenly realised that she was travelling with a recently married novelist, but also poet. This in fact is what I was, a happy man, still unaware – I would find out on this trip – of Rosa's hatred for poetry. I found out on a night with full moon, frankly poetic. I found out when we were floating along the Grand Canal, past the railway station and Tronchetto Island, out to sea, and Rosa the poet-breaker, no doubt abetted by the large amount of grappa she had imbibed, began to tell me, inserting the occasional sinister detail, how she had cruelly cut short the poetic life, and sometimes even the life, of more than one poet. I was horrified, unable to utter a word, there on the Grand Canal. I was dumbstruck as she let out a chilling guffaw that tore up any future attempt to publicise my poetry by the roots.

'Wretch, we're lost because of you!' I told her, pretending that I was joking. It was the least I could say. I knew that, apart from confessing to her that I wrote poetry, I had to tell her something and I told her this, but I did not go on, purely afraid that I would end up composing an ode to Venice before the sea of theatres.

How fragile I was back then, I wonder why.

Rosa has not come out of this biographical sketch very well, nor should Monsieur Tongoy hope to emerge from his unscathed. Here in Budapest he chose a miserable life for his life as a bat. Chilling shadow of the vampire Lugosi, Monsieur Tongoy's presence among us this evening ought to inspire us all with horror. Since I am unwilling to waste energy by criticising him too much, in this theatre-lecture I shall simply reproduce the miserable monologue that our vampire delivered today, when he proposed leaving the 'cabin' and installing himself, at my expense – he achieved this – in the Kakania Grand Hotel.

'For days now I have eaten,' he said with a sleepless beggar's pomposity, as if he wished to mimic a character from Beckett, 'I have drunk, I have dressed and undressed, in this medium-sized cage facing Budapest's north-west, which has a marvellous view of medium-sized cages facing south-east. But soon I will have to get by in some other way, because the landscape is fatally doomed to demolition. Soon I will have to pack up my belongings and begin to eat, to drink, to sleep, to dress and undress, at the Kakania. With you, master. I will be the Sancho Panza you have always wanted me to be, but invite me to the Kakania, Rosario. Your squire is homeless. I've nothing left, only a cow-pat and some red wine and these eyes that I open and shut, two central European eyes, I've nothing left, except my tongue and eyes, my tongue that allows me to say that I will talk about myself when the repulsive vagrants have stopped, though in fact I won't even talk about myself then, why if what I really want is not to talk any more, to rest at the Kakania, to be your squire, your monsieur.'

THE VAMPIRE'S TURNING

You must be thinking that it's high time I told you that neither Rosa nor monsieur exist, since there is nobody in the front row and what's more, had Rosa and monsieur been seated there, they would be so indignant that they would have prevented me continuing some time ago.

Tell us, you must be thinking, that the two of them do not exist and, while you're about it, confess that you're not hungry after the banquet that was given today at the Kakania in your honour.

OK, ladies and gentlemen, distinguished Hungarian public, I am going to make an about-turn, a vampire's turning. I shall tell truths, having lied to you slightly. I am not at all hungry and you're absolutely right that there's nobody in the front row and the only one who looks like a vampire – I know that I resemble Christopher Lee – is me. But this does not mean that neither Rosa nor monsieur exist, that they aren't in Budapest, that they aren't now hung-over having gone out last night, resting in their respective rooms at the Kakania.

Those of you who have already accepted that Monsieur Tongoy exists may be wondering if he and I look very much or a little alike. Well, the answer is: we bear an unmistakable family resemblance. That said, Monsieur Tongoy is not happy when he is placed in the bloody tradition of vampires. Unlike me, monsieur does not like to be connected with that depraved count who derived pleasure out of horror. I, however, feel the vampire's pride. For example, for years I behaved in literature like a complete parasite. Later I began to lose my attraction for the blood of other people's work and, with their collaboration, I even cultivated a distinct style of my own: discreet, cultured, a little bit secret, perhaps just eccentric, but that belongs to me and is a far cry from the uniform modern army of the identical. All the same, I have periods in which I relapse slightly into the vampirism of previous years. Today, to go no further, I have been behaving in this theatre-lecture like a parasite, living off Monsieur Tongoy's ideas, since it was he who designed the script, the outline of my speech this evening.

THIS THEORY'S LIFE

Monsieur Tongoy was born of chance. Like Monsieur Teste. Like everybody. The lecture he dictated to me is as extraterritorial to the conventions of any lecture as the characters are eccentric in the story I have told you about the mendicant vamp, the hungry quack – me myself – and the theoretical vagrant: erratic characters who arrived in Budapest a few days ago and went to see *Detour* and fell into the fatality that pursues those who watch this strange, extremely bizarre film.

I invented the vagrancy of these three characters on monsieur's instructions. His lecture design required one fictional part – unusual for a lecture – that could be mixed, in the name of theatre, with the essay part.

Monsieur Tongoy gave me two initial pointers for this lecture, two pointers he considered of paramount importance: 1) That I should not fail to emphasise the relationship between him and me, that I should not forget that Dracula – along with Faust, Don Quixote, Don Juan and Robinson Crusoe – is one of the myths that founded contemporary man's consciousness and, like other myths, he did not marry or maintain stable and lasting relationships with women and, like the others, he had a male servant or accomplice, which demonstrates his enormous self-centredness. 2) That my lecture should be a microcosm of what I am writing in Barcelona and should, therefore, combine essay, private memory, diary, travel book and narrative fiction. And even copy the structure of my manuscript in Barcelona, going from fiction to reality, but without ever forgetting that literature is invention and, as Nabokov said, 'fiction is fiction. To call a story a true story is an insult to both art and truth. Every great writer is a great deceiver.'

Monsieur Tongoy really is a distant relation of Bela Lugosi. He comes from a family of Hungarian Jews who went into exile in Chile. He has travelled to Budapest to trace his roots. Don't tell me it isn't moving . . . It is also Monsieur Tongoy who gives life to this lecture's theory. A few days ago, when I had just arrived in this city with Rosa, he was perplexed when he understood that I had nothing prepared to say here this evening, and he asked me, 'So what are you going to do? Not say anything? Make word in the treasure of silence.'

I make word. I make theory as well and inform you that I share monsieur's idea that the world can no longer be re-created as in novels before, from the writer's *unique* perspective. Monsieur and I believe that the world has *fallen apart* and only if you dare to show it in its disintegration can you hope to offer a credible image of it.

I make word, therefore, and announce that, because of monsieur, my relationship with Rosa has not been stable for some time. It is also because of monsieur that, seeing me now, you may be thinking of Faust, Dracula or Don Quixote. I'm not sure if it's a very good idea, I'm not sure if I should thank him for it.

But in the meantime I make word and also theatre-lecture and keep going and, guided by the chance of monsieur's mind, I see how the theory takes shape as it chooses, with rhythm and mystery, all by itself.

MONSIEUR TONGOY'S DIARY

Were monsieur to keep a diary, I would find it extremely interesting, since no doubt Rosa and I would figure in it quite a lot. Were he to keep a diary, I wouldn't hesitate for a moment to steal it for a few hours, without him realising, and to read the thoughts he would have consigned to these pages, fascinating for sure, since I am convinced that Monsieur Tongoy is a keen observer and a remarkable thinker. He is also, though you may not have imagined it, the ugliest man in the world. Yes, that's right. And yet this isn't a problem for him, it never has been, he thinks that his intelligence makes him beautiful. However, I do not wish to mislead you: he is horrible, he is the most monstrous, the ugliest man in the world.

Monsieur would like to think like Valéry and continue

Musil's work, that's why you'll see him sometimes looking lost in the streets, searching for Musil. He doesn't look so lost when he tackles the corridors of the Kakania Grand Hotel, though I don't think he'll be tackling anything right now, he'll probably be sleeping off yesterday's drinking bout, though, who knows, perhaps he's already feeling better and is on his way here or opening a private journal. If he's started to write one, I shall pinch it straight away. Though, on reflection, it's absurd. Why steal his diary if I can imagine what he writes there: 'Rosa likes Rosario because the poor man resembles a lesser Dracula. It would be much more natural for her to be drawn to me, since I am the most classic of Draculas, albeit I do not like to be connected with a vampire at all.'

In short, ladies and gentlemen, distinguished Hungarian public, I believe everybody should keep another's diary. It's an enormously healthy exercise.

BASER PASSIONS

You have already seen me improvise from time to time, depart from Monsieur Tongoy's script, so now I leave these sheets behind and inform you that at the start of the twenty-first century, in February this year, Rosa, monsieur and I travelled to the Azores. We had met in Chile, in Valparaíso, where we saw monsieur cruelly drown a fly in a pool of dry Martini. A bird went by, we followed it, we deduced that it was heading for the Azores and, two months later, the three of us set foot on these islands. On the island of Pico, inside its imposing volcano, I thought I saw some tireless moles working away day and night, in the service of the enemies of the literary. I thought I saw them, I imagined them, I suspected that they were there, in truth I saw them . . . I couldn't say now exactly what it was that happened, all I know is that I obtained a valuable image for the fictionalised diary I was, and still am, writing. The image, possibly visionary or simply intuitive or real, burrowed deep inside me. Hijacked as my mind was by the obsession that literature is under threat and runs the risk of extinction, this vision of the moles had a powerful effect on me.

It still does. Allow me to explain that real, true literature has always evolved serenely until reaching the point where it can be classed as lasting. That of the owners of Pico's moles, on the other hand, is mere appearance, practised by animals who claim to be writers and whose literature gallops across the noise and shouts of its practitioners, and every year launches thousands of books on to the market, although, as the years go by, one ends up asking where they are and what became of their brief and noisy renown; it is, therefore, a transient literature, unlike real literature, which is permanent, although, at times like this, real literature has to make an increasingly hard effort to withstand the assaults of the moles' owners.

The day we travelled on the ferry from Fayal to Pico, with bad weather in the channel connecting the islands, I did not know that Monsieur Tongoy was so irritated by what he understood was an exaggerated tendency on my part to think about the dangers threatening real literature. I found out when we had just disembarked in Madalena, Pico's harbour, with Rosa lagging behind us, and – I admit somewhat inopportunely – I remarked that the tragic, silent and deserted scene – there was not a soul in sight in Madalena – was like a metaphor for the death of literature. He answered rudely. He got so worked up that he seemed to have gone mad. I shall never forget his reaction, most of all because, shortly afterwards, he said something that had quite an impact on me and I had a first, fleeting intuition that there could be something between him and Rosa that I was not noticing.

It was an odd moment. As if he had suddenly revealed both how much my Montano's malady or sickly obsession with literature infuriated him and the excessive intimacy he shared with Rosa. In fact it was the prelude to what has finally exploded here in Budapest, where something like a fatality has appeared in our relationship, originating from some miscarriage, some wrong turning, and it is impossible today to know exactly when it took place, but it did take place, and it is dramatic.

I said that Madalena's silent and deserted scene was like a metaphor for the death of literature, and Monsieur Tongoy, out of Rosa's hearing, told me that, if I carried on being obsessed with what I was writing and above all obsessed with the death of literature and scarcely able to enjoy the trip and the scenery, he would feel obliged to warn Rosa that I was confusing what I was writing with reality and that I thought I was Don Quixote in the Azores.

At this point Rosa joined us and we both fell silent. A little later, we hired a taxi – a taxi-driver was the only person we saw in the whole of Madalena – and drove down the gloomy and solitary Lajes road, the road that would take us to a small hill a short distance from the island's volcano, where a secret writer lived, who turned out to be as secret as he was invisible, but who helped me to create a sinister character – it was in front of his house where I saw or thought I saw the tireless moles – which I incorporated into my diary that night in Fayal, after we had returned from Pico and had all drunk a fair amount of gin. It was then I reached a conclusion and, still with the echo of monsieur's words about Quixote, I decided that in my fictionalised diary, to save it from extinction, I would embody literature itself, never so seriously threatened as at the start of this century.

When, on leaving Café Sport that night, I told Rosa and monsieur that in Pico I had witnessed a battalion of tireless moles in the service of the basest of human passions, Monsieur Tongoy reacted abnormally. 'And which is the basest of them all?' he asked obscenely and lasciviously, like an idiot, more drunk than I was, his central European eyes those of a dirty old man.

I thought for a moment. I gazed at the moon, listened to the murmur of the sea, thought how little thought takes place nowadays. The lack of culture, I said to myself, is suffocating thought. As is alcohol, you only have to look at monsieur. I'm not going to talk to him about sex, which is what he expects, I'm going to crush him with the danger posed by the enemies of the literary.

I thought about merchants and the emissaries of nothingness and other enemies of the literary.

'The stink of money and its proud stench,' I answered him, 'and the deliberate lack of culture they generate, which goes against life, against real life.'

There was no immediate reply, only surprise. Then I told them both that for the book I had the idea of embodying literature's complete memory. And this triggered a violent response from the two of them. Monsieur Tongoy looked at me angrily. 'Go fuck yourself,' he told me. 'You see everything in literature, I'm not surprised you even want to merge with it,' Rosa upbraided me. I tried to explain to them that I wanted to embody literature only in fiction. But they were too drunk to heed such subtlety. What bothered me most was that they did not share my concern for the future of real literature. I should have liked to admit to them that I was prepared to organise a movement of world resistance to the masters of Pico's moles, but, given the circumstances, this would have been almost like putting my life on the line. I began to understand that I was alone on that island and that the only consolation left to me was to think that I was in paradise. I said this to myself so as not to lose heart completely. But their lack of solidarity with me so enraged me that I could not contain myself and I told them that, if they did not change their attitude, I would abandon them right there on the island. They were stunned at first, but then they began to titter. This was the famous beginning of the end. 'At the start of the twenty-first century, I am alone and without direction on some by-road,' I remarked reprovingly, testing to see what would happen. And it happened. First they started to giggle, but they ended up laughing their heads off and losing their balance, shaking the two of them, they thought it was so funny, and then holding on to a boat they had bumped into and trying to catch their breath. This was the limit, especially when their laughter expired and, to my surprise, I discovered that monsieur could read my thoughts.

I hate the love stories readers today continue to demand from novels. All those blessed readers complain, I am told, when they see that love stories barely figure in the novels they buy. Since many of you may be such readers, who demand love stories in what they read or listen to, I have come here this evening with a commission from Monsieur Tongoy not to deprive you of a love story.

'The day will come,' monsieur told me yesterday, 'when cold ideas will cross the minds of future beings, who will not be dependent on the romantic warmth of yesteryear, a warmth that will strike them rather as extraterrestrial. But since this day has not yet come, the best thing you can do tomorrow is to make concessions to the public and in your Theory of Budapest to include a love story. Between tramps, for example.'

Rosa and I arrived in this city, we visited monsieur in his cabin, we went to the cinema, we saw *Detour* and, on coming out, I witnessed too many looks from her to him and realised that we made up as devilish a triangle as the one that appeared in the film we had just seen, that film so charged with fatality. And intuition made me afraid that any of the curses this strange film seemed to contain could easily affect us. For a start, I began to confirm that Rosa seemed to have eyes only for the horrendous monsieur. And yesterday I became totally convinced, yesterday conflict broke out. Last night we inspected all the bars in the city and got very drunk, they did especially. I looked at them and thought how strange always is the laughter of those who are going to die. I wanted to kill them, yes, but

I'm not a murderer, I'm a writer, a lecturer, a poor vagrant wandering along some by-road.

We visited all the bars in Budapest and ended up in the New Belvàrosi, where some gypsies played the Rakoczy March as a farewell to the customers. I shan't deny that it was emotional. Rosa did not realise, but it was even a poetic moment, with those exciting tones of the Zingaro cymbals bringing the night to an especially poetic dramatic close . . .

Monsieur Tongoy did capture the poetic tone. 'The three of us are also gypsies, vagrants, and you are wonderfully riddled with jealousy, you should talk about it tomorrow in the lecture,' he said to me.

At that precise moment, the Rakoczy March stopped.

At this precise moment in the lecture, according to monsieur's script, I should drink a glass of water, a normal gesture in such proceedings. But I am not hungry, I am not thirsty, I have a premonition, a theory, the Theory of Budapest: at this precise moment, knowing that I am most probably giving this lecture, Rosa and monsieur are in bed together.

There are proud men broken inside by invisible misfortune. This is not my case, it is easy to see how ridiculously cuckolded I look. But have no fear, ladies and gentlemen, I am not going to burst into tears or utter a cry of cosmic pain, or collapse at this desk as if I were Professor Unrat in the film *The Blue Angel*, and I'm certainly not going to ruin the rest of your evening. A strange sense of professionalism tells me that I must go on with my lecture. And this is what I do. I go on. I know I must go on, not cry, observe how life goes on and watch how the evening light bathes the quiet façades of the historic buildings opposite. I know I must not forget that deep down I always wanted to say goodbye to love in life and in novels, to lose everything except solitude. And to continue. All I have done in life is to continue. I would finish one book and start another, always continuing. To lose everything except solitude. And to have presence and dignity and not to cry, to justify myself before death with a job well done, to lead the unhappy, irreproachable life of a deceived man.

THE MILLIONAIRE BARNABOOTH'S DIARY

This morning I sensed very sharply the romance between them both. I saw it very clearly when both she and he, in their respective hovels at the Kakania, had or said they had a hangover that was literally boring a hole in their minds. I have spent the day in a nervous state and with the impression that a being on high allowed me to be so. I wondered if I would be able to see the lecture through. I have the admirable endurance of those clowns who, after a tragic piece of news, go out into the circus arena to ply their trade, but what I didn't know is whether, feeling so deceived, I would end up deceiving myself, thinking that I could carry it off in public. I see that I have managed it, but I'm not relaxed, all the same; I haven't been relaxed since this morning, when I ate breakfast alone and realised that Rosa and monsieur planned to go to bed together as soon as I was at this lecture. Terrible panorama. It struck me that this breakfast could be the first in a long line of breakfasts alone.

I also felt under the influence of the dream I had suffered in the night, in which I had been mercilessly deafened by the drone of the Rakoczy March played by some gypsies on the terrace of a luxury hotel. I have never felt so on edge as I did this morning in the Kakania Grand Hotel, especially when I saw that the two fried eggs I had just been served – a kind of sinister metaphor for my soon-to-be-cuckolded condition – were staring at me from the plate and I saw in them the eyes of the Chilean millionaire Barnabooth, that brilliant heteronym created by the French writer Valéry Larbaud. This vision lasted only a moment. Barnabooth looked at me and smiled, and then vanished from the fried eggs, but the truth of the matter is he was there for a second, I cannot be more certain, I mean I am convinced that the fried eggs undoubtedly contained the presence of the Chilean millionaire's spirit.

I was so thirsty for revenge that I took my own revenge when I realised that Monsieur Tongoy is also from Chile, with the difference that he'll never be fit to hold a candle to the young *riche amateur* Barnabooth, author of a fascinating private journal, the journal of a happy traveller, who crossed the enlightened, nocturnal Europe of the inter-war period in luxury trains: 'Lend me your vast noise, your vast and ever so sweet march, your nocturnal slide through enlightened Europe, o luxury train! and the anxious music that sounds in your corridors of golden skin . . .'

The anxious music reminds me of the gypsy songs in my dream last night. I have explained it in several of my novels, though many of you cannot know this, I shall tell it again: for the last thirty years I have had a recurring dream in which I have always lived in a luxury hotel and have never paid the bill, which over time has grown and is now sizeable. Often the receptionist is about to hand me this impressive bill, but, conscious of the fortune I owe, I escape down a ramp in the garage, which I know very well and which is next to a service lift that only exists in my sleepwalking imagination. The dream recurs, but it is not always the same, it has all sorts of minor variations. In the version I had last night, it was a bellboy from the hotel, a young man named Montano, who led me stealthily to the ramp down which I could effect my escape. He was a bellboy who seemed to have emerged from one of the illustrations in the first edition of the millionaire Barnabooth's diary.

Last night, when I had escaped down the ramp and was in the street, the bellboy Montano suddenly came up to me and, in a parody of Shakespeare, whispered in my ear, 'To be again, that is the problem.' After that, as if he were going to pay my millionaire bill, behaving as a good son would, he went back into the hotel. 'Montano!' I shouted. 'One moment, I'm looking for the Pope of Rome,' the strange bellboy answered. 'But, Montano!' I said. Rosa, who may have been awake or asleep, murmured, 'Leave Montano alone.'

Some of you must be wondering if Barnabooth was really Chilean. Well, I have to say he was always thought of as a South American millionaire of no fixed state. But he can be considered Chilean because, when he was created – when he was 'written' by Larbaud – his place of birth belonged to Chile, hence it can be said that he was from Monsieur Tongoy's country, though in fact Barnabooth was from everywhere, and this was his grace, he was stateless but also Chilean, because he was born in

1883 'in Campamento, Arequipa Province, *today Chile*, just when a war was being waged between Peru, Chile and Bolivia over this territory.'

Revenge, Hamlet.

You don't know how good it makes me feel to talk about this stateless millionaire, so vastly superior to the ghost of Monsieur Tongoy.

Barnabooth wrote an elegant private journal that begins in the Carlton Hotel in Florence and ends in London, where he takes his leave of Europe and decides to abandon the diary: 'I shall leave these pages, this book. I shall leave it tomorrow afternoon, in Paris, where it will be published, I don't care how or when. It is the final whim I permit myself.'

In truth Barnabooth wants the diary to be published so that he can lose sight of it, unburden himself. He says that when the diary reaches the bookshops, that will be the day he ceases to be a writer. Just like that. He wants nothing more to do with writing. And even less with the diary, about which he says, 'It is over, I begin. Do not seek me in its pages, I'm somewhere else, I'm in Campamento, in South America.'

How superior is Barnabooth to Monsieur Tongoy! Revenge, Hamlet. And goodbye, Monsieur Tongoy. I use Barnabooth, who was Chilean like you, to send you packing to the Chilean Patagonia from where you mustn't return. Goodbye, monsieur. I cease to give the lecture following your dictatorial dictation. I choose my own route, a decision as serious as in fact it is trivial, because in fact the difference between following monsieur's dictation and ceasing to do so is the same as that between repeating the words of your dog and taking it for a walk.

DIARY OF THE CONVENT OF THE PRECIOUS BLOOD

Goodbye, Rosa, goodbye. I knew the day would come when I would have to separate from you and I would write it here. Goodbye, Rosa. You'll even end up missing those mornings when we ate breakfast together and I saw that the fried eggs were staring at me from the plates you served me sweetly, although sometimes they ended up glaring at me from the floor: plates that broke when you hurled the fried eggs at my head and said you felt weighed down by the lack of intimacy and said you wanted to be on your own for a while. Goodbye, Rosa, goodbye. Now you will have all the time to enjoy your precious intimacy. After all, Monsieur Tongoy is a dirty old man with one foot in hell, already the slow Chilean train that will run him down is approaching. Soon, Rosa, you'll have all the time in the world to miss those wonderful mornings when the fried eggs figured so prominently between us. Soon you'll be hit by nostalgia even for the morning you spilled your blood over breakfast. It all began when I asked you if I could make some toast and you told me to wait until you had finished making yours, and shortly after saying this you started to cry, and I asked myself out loud what I had done to deserve this, and you called me a pig, and I told you to stop crying, for God's sake, don't cry any more, I just wanted to make some toast, I told you, just some toast for the fried eggs, and you ordered me to make a boiled egg and to go to hell because I had spoiled your day, and then, when I told you that I didn't want a boiled egg and that this argument was grotesque, you hurled your plate at my head and started crying again and bent down to pick up the remains of the broken plate and ended up cutting the surface of your hand, you spilled your precious blood.

That's where I wanted to get to. To the precious blood, which allows me to think about Chile, to recall the Convent of the Precious Blood, in the city of Santiago, where the extremely beautiful writer Teresa Wilms Montt, enclosed against her will, wrote part of her private journal, which today is named after the convent.

Teresa was a great and you, Rosa, will never be. Revenge, Hamlet. Teresa was a real woman and you are just a flesh-and-blood character in the tragic novel of my life.

Teresa was born in 1893 in Viña del Mar, she was educated for marriage and for high-society parties, but from an early age this young woman of good family showed a tendency to rebel. She married the first man she met, Gustavo Balmaceda, with whom she shared a passion for the opera. The couple – she was only seventeen – had to leave Viña del Mar's closed society and settle in Santiago, where Teresa became literature-sick while her husband became sick with jealousy and gave himself up to alcohol. Shouts, fights, blows. They moved to Iquique, where matters became even worse for the couple when she sought out the company of trade-unionists and feminists who consolidated her Masonic and anarchist thinking.

Teresa had two daughters from her marriage, but was violently separated from them when her husband found out that she was unfaithful. He shut her up in the Convent of the Precious Blood in Santiago, where Teresa began to write her angst-ridden, terrible, bloody diary: 'Stupid clock, continue loathsomely! Your black hands like a crow's wings park on each endless minute. I feel an impulse to throw you far away, to stamp on you! Ironic, biting, impassive enemy of those who suffer, you are without mercy! When you see that we are happy, you become light and your minute-hands fly . . . You're perverted, infested with the devil!'

During her angst-ridden enclosure, she clung to her diary, she acted as if she knew these words by John Cheever: 'Literature has been the salvation of the damned, literature has inspired and guided lovers, routed despair and can perhaps in this case save the world.'

Teresa escaped from that convent and fled with Vicente Huidobro to Buenos Aires, where she entered the literary circles and became one of the few women who frequented Bohemian life in the capital. These words by Huidobro remain as a testament to those Argentinian days and have become an immortal eulogy: 'Teresa Wilms is the greatest woman to have come out of America. Perfect in face, perfect in body, perfect in elegance, perfect in education, perfect in intelligence, perfect in spiritual strength, perfect in grace.'

But Teresa Wilms fled from Buenos Aires as well: 'I have left Argentina because my destiny is to wander.' New York, Seville, Paris, London and Valle-Inclán's Madrid – she was his muse – all saw her go by. Go by and leave. Teresa fled from every city. And ended up fleeing from herself, she began not to eat and to take all kinds of sedatives to dull her overflowing senses. She carried her wandering life, her journey along some by-road, her destiny, to its logical conclusion. At the age of twenty-eight she killed herself with an overdose of barbiturates. Her language reminds me of Alejandra Pizarnik's, and therefore also of my mother's. Teresa Wilms killed herself and in her diary left passages like this: 'Naked as I was born, I leave, as ignorant of what there was in the world. I suffered and this is the only baggage of the boat that leads to oblivion.'

You who in respectful silence follow the staging of my extensive personal drama will hardly or not be surprised if I tell you that Teresa was a very superior being to Rosa. Revenge, Hamlet. One Chilean millionaire and one poet from the same country have sufficed for me to fulminate monsieur and Rosa. Thank you, Chile. Thank you, Hamlet. And goodbye, Rosa, goodbye. You are a toad for me this evening, and so is monsieur. Goodbye, both of you. I shan't say now that a toad like you is the truth of the other toad, monsieur's toad. I shan't say that, Rosa, but I will say that it is a pleasure to lose one toad, and to lose both even more.

A TURNING TOWARDS DESOLATION

John Cheever was a tireless writer of private journals over forty years, during which he scarcely took a break when it came to trying to explain his complex conflict with life, because deep down, beyond appearances, the problem was life, as his son, Benjamin Cheever, writes in his foreword to the journals: 'A simpleton might think that bisexuality was the essence of his problem, but of course it was not. Nor was alcoholism. He came to terms with his bisexuality. He quit drinking. But life was still a problem.'

There is an entry in his journals that I mentally carry permanently sewn in the left-hand pocket of all my trousers: 'Hurricane watch, they say. Heavy rains after midnight. Gale winds. I wake at three. It is close. No sign of wind and rain. Then I think that I can do it, make sense of it, and recount my list of virtues: valor, saneness, decency, the ability to handle the natural hazards of life.'

Since reading this entry from his journal, I have carried it permanently on me, it is a list of values that has been decisive in my life. In the absence of other beliefs, I have had this list, which has served me never to lose my sense of direction. This past night, for example, it has helped me to deal with my problems and to save all of you the unpleasant cries of a wounded animal, the unpleasant signs of desperation.

The problems were always there, which enabled Cheever – this is the positive side of the matter – to write masterly pages in his journals, like this one that I carry loose in my pocket and shall now read you: 'When the beginnings of self-destruction enter the heart it seems no bigger than a grain of sand. It is a headache, a slight case of indigestion, an infected finger; but you miss the 8:20 and arrive late at the meeting on credit extensions. The old friend that you meet for lunch suddenly exhausts your patience and in an effort to be pleasant you drink three cocktails, but by now the day has lost its form, its sense and meaning. To try and restore some purpose and beauty to it you drink too much at cocktails you talk too much you make a pass at somebody's wife and you end with doing something foolish and obscene and wish in the morning that you were dead. But when you try to trace back the way you came into this abyss all you find is a grain of sand.'

Last night, distinguished public, I remained alone, alone and lost in Budapest, you yourselves have been witnessing my tragic process of separation from the others. This plunges me into a state of confusion that takes me even closer to the world of Cheever, who opened his extensive journals on a disconsolate note in which he talked of loneliness and of how the beauty of the visible world seemed to crumble before him, even love crumbled. And Cheever spoke in this opening of some miscarriage, he had the impression that he had taken some wrong turning: the same impression that I have today, here in Budapest, the sensation that, since seeing *Detour*, I have wandered from my road. I should never have gone into that cinema, the beauty of the world has crumbled in me, and fatality has left me broken, alone, wandering along some by-road.

'The most I can make out of this hour is a kind of loneliness.' This is how Cheever's journals begin, this is how I should begin my diary of a deceived man, because this is what my diary is turning into – that of a deceived man – after having told you the story of my turning towards desolation, the desolation I have come to know here in this city of Budapest, where I have undoubtedly taken a wrong turning, as if Cheever's loneliness – the journals' opening reminds me of the start of Robinson Crusoe's diary: 'And now being about to enter into a melancholy relation of a scene of silent life . . .' – continued to affect me.

I'm not going to sink further before you, I shall simply

draw to a close with the spectacle of someone who is not really hungry, who in the course of this lecture has gradually transformed into a deceived man, the composition of whose diary you have witnessed live, a diary that will continue even if the lecture finishes, that will go beyond this historic room and follow its course out of your sight, reflecting like Cheever on loneliness, on the weight of despair and dejection, on the painful attacks of unfounded anxiety, on love and hate, on the need for a writer to give words especial importance, to move among them as comfortably as among human beings, if not more so; to dethrone words in order to show them to better seats, to squeeze them and question them and stroke them delicately and even paint them with the colours of the impossible and, after so much intimacy with them, to know also how to be able to hide out of consideration for them.

RUSSIAN DIARY

It is not the revelation of some truth that my diary pursues, but information about my constant mutations. My diary has existed for years, but only started to turn into a novel a few months ago, in November last year, when I travelled to Nantes and imagined that I was visiting an invented son. I started to turn my diary into a novel being the narrator that I am, but pretending to be a literary critic, later I began to construct a fake biography by injecting myself with fragments from the lives or works of my favourite diarists and I discovered how right Gabriel

Ferrater was when in 1956 he wrote in a letter to Jaime Gil de Biedma, 'Have you noticed how curiously impersonal we letter-wounded are or, perhaps better, how lacking in intimacy our personality is?'

In short, I built myself a timid biography and later, here in Budapest, I transformed into a hungry lecturer whom I see now turning, after a new mutation and because of his treacherous wife, into a lonely man, into a man who wanders along some by-road, into a walker who tries out the identity of a deceived man.

The different characters I have been all suffered from literature sickness, they needed to cling to literature in order to survive. The deceived vampire you see now before you is, of all those characters, the one who most needs literature to survive. This may be because in fiction he has just discovered a moral of life.

This deceived vampire's diary is turning Russian since he connected it with another diary, that of Pierre Drieu La Rochelle, called *Diary of a Deceived Man*, no less. This man, by which I mean this vampire, remembers well a passage from the anti-Communist Drieu La Rochelle's diary; two sentences written nervously in the days when his compatriots were asking him to commit suicide so that they would not have to shoot him for his collaboration with the Nazis: 'It is said that in Russia they no longer know what jealousy is. I am Russian.'

The deceived man I have turned into is Russian, he no longer knows what jealousy is. So he's not going to cry out here with pain and terror. But I feel rage and infinite resentment, I cannot hide it. I should like to destroy the world. I'm afraid that from now on I shall keep the diary of a deceived, resentful, vindictive man. Life has treated me badly. Nobody likes to be deceived. I am not deceiving you if I tell you that I am Russian and am not jealous, but I'm thinking of planting mental bombs in all the homes of all those swines who are destroying literature, of all those businessmen who publish books, of all those departmental managers, market leaders, marketing funambulists, economics graduates. I'm after them, I've already located where their lackeys hang out on the island of Pico, and now I'm after them. What they do lacks spirit and grace. I'm becoming increasingly like the protagonist of *Detour*, that character we see at the end of the film lost and alone on a road at dusk, without direction, subject to an abstract freedom he can do little or nothing with, except to try to disappear or hide or dissolve in the last corner of the world.

I want to delve deep into unreality, to flee from so many hateful ghosts, so much falsification and masquerade, to flee from a reality that has lost its meaning. 'One does not grow old in the space of an afternoon,' John Cheever remarked in his journals with reference to his story 'The Swimmer', whose protagonist crossed swimming pools in the course of a few hours that ended up turning into months, and finally years; he was an old man by the time he made it home. 'Oh, well, kick it around,' I recall Cheever adding. And yet you have been able to see how it is perfectly possible to grow old in the space of a lecture on the private journal as narrative form. You have witnessed my unsightly mutation and know that I'm in an understandably bad mood. I shall leave this Literature Museum twenty years older, I have transformed into one of those terrible and very dangerous old men Macedonio Fernández talked about in one of his notes.

George Sand had already talked about this phenomenon of ageing live, in front of everybody. In one of her novels, she describes a French drawing-room in which she observes the gestures and faces of the stale aristocracy and sees all the ancient aristocrats *ageing right there*. And Marcel Proust uses this idea for his *Recherche*. And now it could be said that the idea has used me, given that, as all of you have been perfectly able to appreciate – and this has formed the core spectacle of this lecture – I have been seen this evening to *age right here*, in front of everybody.

I feel bad for you, since you came to this museum to hear a lecture and have ended up witnessing the spectacle of a poor cuckold who has aged twenty years in an hour. The truth is that I never thought I would leave here so ancient and so dangerous, full of resentment, having just joined a band of imaginative elders, of wakeful monsters, although almost all have a cough, almost all are stooping, almost all are drug addicts, almost all are single, almost all are childless, almost all are in strange nursing-homes, almost all are blind, almost all are forgers and fakes; and all, absolutely all, are deceived.

IV
Diary of a Deceived Man

25 SEPTEMBER

At the start of the twenty-first century, as if I were walking to the rhythm of literature's most recent history, I was alone and without direction on some by-road, in the evening, heading inexorably for melancholy. A slow, enveloping, increasingly deep nostalgia for all that literature had once been merged with the mist at dusk. I considered myself a very deceived man. In life. And in art. In art, I saw hateful lies, falsifications, masquerades, frauds all around me. And I also felt very lonely. And when I looked at what was in front of my eyes, I always saw the same: literature at the start of the twenty-first century, in agony. I sensed that, like the castaway Crusoe at the start of his diary, I was reaching the point where I had 'to enter into a melancholy relation of a scene of silent life'. I was wandering without direction along the by-road. And the mist was becoming increasingly thick and mysterious. I might bump into Musil, I told myself. In its decline, literature, like the day, was growing pale, dying. I wanted to discuss it with someone, but the by-road was empty. I kept going for a long time, night fell. Suddenly I saw a shadow move next to an empty house. It was Emily Dickinson. She was wearing a white nightdress and walking a dog. I asked after Musil and she looked at me in surprise. That place resembled the end of the world, the end of the earth. 'Fog,' she remarked. I carried on walking, all night I heard birds passing, I flew with them. At dawn, as I turned off the by-road, I saw Musil next to an abyss. White open-necked shirt, very black coat down to the feet and red broad-brimmed hat. He was staring thoughtfully at the ground. He raised his head and looked at me. Before us there was only void. 'It is the air of the time,' I said to him. He gazed towards the blurred horizon. 'Let us not just hand ourselves to the age as it covets us,' he said.

When I went to Nantes in November last year, I still hadn't aged twenty years in a single evening in Budapest. And literature was in a bad way, but not so much as now, when it isn't that it has aged a lot as well, it's that it resembles the Austro-Hungarian Empire hurtling towards its destruction.

I went to Nantes and was still young. Ten months later, the hand of the person writing this diary is that of an old man who was deceived in Budapest.

Two weeks ago, on Tuesday the 11th, Manhattan was attacked. The news affected me, but not so much as having aged twenty years in the course of the lecture I gave last June, one evening in Budapest. As is to be expected, I don't have very happy memories of that Hungarian evening. The worst bit was perhaps at the end, when I had already gained twenty years and I realised that, at the rate time was passing, if I didn't end the lecture soon, I would come out of there dead. The trouble was I didn't know how to round off that lecture, which was gradually turning into something like the *Museum of the Novel of the Eternal*, that book Macedonio Fernández could never find an ending to.

I didn't know how to finish, it only occurred to me to ask the public to leave me alone on the stage, silently to acknowledge my drama as an old, defeated man of letters in Budapest and for them all to go. This is what I finally did, I begged the public to leave me all alone in that room.

They didn't budge.

'But don't you see I've aged twenty years? Please go, all of you, disappear, I can't face anybody right now, the lecture has ended, we mustn't let it turn into the Museum of the Eternal Lecture.'

'What will we do to disappear?' asked Blanchot. I didn't know what I would do to disappear, but I knew that the public could go, could disappear, and that this could be a good ending.

They began to leave.

After their initial hesitation, they started heading for the exit, they all filed out, emptying the room; the last to go was the writer Imre Kertész, who came towards me as if he wanted to say something, but I cut him off with two sentences that were sufficiently extravagant to make him arch an eyebrow and to stop him in his tracks: 'I want to be alone, Kertész, my friend. I want to know whether I am not when I am alone.'

Finally I was left alone, with a half-empty jug of water and the script dictated to me by that wretched Tongoy, who throughout the lecture I had always referred to as monsieur, as if eager to turn him into a kind of personal Monsieur Teste. I remained alone on the stage, telling myself that no doubt in the world of the theatre – or in that of lectures like mine, with a theatrical slant – there is a closely guarded secret: that, when everything is over, the authors, the people responsible for so many words, *carry on living there*, remain in the theatre and their words carry on living beyond the moment at which they were spoken.

Everyone left and for a few moments I remained *living there*, experiencing a strange and highly paradoxical sensation, since on the one hand I felt that I was living in the Literature Museum and on the other that, on remaining alone, *I was not*. It was during those moments of loneliness and life that wasn't, but was life, that I decided, in view of the nonsense of reality at that point, I would delve into unreality.

I had just made up my mind when the museum's administrator appeared out of nowhere and immediately returned me to my condition as a deceived man, returned me to the brutalised, debatable, muddled, hateful, meaningless reality.

'Mr Girondo, your wife is waiting for you in the hall,' she informed me.

You are abandoned, but told that it's not like that, it's absolutely not true that you've been left.

'Tongoy? Oh, come on . . . He's just a friend, you're crazy if you think that I'd sleep with a dragonfly,' Rosa tells you.

Then you decide to be the one who abandons, but you

won't do it in Budapest, you'll arm yourself with patience and wait until you reach Barcelona.

One morning, you suddenly up and leave, without even writing a note. You take nothing with you, only your private journal. You put on a dark suit and walk along the Catalan streets in the rain: the trees, the pavements, the odd pedestrian. On reaching a square, you spot a bus. You quicken your pace, run across the avenue and board behind the other passengers. The bus moves off. You sit at the back for a better view of the human panorama. You contemplate the rain on the windows. A few hours later, you cross the Seine by Austerlitz Bridge, still on a bus, and at each stop you watch the people boarding. At Orly you pass a small police control, you don't even have hand luggage, only your private journal. You board an aeroplane that cleaves the air and lands in Santiago de Chile, where you take a taxi for Valparaíso and, once there, you race towards the Brighton Hotel's terrace, where you notice that it will rain soon and in any case you do not commit the idiocy of asking yourself what you are doing there, as you do not ask yourself whether you should put your scarf on the radiator in your room to dry, that is if you had a scarf, radiator, room, which you do not.

Later, you recall Tongoy on that very terrace the year before, all that disgusting business with the fly he drowned in alcohol, the end-of-century party on this very terrace, deserted today, terribly empty, without anybody. The hotel seems closed. It's amazing to see a place so alive in your imagination and so dead in the world of reality. But this is not the time to be amazed. After all, you're the one who sought the tremendous loneliness of this terrace, previously full of joy for you. It would be absurd to complain about anything now. You say this to yourself and suddenly a waiter appears. You're slightly disappointed, you had begun to like the idea of walking alone through a space that is one of the central axes of your diary, as regards both your real life and your imagination. But, to counteract your disappointment, you realise that interesting possibilities are opening up for you and one of them is to order a pisco sour, which is what you do. A little later, as you are served, you think about life and you feel proud of yourself, you ask yourself what you have turned into since your escape. And you answer, I am a man of leisure, a sleepwalker, an oyster. You play alone, you're content, a fugitive's happiness. You're far from the world's uproar: Rosa, extravagant projects, friends. You've left it all behind. You tell yourself that there was nothing else you could do and, for everything now to be perfect, all you need do is completely disappear, really disappear. It's not so simple, you think. You look out over the bay of Valparaíso. What will I do to disappear, you ask yourself. You find no response and change the subject, you tell yourself that there's a lot of poetry in abandonment and you recall the envy you felt one day when you heard somebody in the street say, 'He chucked up everything and just cleared off.' Since hearing that, you've been obsessed with the idea of escaping and have ended up doing it, you can feel satisfied, even if you're very alone when before you had so much company. There's a lot of poetry in abandonment, you think again as you listen to the Pacific's deep, warlike roar. And you recall some verses by Philip Larkin, where the author says that deep down we all hate home and having to be there, we all detest our rooms, their specially-chosen junk, the good books, the good bed, and our lives, in perfect order.

Take that! (you think), you bastards, you can have your soft houses, with the Mediterranean's tame, miserable murmur, this pisco sour's damn good.

It is evening on 25 September. In a break from writing this diary, I flicked through a book I bought yesterday by Robert Walser, *The Walk*, and was surprised to find some lines that inform me that the Swiss writer also wandered in the mist, along some by-road: 'Often I wandered of course perplexed in a mist and in a thousand vacillations and dilemmas, and often I felt myself woefully forsaken. [. . .] Proud and gay in the roots of his soul a man becomes only through trial bravely undergone, and through suffering patiently endured.' I told myself that now was a good time to identify with Walser. After all, my grandfather, my mother's father, was very like Walser, and also his sons, the Girondos, my mother's three brothers, bore a certain spiritual resemblance to Walser. They spent their lives bravely undergoing the hardships set by life and silently enduring the suffering that continually came their way, they suffered life without fuss, which always struck me as admirable. They were what we understand by blessed souls and sometimes seemed like people made of wood, functioning automatically (like Felicity, the servant Flaubert wrote about). They possessed an enviable simplicity and, as an example of how they viewed the world, they would gaze at the sea and think that it had no bottom, that it was an image of the infinite, and that next to it one should always be very far-sighted and, contemplating it, should say, 'So much water, so much water!' They were discreet, extremely modest, simple, kind; I feel very sad but peaceful when I can identify with the Girondos, it's as if I returned to the land I came from. They understood perfectly that it will always be a fine thing to fight and to know what it is to be gay in the roots of one's soul through certain hardships bravely undergone. It's a fine thing to fight and to be, for example, literature itself, to fight for it, to embody it in your own person when it is in agony and you lead the pleasant existence of a deceived man. It's a fine thing to fight, to challenge the abyss there in front of the void, to seek Musil.

You literally left with what you had on, with the dark suit and the private journal. On the Brighton's Victorian terrace, where one day you were with friends, today you are extraordinarily alone in a space where for you real and invented life meet. You left with what you had on – that said, inside the dark suit, not by chance, was your credit card. Since it's Sunday, you'll wait until tomorrow to buy new clothes, socks and pants, toothpaste and slippers, all that prosaic stuff that ruins your romantic escape and makes you a poor, lonely credit-card holder in a dark suit. So you change your mind and tell yourself that your loneliness is not such an agreeable sensation as it seemed a moment ago. But you mustn't lose heart. Fortunately you have your diary with you, which can fill the dangerous hole your life as a deceived man has occupied. You instantly smile out of pure pleasure when you tell yourself that basically you're hiding from your many friends

– an entire life devoted to the noble nurturing of friendship and all that now thrown overboard – you're hiding from your friends and you experience a peculiar delight in this new, lonely lifestyle you have chosen and you recall Walser when he said he found strange the depravity of secretly rejoicing when one confirms that one is hiding a bit.

You have your diary to fill your deceived man's dangerous hole. You order another pisco sour and ask the waiter if he remembers you, if he remembers the Catalan who came here at the end of last year. 'I'm new in Valparaíso,' replies the waiter grudgingly. It may be that, apart from what you've written in the diary, there is no human testimony left to corroborate that you were here and you were happy.

The waiter was so unpleasant that, when he brings your second pisco, you ask him if he can offer a fly on the side, a fly to martyr and drown.

'Martyrdom by Martini,' you remark.

He thinks you're mad or drunk and disappears, you are once more alone with your diary, you decide to record in it everything that is happening to you, therefore you decide to be sincere and realistic, that is until you remember that the anti-artistic and naive artists you so detest do something similar. And then you also remember that, in view of the nonsense of the reality of your age, you were going to delve into unreality. You bring all this to mind and pull your diary out of the bag and propose to renounce stupid sincerity, to write images and situations that, like the landscapes in Italian metaphysical painting, are described in a very clear, very exact, very accurate and yet very unreal way. But you soon decide not to be a kind of metaphysical painter, in the same way as you decided not to be a silly and sincere diarist. And you end up writing this: 'I think I've been on this sumptuous hanging terrace before, but I couldn't say when. I have the bay of Valparaíso at my feet and tell myself that I should go back through this diary and try to find out when I was here before, supposing it to be certain that I have been in this city with all its winds and all its funiculars, in this city where the customs officer Rubén Darío wrote *Azul* . . .'

You interrupt what you were writing, it strikes you as stupidly literary and stupidly false. For this you'd do better to be faithful to reality and tell the truth about your anomalous situation here in Valparaíso, tell how you're very alone and you don't know what's going to become of you and you don't understand what you're doing on this Brighton terrace, on this terrace so far away from your home in Barcelona, although, that said, it's also true that you've done well to delve into a poetics of abandonment and escape, no doubt you've acted correctly in chucking up everything and certainly the best thing you can do is not lose heart, since you need to feel very complete if you're going to devote yourself to the fine fight you've got into, to the fine gesture of embodying literature in your own person in order to protect it from its desperate situation in front of the abyss.

You are a man of leisure, a sleepwalker, an oyster.

You are literature itself, you embody it this afternoon on this terrace. And you feel proud of your new life.

You have banished every kind of sincerity and any

temptation to become poetic or to make literature from the diary. And you discover that, alongside the options the diary was offering you here in the Brighton (to record reality, delve into the unreal, be sincere and confess your anxiety, etc.), alongside the traditional options, a new and very attractive path has opened up, no less traditional even if you hadn't thought of it before: to transfer what you would like to happen to you right now on this deserted terrace to the diary. And what you would like to happen is really tender, simple, pure filial love: for your mother to revive and be here with you now, to keep you company in your loneliness.

You think that to favour what isn't happening is also a way to keep a diary. And then your deceived man's aged hand does not tremble when you write that your late mother is at your side, she is there on the terrace, her eyes open to the void, and quite different from when she was alive.

You would proceed to ask your mother what life is like in the hereafter, you would ask her this, except that you've often asked the dead in your novels this question and all of them have replied that life in the hereafter is like swimming in the pampas at night.

To avoid eliciting the same response from her, you decide to vary the question slightly and you express an interest in how things are with her, meaning that you do not give her any ideas by naming the hereafter and you simply ask her:

'How is everything, mother?'

'How do you think? Bad, son. That's why things are bad for you as well, and they'll get worse, you'll see.'

'What shall I see?'

'You'll see they call you Eternity like me.'

Your mother begins to sob and seems to you to do so in the coarse manner in which Lewis Carroll's Caterpillar wept. Although the wind starts to blow, you do not ask yourself whether this will finally help you to disappear, completely disappear, as has been your objective for some time. You do not question any of this because actually you feel wonderfully well and you don't want to ask anything, being as you are with your pisco sour next to Eternity Girondo, your late mother.

You point to the sea and, like someone made of wood, functioning automatically, you feel like a Girondo when you remark:

'Lots of water, lots of water.'

She nods and the wind picks up, and you feel increasingly well being carried along by the life of your mind.

You leave Valparaíso lonelier than when you arrived and go round the world a few times, you pass through strange cities in various continents and end up returning to Europe, and by train from Munich you arrive in Budapest, where your first impulse – as if you were one of those stupid ghosts in Dickens which, having the whole of infinite space at their disposal, always want to go back to the exact place where they were unhappy – is to visit the city's Literature Museum and wander round the room where two months previously you gave a lecture, but at the last moment you withhold the impulse and remind yourself that you are in what was once 'the city of the cafés' and you take refuge in the Krúdy, a literary café, and pretend to be Dezşö Kosztolányi, the great Hungarian writer and great sufferer of literature sickness who in the old Sirius, instead of ordering a coffee from the waiter, would ask for ink.

'*Garçon*,' he would say, 'ink *s'il vous plaît!*'

You're in the Krúdy and you write in your diary what you would like to happen now, and your deceived man's aged hand does not tremble when you write that you have just remembered that Nabokov wrote that 'the soul is but a manner of being – not a constant state – that any soul may be yours, if you find and follow its undulations'. You also remember that he wrote 'the hereafter' – something your mother, Eternity, seems to know a lot about – 'may be the full ability of consciously living in any number of souls, all of them unconscious of their interchangeable burden.'

Nor does your aged hand tremble when you write that a kind of grey cloud slowly dilutes the darkness inside the Krúdy and a snowy exterior becomes faintly perceptible through the café's windows, and you feel you have taken possession of the soul of Robert Walser – that eternal walker along roads of fog and snow – and at the same time you think you see Robert Musil outside the café with a thermos of coffee, wearing a metalworker's overalls that evidently are not sufficient to protect him from the cold, which leads you to rap with your knuckles on the window-pane and invite him in.

Musil comes in, you shake his hand.

'My name is Robert Walser,' you say, 'and I'd like you to forget about the thermos so that I can buy you a proper cup of coffee.'

'I'd prefer something solid, a proper steak, for example,' replies Musil. 'So your name's Robert Walser, just like the writer? Funny that. Do you know you even look like him? Though, to tell the truth, with an air of Dracula.'

It being Musil, you allow him to pull your leg, but ask him why he is dressed in such horrendous fashion, why he is disguised as a metalworker.

'Volume one, chapter twenty. Of my unfinished book. Do you remember that the title of this chapter is "The touch of reality"?'

You think you more or less understand what he means and call the *garçon* and order a steak for your guest and you ask him if he wasn't very cold and hungry standing outside, dressed as a metalworker in touch with reality.

'I had spent,' he replies, 'three days and nights on endless roads of snow. Finally I reached the place I wanted to get to, Budapest. But no sooner had I set foot in the city than I decided this place was unreachable. So I stopped to think and did so here, in my overalls, in front of the Krúdy. And I thought that, if this was the city I was seeking and I had reached it so easily, then I was an insignificant being. Or else this couldn't be the place. Perhaps, I now tell myself, it is the place, but I may not have reached it.'

'Allow me to say that your reflections have an air of Kafka about them,' you comment, thus taking revenge for the bit about Dracula.

He behaves as if he hadn't heard you and carries on talking in Kafkaesque mode:

'Or perhaps it's that there's nobody in this place, and

I am simply of the place and in the place. And nobody can reach it.'

A great writer is seated before you and at no point do you forget this. You know that to have someone like this before you is not normal in an age like today's, which has hardly any great writers. You suddenly recall a novel by Hemingway you read years ago, *Green Hills of Africa*, in which the author, next to the palm trees, in the middle of lion and rhinoceros tracks, abruptly falls to thinking about James Joyce and the days he saw him in Paris, and he writes, 'When you saw him he would take up a conversation interrupted three years before. It was nice to see a great writer in our time.'

But you're not in Africa, you're in the Krúdy, you don't have Joyce in front of you, you have Musil.

'What was that about Kafka?' he suddenly asks you.

'Oh, nothing.'

'I was thinking about him a lot only today. Were Kafka still in Prague, I would go to this city and ask him to join Action Without Parallel, I'm thinking of gathering my resistance friends in some place in the world.'

You immediately think of the island of Fayal, in the Azores, as an ideal place for this gathering. But you don't say this to him because you realise in time that you don't know what kind of resistance he's talking about, nor do you know what Action Without Parallel might be.

Musil seems to have guessed what you're wondering.

'Resistance,' he says, 'people of letters and catacombs. Fighters against the destruction of literature. I'd like to gather them together and start planting mental bombs against false writers, against the rogues who control the culture industry, against the emissaries of nothingness, against the pigs.'

Instinctively, with great enthusiasm, you think of mental bombs that you would carefully plant in the offices of certain pigs, enemies of the literary. And it brightens your day to dream about the triumph of literature. But you don't say any of this to Musil, you're afraid that he considers you too naive or a subversive infant, you prefer to hand him the initiative, for him to propose – you'll soon find out he won't – that you join Action Without Parallel.

When his steak arrives, you decide to clarify something he told you before and you ask him what exactly he understands by touch of reality.

Musil stares at you for a good while and finally says:

'What you're seeing now, that's exactly what I understand by touch of reality. And what are you seeing now? Well, what you see, a man in overalls preparing to tuck into a steak. For unreality, Walser, my friend, to invent, for example, that today is snowing and is a beautiful day in August 1913, for this and to do those things, we've plenty of time,' says Musil.

At which point he tucks into his steak.

You leave Budapest on the following day without going anywhere near the museum where you displayed your cuckold's horns, you leave without even going back to the cinema where your life took a detour on to some by-road, you leave Budapest without Musil, whom you lost sight of in the baths of the Gellert Hotel. You leave Budapest and barely ask yourself what can have happened to Rosa these past two months – before now you would ask yourself this from time to time, you would play at imagining that she had given you up for dead in a ditch by some by-road – you leave Budapest for Vienna in a boat that travels along the Danube and reminds you of the *vaporetti* in Venice, you leave for Vienna and there you take a taxi for Kierling, where is the building with three floors – once a nursing-home – that Kafka died in.

You reach this modest building at 187 Hauptstrasse, Kierling, a small town near Klosterneuburg. Here, on 3 June 1924, Kafka died when the place was Dr Hoffmann's sanatorium. It is now a block of flats, which you have reached easily, having found the exact address in *Danube*, the place is more or less as Magris describes it in this book after his visit there in the 1980s. Kafka's room on the first floor looked out on to the garden. It was a room covered in flowers. On that same first floor, in the exact space Kafka died in, a very pleasant old lady allows you into her flat so that you can see the garden below from the balcony. The lady is dressed in a kind of white night-dress embroidered with ivory; it almost seems she had dressed up to receive you. In the garden there is now a wooden shed full of wheelbarrows and sickles. From his rocking-chair, Kafka contemplated this garden, it was the last garden he saw. A neighbour's dog barks, you try to imagine this landscape in winter, the sky grey with ice and snow stains. You're quite impressed, you're in the exact place where Kafka took his leave of life. Depending on how you look, you might see what he saw at the end of his days. 'He saw,' writes Magris, 'the greenness which eluded him, or rather the flowering, the springtime, the sap, everything that was sucked out of his body by paper and ink, desiccating him into a feeling of pure, impotent barrenness.'

'Will you have some tea with me, Mr Walser?' the pleasant lady suggests.

You say of course you will and you're delighted with her hospitality. Kafka died here, you think. And you think that, if you told the lady this, she would tell you that she also plans to die there. And you recall something else Magris wrote about this room: 'Here truly, as in the old medieval morality plays, died Everyman.'

When she serves your tea, you ask her if she has read Kafka. If you could, you'd go on to ask her what it's like living where Kafka died, but this second question seems rather inappropriate to you.

'I don't read, Mr Walser,' she replies.

'Don't you?'

'It's not a habit of mine, I need to do things with my hands, to keep them busy, you see. Books leave them static. No, I haven't read Kafka.'

'Don't you read at all?'

'No, though I admire Stephen Hawking a lot, I adore him, I hear him say amazing things on the TV and also on the radio' – she points to an old Marconi set from the 1950s – 'he's an extraordinary, moving person. I'm fascinated by everything he says, that we live in a universe with thousands of millions of galaxies, which in turn contain thousands of millions of I don't know what other galaxies, which make it all infinite . . . And all those opinions about God. Believe me, I admire Hawking a lot, he's an amazing man, he's like God. The other day, I heard him talking about Ur, in Chaldea. Have you heard of Ur, in Chaldea, Mr Walser?'

'I must confess I haven't.'

'In Ur, Hawking says, they already knew about the cubic root and I don't know what about the square root. That's right, Mr Walser. The cubic root! In Ur they already knew about it. Abraham and his lot were aware of it. Isn't that incredible?'

You ask her who Abraham was, you recall having studied him at school, but you don't remember any of it. She seems surprised that you don't know who Abraham is, but then hesitates a little when it comes to explaining who he was, she doesn't seem to know so much about him:

'He was the father of the present-day Israelites, or the God of the Jews, or something like that. He was Abraham, you must have heard of him. The point is I admire Hawking and everything he says, he's someone who encourages you to live when you see him like that, overcoming all his physical problems with an iron will.'

You discover that this very pleasant old lady, unlike you, is far removed from any Montano's malady. And you tell yourself that you wouldn't mind staying here for a long time, the conversation is agreeable and the tea is excellent. No doubt in a few days you would cease to be seriously literature-sick. That said, of course – the thought comes into your mind – you shouldn't abandon your catacomb warrior's militancy against the enemies of the literary, don't forget that, even if it's only out of loyalty to Musil, think that the likeliest outcome is for you to join Action Without Parallel, think that one mustn't abandon one's convictions, think that you're almost obliged to stand by those who put up a fight against those who try to avoid the triumph of literature.

You again look out on to the garden that was the last Kafka saw, and you hear the lady say:

'We live not to live, Mr Walser, but to have already lived, to be already dead.'

You wonder what she can have meant by that. You can scarcely believe that this room where you are now, with its Marconi radio set and four pieces of petit bourgeois furniture, was once a room in a sanatorium, a room covered in flowers, in which a moribund Kafka was at times delirious: he no longer read, he played with the books, opened them, flicked through them, looked at them and closed them again, with the same old happiness. Pietro Citati relates how, after Kafka read the final proofs of his final book, tears came into his eyes as never before. What was he crying for? Death? The writer he had been? The writer he could have been, that he may have glimpsed in this final fire? He praised wine and beer and asked the others to drink, to swill the liquids – beer, wine, water, tea, fruit juice – he could no longer swallow.

You can scarcely believe that in this room where you are now, with a single vase, there used to be lots of flowers and a doctor and a nurse, and Kafka died here. You wonder what would happen if this room were once again full of flowers, covered in all the world's flowers. And you tell yourself that you would hardly be able to breathe, like Kafka in his final hours here, in this world.

Kafka, in his final minute in this world, made a

brusque, unusual movement and ordered the nurse to leave. All this happened here.

'A little more tea?' the lady asks you.

All this happened here. Kafka gave this order and yanked out the catheter he was wearing and threw it in the middle of this room and said he had put up with enough torture. When the doctor moved away from the bed for a moment to clean a syringe, Kafka told him, 'Don't go.' The doctor said, 'No, I'm not going.' In a deep voice, Kafka replied, 'I am going.'

1917 was an intense year in Kafka's life. He began it in January by writing 'The Hunter Gracchus', his best story, in which he wrote a sentence so perfect that he had to finish the narrative with it, it's not that he couldn't find an ending to the story, but that the ending was in this perfect, terrible, icy sentence. The burgomaster of Riva asks the wild hunter Gracchus if he intends to remain with them in the town. The hunter has just arrived in his boat and, to make up for his mocking tone, lays a hand on the burgomaster's knee and says, 'I have no intentions. I am here. I don't know any more than that. There's nothing more I can do. My boat is without a helm – it journeys with the wind which blows in the deepest regions of death.'

In March that year, he wrote 'The Great Wall of China' at the same time as he began to lose himself in a maze of mysterious roads that he journeyed along all his life without ever finding a way out, though now he would always have the hunter Gracchus' final, perfect sentence.

In July he got engaged for the second time to Felice

Bauer. In August he spat blood. On 4 September he was diagnosed with tuberculosis and on the 12th he was granted sick-leave from the office. In October, in his diary, he compared Dickens to Robert Walser and said that they both hid their inhumanity behind styles of overflowing sentiment.

This is a brilliant intuition by Kafka and still today absolutely difficult to accept for those illustrious minds that believe in warm culture and have always regarded Dickens as the founder of some kind of vital realism, sympathetic towards poor humankind, when in fact he was someone, like Walser, with a cold, crushing intelligence, which behind closed doors, for all who came into contact with him, made him a terrible, secretly inhuman being, obliged only by the dumb circumstances of the age to hand out false, good sentiments left, right and centre.

On 10 November Kafka wrote in his diary, 'I have yet to record the crux, I'm still flowing in two channels. The work awaiting me is enormous.' At the end of November, he burst into Max Brod's house reading Walser aloud, reading him and laughing. 'Oh, come on, listen to what this man says completely seriously,' he remarked to Brod. In December his second engagement to Felice Bauer was broken off.

That's about enough for today, night has closed in and this 25 September is reaching its end and I – call me Walser – take my leave of the day and also of this recollection of a year in Kafka's life, this recollection that has turned into a digression that has diverted me from the narrative of my vagrant steps along the by-road. That's about enough, but I shall keep going a while longer, I shall continue telling the story of my intimate, minimal escape, I shall carry on journeying without moving from home, and at the same time being on the by-road.

You mustn't say you understand me.
KAFKA in a letter to MAX BROD

Two days after visiting the house in Kierling, after stopping over in Lisbon, you're on the island of Fayal in the Azores and the pulse of your aged left hand does not tremble when in Café Sport you write that you're back in your favourite bar, opposite the volcano on the island of Pico, in a lively gathering of your favourite authors of private journals; they're all there except for Musil and Kafka, two forces whose whereabouts are unknown, apparently they're on a secret mission, or perhaps they're in reserve should some catastrophe befall the conspiracy in Fayal. In any case Musil and Kafka are not with you as you formulate your initial strategies for halting the advance of Pico's moles. You call yourselves 'the conspirators of the Great Wall' in memory of Kafka's story that talks about a great wall, a great work involving builders and labourers scattered all over the geography of China: a story that essentially evokes Kafka's own work, since this also resembles a wall and, like the conspiracy of diarists in Café Sport, has holes and cracks, gaps that other groups seek to fill.

You're in Café Sport, in your favourite café, and you're one of the pioneers of the walled plot, you're on the alert against any movement by the enemy, though you've no plans to sit back and wait in some legendary desert for the Tartars to turn up. Like your fellow conspirators, you're going to take the initiative and tomorrow, without further delay, you will disperse after the brief but decisive meeting. You'll disperse as one day the hidden forces of this diary you're writing today with an already aged hand will disperse.

Café Sport appears to have endless galleries, like the whole of Kafka's work and his Chinese wall. These galleries – of Kafka's work, of Café Sport – being still under threat, have been equally perfectly articulated as a challenge against the wear and tear of time and, in the case of the conspiracy, against the wear and tear of the literary at the start of the twenty-first century as well.

You're gathered here, but tomorrow you'll disperse all over the world and join other conspirators and recognise each other by means of a simple password for Chinese conspirators that you have read before – it's in Kafka – and now you can hear in any part of the world, on the lips of accomplices, it's a simple password, which Max Brod failed to understand at the time, all you have to say is:

'You mustn't say you understand me.'

You leave the island of Fayal and your favourite bar behind and return to Lisbon and sleepwalk through the Baixa and Barrio Alto and visit the British Bar and like Alexandre O'Neill, without ruffling your hair, you ask yourself, 'What are we doing here, Lisbon, the two of us, / in the land where you and I were born?' '*Fazer horas*,' the people of Lisbon say when they don't have anything to do. Making time. Bars are ideal for such activity, though, as Cardoso Pires said, time out in bars often becomes time in and can even cease to be waiting time: 'In reality only the unsuspecting drinker believes he is deceiving the hours, since it's often the hours that deceive us, with a firm and steady step marking a time beyond numbers.'

You're in the British Bar with its clock that goes backwards and strikes very punctual hours, you're drinking right under the clock that advances in the other direction and you also think you've deceived the hours and the days when suddenly, when you're least expecting it, Alfonso Dumpert, a friend from Barcelona, wanders casually into the bar and is very surprised to see you there, since in your city they think you've disappeared, or maybe even died.

Dumpert asks you if you've come for tomorrow's tribute to the ill-fated Manuel Hermínio Monteiro. You weren't aware of this tribute, you're lost in the world, in endless flight, and in the British you were only 'making time'. You say this to him and suddenly receive the impression that, now you've been discovered, from now on everything may be different in your life and you tell yourself that it's as if the clock of the future, its hands also turning the other way, had returned with stupid punctuality to an appointment with your life before you escaped.

Perhaps you have made the mistake of going too near Barcelona. You've been spotted in Lisbon and your escape has entered a new phase, it may be drawing to a close. You disguise the bad temper this setback has caused you and tell Dumpert you'll see him at the tribute tomorrow. And in the evening of 10 September you walk towards Fórum Lisboa, where the tribute is taking place, and embrace your dear friend Manuela Correia, Hermínio's wife, and witness the recital of music, poems and images opened by the actress Germana Tánger with *Aniversário* by Álvaro de Campos: 'At the time they were celebrating my birthday, / I was happy and no one was dead.'

At midday on the following day, in the reasonably pleasant restaurant without television on the rua das Janelas Verdes, you have lunch with Manuela Correia and your friend Dumpert. One minute before the latter's mobile phone rings and you find out about the attack on Manhattan, a group of ugly, noisy people enters the restaurant and the three of you are dumbstruck, horrified, until Dumpert remarks that the barbarians have just arrived:

'The world does not change.'

You understand that he means that the world can't be helped. The world does not change, the world is *like this*, as Baroja would say. But isn't it perhaps the other way round and the world, with its dizzying succession of images, is changing? You're wondering about this when Dumpert's mobile rings and in Barcelona they're surprised that you still don't know about the attack on Manhattan and the outbreak of the Third World War.

After lunch, when you emerge on to the extremely beautiful and serene rua das Janelas Verdes, you're surprised by the idea that war has broken out. In the white of the breeze and the light of Lisbon, greys are greens and the world, immersed in the course of time, seems perfect.

The radio of a red convertible abruptly disturbs the calm of the street and an excited announcer speaks of spectacular images that surpass any fiction out of Hollywood.

You think about Franz Kafka.

You see the images of the attack on the television of a bar and you think again about Kafka, who imagined something that in its own way also changed the world: the transformation of a clerk into a beetle. What would he have thought, watching the spectacle of aeroplanes and fire in Manhattan?

Kafka was an enormously visual person who could not bear the cinema, because the speed of movements and the dizzying succession of images subjected him to a continually superficial vision. He said that in the cinema it's never the look that chooses the images, but the images that choose the look.

You've been spotted in Lisbon and the clock of your life advances in the other direction. Somehow you have begun your return to Barcelona. What a shame. You would have liked to go back with your lungs burned by the sea air, tanned by distant climates, go back to your city having swum a lot, having mown the tall grass and having hunted lions and, above all, having smoked like nobody before and having drunk strong liquor like molten metal, and you would also have liked a lot to return with iron limbs, dark skin and furious eye, Rimbaud of the twenty-first century, you would have liked to return and, because of your mask, for all to think you belonged to a strong race and came with a lot of gold, with gold and more gold, transformed into a brutal creature of leisure, whom women would be eager to look after, because women like to look after such fierce cripples back from hot countries. But the reality is other and says you won't return with iron limbs or dark skin or furious eye, you'll return with a dark suit and a credit card.

You wonder what Kafka – who could not bear the cinema – would have thought about all this visual spectacle of the attack on Manhattan. And you ask yourself this in Seville, on the night of the 11th. You ask yourself this as you open Kafka's diaries at 11 September 1911, exactly ninety years before the attack on the Twin Towers. You're in Antonio Molina Flores' home, in the Alameda district. You're going to sleep on his sofa tonight, until you decide tomorrow whether or not to return to Barcelona.

You open Kafka's diaries at this date ninety years ago and see that on this day he wrote a detailed description of the collision between a motor car and a tricycle. It was a minor crash that Kafka had witnessed that same day in the streets of Paris.

You're in Molina Flores' home, seeking refuge, before falling asleep, in Kafka's diaries. On 11 September 1911, in connection with the collision between the motor car and tricycle, he wrote, 'The bakery employee, who before that had been pedalling along without a care, wobbling in the way that people on tricycles do, on this vehicle that was company property, dismounts, approaches the motorist, who also dismounts, and begins to launch recriminations at him, lightened by the respect due to a motorist and heightened by the fear of his boss.'

This 'pedalling along without a care' reminds you of the people of New York, without a care this morning before the double collision of the aeroplanes with the Twin Towers. You carry on reading.

Cyclist and motorist argue. And people begin to congregate around the motorist and bakery employee, foreshadowing Guy Debord's Society of the Spectacle. They are anxious to know the possible consequences of the crash, many approach the tricycle to take a closer look at the damage that is the subject of so much discussion. The motorist, Kafka tells us, does not think that what has happened to the tricycle's misshapen front wheel is so serious, despite which he is not prepared to cast a cursory glance, but circles the tricycle and examines it above and below.

'A large number of new spectators turn up,' Kafka goes on to say, 'people who will have the enormous, cheap pleasure of watching the taking of the statement.' If the spectacle has continued to grow, it is because a policeman has arrived on the scene, who writes down the names of those involved and the bakery's business address. In the crowd that has gathered around the spectacle, Kafka reads 'the unconscious and candid hope of everyone present that the policeman will immediately resolve the matter with complete impartiality'.

You read this commentary by Kafka and think that everything seems to indicate that you are living now in just such an unconscious and candid hope. Like so many people in the world, you want it to be known soon who the enemy is, you want the FBI to shed some light and resolve the matter of Manhattan with impartiality. You share with Molina Flores the impression of having suddenly started to live in those barracks in *The Tartar Steppe*, Dino Buzzati's novel, in which a military contingent spends its life trying to ascertain who the enemy is.

You think to yourself that at least the conspirators of

the Great Wall have a better idea where their enemies are and can even name them.

You are confused, there's no denying it. To your amazement at what has happened in New York is added, on a strictly personal level, the impression that the time for being like Musil and Kafka, whereabouts unknown, is over. You have gone so near your city and your old home that you've been caught out. You've been spotted under the clock in the British and there everything has ended. Everything? Yes, everything. But think that it's not so serious, remember that in the end, as Amália sings, all this is only destiny, all this is *fado*.

And the world turned into a foreign country where it was no longer necessary to flee or to return home.
PETER HANDKE, *Slow Homecoming*

You've been tracked down better than you thought. From Barcelona, by telephone, Julio Arward explains that your editor has known about you for days. Someone from the Spanish embassy in Budapest saw you in Café Krúdy and passed on the information. It's public and perhaps notorious that you've gone walkabout and could well return. Everything seems to push you into returning, even Monsieur Tongoy's muffled – others call it inner – voice recommends you go back. And in the morning of the 12th you try to forget this and walk in the vicinity of the Giralda, the weather is magnificent, the conversation with Molina Flores very lively as you head towards the Hospital of Holy Charity, where legend has it that Don Juan, Seducer of Seville, is buried.

You see the tomb of Don Miguel de Mañara, the repentant sinner who for many was the real Don Juan invented by the Spanish genius Tirso de Molina. 'Here lies the worst man that ever existed in the world,' Mañara had inscribed on his tombstone, at the entrance to the hospital. Everyone, as they enter, is obliged to step on that tomb, to trample on it in fact, which is what the penitent ladykiller demands from his stone.

Inside the church is a painting by Valdés Leal, carried out according to Don Miguel de Mañara's instructions, it is a dramatic depiction of death. *In ictu oculi* (In the Blink of an Eye) is the title of the seventeenth-century funereal painting. This Latin inscription is written around the candle in the upper part of the painting, where the scene is dominated by the figure of a skeleton carrying its own coffin and a scythe as it extends one of its arms to quench the light of the candle, a clear symbol of life.

Molina Flores, who has never heard of Tongoy, abruptly remarks that the skeleton travelling with its own coffin is a seventeenth-century forerunner of the Nosferatu in Murnau's film. You are delighted to discover suddenly that the wretched Tongoy's skeleton is depicted there, and delighted also to feel that you're in the place where Don Juan died.

This is where Don Juan Tenorio died, you tell yourself. You're not as impressed as when you were in the room where Kafka died. In the Seducer's mortal space, you're more relaxed. Molina Flores notices this and asks you why you let out a laugh. 'This is where Tongoy died,' you tell him. He gives you a blank look and asks you who Tongoy is. 'A Nosferatu from Chile,' you reply, 'and the worst and ugliest man that ever set foot in this world, I didn't want to see him even in painting, and look where I see him now, here in this church, poor second-rate Don Juan, he had the face of an empty train.'

Two days later you arrive in Barcelona by night and go to the home of Julio Arward, who has promised not to tell anyone that you've returned to your city and lets you sleep at his house today, until you decide what to do with your life.

You're in Julio Arward's home, in the claustrophobic sitting room where you'll sleep tonight, a sitting room adorned with lots of reproductions of Edward Hopper's paintings, whose protagonists always seemed to Arward to have just emerged from a Chinese tale. You also, recently landed in your city, remind him now of a character who has just escaped from a Chinese tale. He says this to you, laughs without malice, asks you what Chinese tale you come from. He doesn't manage to surprise you, whereas you could give him a big surprise if you talked to him about your friends, the conspirators of the Great Wall. I'm from that tale, you would inform him. And you would leave him perplexed. But you prefer not to say anything. The conspiracy is secret. You simply ask him if he has Kafka's diaries, you'd like to read them for a bit before turning out the light and being left in the dark with all Hopper's characters.

He has the diaries and gives them to you, takes his leave until tomorrow. You search for what Kafka did on 11 September 1912, exactly one year after witnessing the collision between a car and tricycle in Paris.

That day the writer dreamed. He was on a spit of land constructed from blocks of masonry, extending some way into the sea. To start with, the dreamer did not really know where he was, he only began to know when by chance he stood up from his seat and to the left, in front of him, and to the right, behind him, saw that the vast sea was clearly circumscribed, with lots of warships lined up and firmly anchored. And the writer who dreams, a visionary Kafka, says:

'To the right you could see New York, we were in the port of New York.'

When you wake up, the curtains of a coarse fabric filter a yellowish light into the room that you find very familiar. You listen to the tick-tock of the clock on the bedside table and, next to you, the steady breathing of Rosa, who is fast asleep. You soon slide a leg out of the bed. You have been home since yesterday; you returned, but not without having first watched the house for some time from the street. You recalled Wakefield, that character in a story by Hawthorne, that man who, after an absence of twenty years – they think he's disappeared or died, though in fact he's carried on living in the area – feels tempted to return to his wife and stands for a long time in front of his old home until finally entering the house as if he had never left it.

Yesterday the same thing happened to you, you felt a bit like Wakefield as in the street you studied the possibility of returning home and recovering your identity as a writer, rediscovering your papers, your books, the vases acquired to keep the books company, your sweet bed, your perfect sedentary life. You were a long time yesterday deciding whether or not to return, watching your home from the street, until suddenly some drops of water fell and it began to rain and you even felt a gust of cold and it seemed to you ridiculous to get wet when your home was right there. So you trudged up the staircase and opened the door and Rosa, on seeing you, did not tell you off for not ringing the doorbell, she simply remarked:

'I've been waiting for you all afternoon.'

It can be said that your escape has ended, but also that you continue to journey at home, along the by-road.

The world for you, after your slow homecoming, has turned into a foreign country where there's no longer the need to flee or to return home either.

Before the world was a foreign country, literature was a journey, an odyssey. There were two odysseys, the classic one, a conservative epic going from Homer to James Joyce, in which the individual returned home with an identity, despite all the difficulties, reaffirmed by the journey across the world and also by the obstacles encountered along the way: Ulysses, in effect, returned to Ithaca, and Leopold Bloom, Joyce's character, also, in his case he did so in a kind of circular voyage of Oedipal repetition. The other odyssey was that of Musil's man without qualities, who, unlike Ulysses, moved in an odyssey without return, in which the individual hurried forwards, never returning home, *continually advancing and getting lost*, changing his identity instead of reaffirming it, dissolving it in what Musil called 'a delirium of many'.

Now you live a double odyssey in a foreign country and

along one of its by-roads you walk in the mist at dusk, seeking Musil. Sometimes you catch sight of Emily Dickinson, who flees from something and whispers the word *fog* as she walks her dog. Sometimes you don't see her, because she is sewing at home, she is the Penelope of the conservative epic.

You continually advance and get lost and change your identity instead of reaffirming it, and you dissolve in a delirium of many along the by-road, in the sitting room at home, amid the fog, under the mist, with the television switched on, but without the sound, so from time to time you lift your eyes and perceive an image, but do not retain it, in a kind of continuous visual track, in the background, as there was background music before.

I am with my favourite homely vases, in front of the abyss, in a directionless present, like the pages of this diary, paradoxically so attentive right now to the calendar. Early morning on 26 September. The world is in flames, up in arms. At the start of the twenty-first century, as if I walked to the rhythm of literature's most recent history, I am alone and without direction on some by-road, at dawn, heading inexorably for melancholy. A slow, enveloping, increasingly deep nostalgia for all that literature once was merges with the thick mist in the early morning.

At the start of the twenty-first century, as if I walked to the rhythm of the Great Wall conspiracy, I notice the cold that is usual at this hour and season in this house and switch on the heater and drape my shoulders in a shawl and wander mentally with my eyes closed and wonder what unknown I carry in me. I'm at home, but also on the by-road. With my homely vases, but in front of the abyss. Call me Walser.

25 OCTOBER

I place my hand on my temple because what I can't believe is that the moles are working away inside my brain as well, injecting me with the sickness of Teste (from the Latin *testa*, skull), an acute and furious, frightful pain caused by the opening of underground galleries in my mind: a wedge of ninety degrees, of burning metal, driven into one side of my head. The wedge is the artwork of the enemies of the literary who dominate my city: haughty illiterates, general managers of publishers that give shape to the black bottom of Nothingness. But the resistance to Teste's disease is under way and gathering strength, it's already here, it's already in this foreign country of the double odyssey where I dig in with my fellow conspirators, it's already here in Action Without Parallel and the wall being built by Chinese conspirators. I'm going to resist, I need literature in order to survive and, if need be, I'll *embody* it myself, if I'm not already doing so. 'To suffer is to give something supreme attention and, to a small extent, I'm a man of attention,' we read in *Monsieur Teste*. The supreme attention I devote to literature and to my Montano's malady has caused me to suffer, has given me a Teste-ache, but it's worth it because Action, the wall and myself have now turned all our attention to the moles and their confident bosses. And both moles and bosses are in a bad way, they have it coming.

25 NOVEMBER

Unable to sleep at four in the morning, I switch on the heater due to the cold in the house and drape my shoulders in a shawl, I remember when I used to like writing at this silent hour of the night and decide to pick up this diary I left off one month ago, to go over the last three days, which have been 'very mountainous', I think it could be said that they have been traversed by the continuous breeze of the most diverse mountains.

The day before yesterday, I had to travel to Granada in the afternoon. I got up as normal at eight in the morning, I got to my feet as soon as the alarm sounded, with its customary stridency, and Rosa turned it off with her no less customary smack.

A wonderful smack.

We had coffee, biscuits and orange juice for breakfast. At nine Rosa went to work. Her first appointment was with a writer of journals who has dared to publish, for example, that the letters always flicker and blur in front of his eyes and he often has the sensation that everything is going to become paralysed inside his body. While this is an idiocy or a poor imitation of some disturbed German writer, the worst part is that he writes such things because he believes they make him look interesting and this may help him to get on in his career and ascend in the social scale, clothed in the purple mantle of a 'tormented writer'.

I felt sorry for Rosa, who was going to meet this sad case, a friend of Pico's moles and of the haughty illiterates. Few writers turn people off literature so much as this one. I felt sorry for Rosa and she did not thank me for it, but became annoyed. 'He's a client,' she said. Some people are very amusing when they get worked up and Rosa is one of them. I live with her due to lack of evidence, and it's not because I haven't searched for it deliriously, but the fact is there is nothing that proves her treachery.

I prepared my suitcase, although it was hours before I had to go to Granada. I started to reread *El quadern gris* by Josep Pla. I was due to talk about private journals at Granada University, most of all about my own, and decided to have another look at Pla's. 'Mountainous' hours and even days were approaching, but I couldn't tell at that moment when I opened Pla's journal and read, 'I don't think it can be denied that the mountains are well made. If somebody disagrees and is of another opinion . . . tough luck! Some people are never happy.'

At midday, I turned on the computer and came across an e-mail in which I was again invited, this time with plenty of warning, to the Literature Festival that takes place every year in June on Matz Peak in Switzerland: open-air readings, all of them after midnight, probable Tyrolese songs and a journey by aeroplane, train, coach and cable-car before reaching Matz Peak and the high climate created every year among writers, all of whom are German speakers. 'You will be the only foreigner, an interesting situation, you might write something about it. Intellectual inspiration and mountain spirit,' it said in the e-mail, this time written in correct English, sent to me by my Swiss-German publisher.

As I went down to the lobby to collect the day's post, I thought about Thomas Mann's *The Magic Mountain* and the kind of young sufferer of literature sickness that appears in it: a young man who, Mann tells us, was sent home from the sanatorium on top of the mountain in an experiment to see if he had been cured. The young man returned to the arms of his wife and mother, to the arms of all his friends and relatives. But he spent the day on his back, with the thermometer in his mouth, and did not worry about anything else. 'You don't understand,' he would say, 'you have to have lived up there to know how things must be done. The essential principles do not exist in this house.' In the end his mother, tired, told him to go back up there, her useless son was now no good for anything. The young man returned to his 'homeland', as all the patients called the bewitching sanatorium.

At about one in the afternoon, I dropped Mann's book on the floor and in a few seconds, without even forcing my imagination, I was on the by-road, walking in the mist over the snowy peaks of Matz. At ten past one, another mountain: I thought about Pico's volcano and its tireless moles. At twenty past one, the telephone rang and I felt at home again. It was Justo Navarro from a chalet in Sierra Nevada. At a quarter to two, I emerged on to the street, went to the bank, where I changed my investment fund and chatted to the branch manager for some minutes. I talked to him about snowy mountains as well, since his two daughters, he told me, went skiing in La Molina every weekend.

On coming out of the bank, I wanted to see myself as a businessman, something I have never been but, like everything I have not been, I like to try to be. Someone passed by and greeted me, 'Hi there, Walser.' I then slowed my businessman's powerful pace and, forgetting about my brand-new investment fund, began to move like a peaceful being, like a walker of Swiss nationality who liked to stop to contemplate all the vistas afforded along the way: a Helvetic walker on a direct path towards the abysses and pagan calm, or perhaps, as Dickens said – not in vain, in the world inhabited by Rosario Girondo, was 25 December approaching – towards 'the Ghost of Christmas Past'.

I bought the papers and, walking along my street's sunny pavement – the other always looks like a by-road in permanent mist – I told myself that my name was Walser, but also Girondo. I was two people, like Kaspar Hauser in the streets of Nuremberg. But in my case, which is not that of Hauser, with all my memory intact.

At the airport I bought *Tales from the Mountain* by Miguel Torga. 'Pursued all day by the mountains,' I wrote on the aeroplane – in the absence of other blank paper, on the bag Iberia provides for passengers who need to be sick.

I had left this diary at home, but carried photocopies of everything I wrote in the last year in my suitcase – I planned to read excerpts in Granada. So Iberia's sick-bag became a scribbling pad of ideas destined for this diary. I jotted down, for example, in microscopic writing and telegraphic style that I elaborate here a little to make it more intelligible, 'The prehistoric wind of the Icy Mountains blows in Walser as in Kafka. In reality both of them were doomed to a journey without a point of arrival. Their prose had something indefinitely extendible and elastic and a desire to comment on life from top to bottom, to comment on it all, to chase after even the most trivial details with a clear tendency towards the infinite, which made it ridiculous to search for conventional endings to their stories. I like novels that have no end. The reader who seeks finished novels – Unamuno said – does not deserve to be my reader, since he himself is already finished before he's read me. In short, I recall that Walter Benjamin maintained that every finished work is the death mask of its intuition.'

In the evening I had dinner in Granada with some friends and we talked at length about Mulhacén Peak, where legend has it they buried the last Nazrid king, who from this magnificent viewpoint could dominate the jagged outcrops of Alcazaba and Veleta, the white villages of the Alpujarras, the meadows next to the Guadix desert and, of course, the Alhambra and gentle slopes of Sierra Nevada rising out of nothingness.

It was a mountaineering evening and, after a few hours' sleep, the following morning . . .

'I have to report that one fine morning, I do not know any more for sure what time it was, as the desire to take a walk came over me, I put my hat on my head, left my writing-room, or room of phantoms, and ran down the stairs to hurry out into the street.'

This is how Walser's *The Walk* begins, and this is how yesterday began for me. My appointment at the university was at noon, but I rose very early and decided to go for a morning walk through the streets of Granada. I symbolically put *il cappello in testa* (as it says in the elegant Italian translation of Walser's book) and went out into the street, *diretto in strada*.

Imaginary blue hat on my head and straight into the

street. As far as I can remember today (as I write this in the cold early morning warmed by the poor heater), my spirits as I went out into the street yesterday were luminous and gay, like the self-same morning. The early world extending abruptly in front of my eyes seemed to me as beautiful as if I were seeing it for the first time. I had not yet taken twenty or thirty steps from a still empty square when it occurred to me to look up, towards the paths of imaginary gravel that led to Sierra Nevada, and suddenly I walked mentally along endless, straight roads, over jagged, red stones seen in childhood, until I reached a solitary, strange and remote valley that, as I scoured it, gave me the sensation that a distant historical age had just returned to the world and I was a medieval pilgrim.

It was hot, and the slightest human trace, the slightest indication of industry, culture or effort, was nowhere to be seen. A marvellous but terrifying sensation. I thought that it was better to be alone than that suddenly, for example, Emily Dickinson should appear in the wake of a strange, thick fog, walking her dog. I was alone and enjoying being so, and from time to time I thought about the art of despising art, which Pavese spoke about in reference to the world of private journals: 'The art of despising art – The art of being alone.'

With this art in mind, I began to traverse rustic, stormy places that alternated with others that were peaceful and, it seems to me, absurd. And so, thinking about this art of being alone, I arrived at Granada University, at exactly midday, dreaming that I was dressed as a mountaineer, with a stick in one hand and a blue hat on my head.

In this way I arrived at Granada University. In one hand,

the imaginary – the stick – and in the other, the real – the photocopies of my diary. Only in my mountain waistcoat did the real and imaginary merge: sewn into this waistcoat, in the form of an impeccable cheque, I carried my savings on the way to the wide, fresh and luminous world of nothingness.

It's not surprising that, arriving in good health, in such an early mountaineering spirit, I should choose first to read the opening pages of my *Diary of a Deceived Man*: 'At the start of the twenty-first century, as if I were walking to the rhythm of literature's most recent history, I was alone and without direction . . .'

I read excerpts from my diary for an hour and, when I finished, a beautiful young student called Renata Cano – I understood she was called Renata Montano – came up to tell me, in a voice as pure as the driven snow, that she had been moved at the end of my *Theory of Budapest* by all those elders who appeared, almost all of them single, almost all of them childless, almost all of them plagiarists and fakes, and all, absolutely all of them, deceived.

I am very old. You see, in Budapest I aged twenty years in one go. In any case, the words of Montano – I have her permission to call her this – comforted me enormously. I can't sleep, possibly because I'm unable to forget Renata's words and yesterday's lunch with her at that inn near Puerto del Suspiro del Moro, where we talked about snowy peaks, in particular those of Kilimanjaro, and also about other peaks, those that are reached only through love, passion.

I'm unable to forget the young Montano as I write now

with the shawl around my shoulders and the heater's silent company and tell myself that the constant presence of mountains in recent hours may be a sign indicating to me that it might be very good for me to accept the invitation to climb Matz Peak and read there excerpts from my diary, read them in the open air at midnight, in the Alps' great silence, as a tribute to Renata.

In short, at eight, when the alarm sounds and Rosa turns it off with her customary smack, I shall answer the e-mail and at the same time – now that I remember – I shall send the critic Stanislaw Wicinsky a letter, the last I send him, I've decided to stop sending letters to this character I invented one day, perhaps to compensate for the fact that I've not been the great literary critic I wanted to be, I'm not going to send him any more letters to which I then have to reply, the game of writing to myself is over, but above all – I hope I don't forget – I shall answer the e-mail, I shall agree to travel to the Swiss mountains and once there to listen to the wind that they say, as it stirs the leaves of the great trees, mimics human voices, the voices of unknown people that up on Matz Peak, in a great high climate, tell the world's secrets.

The alarm rings, it's eight o'clock, end of snores, the day awakes and with it its poetry, I hear the almighty smack.

25 DECEMBER OR LE RICORDANZE

The memories of various lay anniversaries dance today.

On such a day, forty-five years ago, in 1956, Robert Walser died. After lunch at the sanatorium, he decided to go for a hike in the snow, to climb to Rosenberg, where there are some ruins. From the top there was a wonderful view over the mountains of Alpstein. The hour was soothing, it was midday, and outside there was snow, pure snow, as far as the eye could see. The solitary hiker set out and began to fill his lungs with the clear winter air. He left Herisau Sanatorium behind. He climbed through beeches and firs up the side of Schochenberg. Two children found him where he dropped down dead in the snow, in perpetual ecstasy over the Swiss winter.

Walser or the art of disappearing.

In one of his novels, *The Tanner Siblings*, there are some lines that presage his own death in the snow, in the mouth of one character he places an elegy to Sebastian, the poet found dead in the snow. 'With what nobility he has chosen his tomb! He lies among splendid green firs covered in snow. I don't want to inform anyone. Nature bends down to contemplate her deceased, the stars sing softly around his head and the night birds caw: it is the best music for someone who cannot hear or feel.'

Walser or the art of disappearing at Christmas, of knowing how on such a sentimental date to leave the writing-room, the room of phantoms.

On such a day, thirty-nine years ago, on 25 December 1962, the Great Snowfall took place over Barcelona. It is one of the most important memories of my early years. That morning the patio of my parents' home appeared covered in snow and I couldn't believe it. To start with, I thought it was part of my mother's Christmas decorations. I remember that 25 December very well. Me with a scarf inside the house listening to my mother say that for a city like Barcelona, so abandoned by the hand of God, it was a blessing that, even if it was only the once, He should have remembered us and brought us snow on the most appropriate day, Christmas Day, with divine punctuality.

For me, Christmas Day will always be the Day of the Great Snowfall. Wrapped in two jerseys and a scarf inside the house, I switched on the radio and suddenly we heard a message of peace and Christmas goodwill from Salvador Dalí, a few emotional words from the Ampurdán painter telling us that, from that day on, he planned to orient all his life towards Franco's Spain and the Family: 'Isabella the Catholic, consecrated hosts, melons, rosaries, truculent indigestion, bullfights, Calanda drums and Ampurdán sardines. To sum up: my life must be oriented towards Spain and the Family.'

We listened to that message in respectful silence mixed with some astonishment. The snow fell stealthily on the patio outside, as at the beginning of a Christmas tale.

'Dalí's turned into one of us,' said my father.

On such a day, forty-five years ago, in 1956, W. G. Sebald's grandfather died, having gone out for a walk in the snow and collapsed on top of it at almost exactly the same time as another walker, Robert Walser, was also struck down on the snow, in a similar landscape.

Two dead for a single Christmas Day.

Eleven days ago, last Friday 14 December, the writer W. G. Sebald died while out driving. He always seemed to have just emerged from another age: a slightly ancient man who, in sight of solitary landscapes, came across traces of a past in ruins that referred him to the wholeness of the world.

I am seated next to the Christmas tree in my home and I remember the Great Snowfall of my childhood and that speech by Dalí and I begin to listen to Vittorio Gassman reciting Leopardi's *Le ricordanze* and I let the memories, mine and others', invade me and tell myself that without them and without those memories' ruins, without memory, life would be even more distressing, though it may be even more distressing to realise that the more our memory grows, the more our death grows. Because man is just a machine for remembering and forgetting, heading for death. And I don't say this with sadness because it's also true that memory, disguised as life, turns death into something subtle and tenuous.

The memories dance for me and I adhere to the indispensable fabric of my memory and my identity – in this case, that reached with my double odyssey – and I tell myself that I am somebody only because I remember, which is to say that I am because I remember, I am the one memory has always helped, preventing him from falling into absolute distress, has helped during years with flashes and luminous sparks in which every day, like a ray of sun, charming and tragic, the tragic dust of time has danced for me.

There are two of me. I have a double odyssey's identity. One is lurking in the Chinese wall and the other, more Christmassy and sedentary, listens to Gassman at home: '*Viene il vento recando il suon dell'ora / dalla torre del borgo . . .*'

The detective's patience to trap a memory can verge on

the ridiculous. One is satisfied with a cake dunked in tea; another, with a drop of perfume at the bottom of an empty bottle; another, with *il suon dell'ora*, a peal of bells swept by the wind from the village tower. Tastes, minimal smells, sounds of the past. I'm ashamed to say so, because it's not very poetic, shall we say, but this is how it is and I can't change it: my dunked cake, my drop of perfume, my music of the wind is a prosaic and vulgar mouthful – as brief as childhood – of a Catalan beverage called Cacaolat, a mixture of milk and cocoa that I used to drink daily during morning break at school.

I only have to taste that beverage for the memories of the past to return. But this word, Cacaolat, could not be more ridiculous and less poetic, which may explain why I have spent half my life hating writers who work with their memories and instead defending those who without the dead weight of memories are in a position to reach the writer's adulthood more quickly. I have spent half my life defending those writers who do not live off the rents of the past and can demonstrate an up-to-date imagination, an imagination capable of inventing out of the present, out of nothingness itself.

Half a life boasting of finding hardly anything in my tedious childhood, just a scarf, a patio covered in snow and not much else. Half a life congratulating myself on never having had to resort to childhood to be able to write, congratulating myself on not becoming emotional when I examined a situation from my early years. And yet all this suddenly collapsed a few months ago in Barcelona's Rovira Square, the approximate geographical centre of my childhood; it collapsed when I visited this square recently to witness the filming of a sequence from *Shanghai Nights*, Juan Marsé's novel that Fernando Trueba was making into a film. The set-designers had turned Rovira Square into what it was fifty years before. It was as if I had pressed the time machine's exact switch. Suddenly everything was the same as fifty years ago; even the posters for the double bill showing at the long-since-disappeared Rovira Cinema were the same; even the atmosphere of the air in the square struck me as identical to that of fifty years ago. I immediately understood – as when I took LSD in my formative years – that Time does not exist, everything is present.

I cried, I could not hold back the tears. I cried before the unexpected return of the past. Something very similar occurs in a passage from Sebald's *Vertigo*. The narrator of 'All'estero', a story in that book, travels with a friend, Clara, who succumbs to the temptation to enter the school she had been to as a child: 'In one of the classrooms, the very one where she had been taught in the early 1950s, the self-same schoolmistress was still teaching, almost thirty years later, her voice quite unchanged – still warning the children to keep at their work, as she had done then [. . .] Alone in the entrance hall, surrounded by closed doors that had seemed at one time like mighty portals, Clara was overcome by tears, as she later told me [. . .] We returned to her grandmother's flat in Ottakring, and neither on the way there nor that entire evening did she regain her composure following this unexpected encounter with her past.'

Here Sebald seems to be telling us that the past, *all* past, is still happening, surfacing, *is there*, doing its own thing. Without handing out a visiting card or needing us to invoke it, the past, our past, *is happening in the present.* It's thrilling, it's terrifying. It reminds me of Emily Dickinson begging the Lord not to leave her alone down here. I believe that she sensed that we are completely alone, without anybody, in a world that is only a dark basement, where we may have been put for good.

23 JANUARY OR MONTAIGNE'S MALADY

You aged twenty years in one go, one evening in Budapest, and now you're lying on the bed and a voice talks to you in the dark. I am not, it tells you, exactly a human voice, I am the one who has always been with you, I am the voice that causes you to be alone, that tells you now there's still something to say, I am Tongoy, I know very well who I am, the afternoon is flat, I am Tongoy, seated beside you, head on hands, seeing myself right now rise and go, go out in search of the by-road, I am Tongoy, I see myself first rise and stand holding on to the chair and then sit down again and then rise again and stand again holding on to the chair, here I am, I know who I am, I am with you, I am alone, I am Tongoy, I have Montaigne's malady, I like to assay, I assay, today I just assay.

24 JANUARY

I am the one who has always been with you, the voice that causes you to be alone, that tells you it may still be possible to name something, there may still be words to say,

I am Tongoy, I know who I am, the afternoon is sad, the afternoon is flat, I am Tongoy, seated beside you, I am the one who has always been with you, look at me, my head is sunk on crippled hands and I see myself right now rise and come closer to you, I am Tongoy, a leaden light illuminates me, I am enormously tired, possibly because I have been conceived by a man I guess is vulnerable in everything except his writing: I'm sure that, if the world collapsed, he would keep up the work he has to do, without changing the subject, he would carry on talking about all that he will identify with until he finishes the book he is writing, he will identify fully with it only until then, so that, if the world collapsed now, he would carry on talking about the threat to the literary and how he conspires against the enemies and survives in the pages of books. He would carry on talking about all this, waiting to come across unexpected frontiers and find in them the prized formula to disappear completely one day. Said formula – the vulnerable man has an idea – may consist in saying disappear, naming the word, disappear, it may consist only in this, in saying disappear, never despair. Or it may consist only in saying that I am Tongoy and I know very well who I am. In saying, for example, leaden light. Or saying leaden light on my body. Or saying head sunk on crippled hands. And then saying that it isn't possible to name or say anything. And then what. I don't know, I am Tongoy, the afternoon is flat, I know, there may not be anything to name, nothing, I don't know, I shouldn't have started. Once something begins, that something can no longer vanish. God, what will we do to disappear? We are immeasurable distances away from achieving it. But I plan to try, I shall go to the limits of the limitless void. With my head sunk on crippled hands.

25 JANUARY

A few minutes ago I was lying on my back, with my legs in the air, as if they wanted to hit the ceiling, my eyes closed, my face full of tears. It was surprising, but even crying and in this pathetic or ridiculous posture I confirmed once again what the great secret of everything is: to feel oneself the centre of the world. This is exactly what every individual does.

23 FEBRUARY

Switzerland: admirable source of energy. If the mountain makes a fir of the tree, it's possible to guess what it can make of man. Aesthetics and morality of conifers.
ANDRÉ GIDE, *Journal*

Aesthetics of cypress, pine and savin.

All morning on the by-road, under the constant weight of what I was reading by Kafka. The vaguely disturbing sensation of being at home and feeling that I wasn't, although I was reading at home.

'So he carried on; but the way was long. The road, that main street of the town, did not lead to the castle mound; it only approached, but then, almost deliberately, it took another direction, it didn't move away from the castle, but it didn't go any closer to it either.'

This is what I read this morning. And all the time I was lost on the by-road, where I got even more lost in the afternoon, when I travelled across a high ridge, where bluish-black boulders advanced in sharp wedges towards the train, and looked out of the window, searching in vain for the peak. At dusk I suddenly saw snow-covered valleys, narrow and uneven, and with my finger I traced the direction in which they disappeared.

To avoid growing more anxious, I thought about the snows of yesteryear, about Christmas past, Christmas in Barcelona in 1962, the year of the Great Snowfall. And I picked up Josep Pla, hoping to find myself back at home, I started reading the Catalan writer, I searched for a passage from his diary in which he spoke of his strange feelings towards Christmas. I tried to put Kafka out of my mind.

On such a date, the 23rd, but in the month of December, in a year long ago, 1918, Josep Pla noted down in his diary his concern for the dryness of his heart and his sentimental sterility at Christmas-tide.

If Pla was worried by this dryness, I have once again been concerned all day with the difficulty of disappearing from the world, of disappearing even from this passage that I sense will always be unfinished, since it has neither a middle nor an end nor any chance of dissolving, disappearing fully from the moment it began.

This, however, did not worry Pla, writer of passages. It was a relief to read him for a while, to cross a street and escape from Kafka. Pla was worried by other affairs. His cold attitude towards sentimental Christmas, for example. Had Kafka heard about Pla's concern, he would have said of him that 'the breath of his coldness towards

Christmas made the faces of the others shudder'.

Although nobody's forcing us to, the diarist Pla and this inhabitant of the Chinese wall coincide in one thing, and that is in our irrevocable – no longer for me worrying – permanent state of literary sickness.

On 23 December 1918, Pla noted down his concern for his sentimental sterility at Christmas-tide and ended by saying that he felt not the slightest impulse to adore anything and it seemed to him objectively disagreeable not to feel any excitement, either about women or about money or about becoming somebody in life, 'just this secret, devilish obsession with writing (with poor results) to which I sacrifice everything, to which I shall probably sacrifice everything in life'.

It was a great relief momentarily to take refuge in a great writer from my native land, but at around midnight I got lost again in my own home and thought I was in Switzerland when I saw wide mountain torrents gushing down, in huge waves, towards some dark, disturbing, almost invisible, foreign hills.

I realised that all this was of deep concern to me, but the fact is I suddenly felt an enormous aversion for everything that concerned me.

6 MARCH

It snowed, no one was expecting it, but snow always arrives like this, everybody knows. After the initial moments of amazement, I began to feel an urge to go out into the street and step on the snow. What did Robert

Walser do when it didn't snow? Where did that question come from? It seems strange to ask myself such things. I sat down in my favourite armchair and repressed the desire to step on the street and snow. For a long time I read Álvaro Pombo, a writer I admire. One of the concerns of his moral life is *salvation*, I would say the spirit's salvation, which is not strictly a literary theme – this comes as a relief – but a universal one, human, which concerns us all. To create a reality distinct from the impoverished, meaningless reality of today's world. To explore the countless, infinite meanings of the uncreated reality we shall only be able to invent *from inside* that reality. To be intelligent and kind. And in others to seek, as Mario Cesariny says, 'a land of kindness and fog'. To see others. And not to carry out market research. To fight against the destructive mechanism of social Montano's malady, to fight against the draining of the human figure brought about by the perversion of the self-same humanist undertaking.

Outside the snow fell as in a song by Adamo.

I read Pombo and then I switched armchair and moved to one with wings, where I used to read novels in the past, I spent hours reading stupid love stories. I put down Pombo to read a book about the *universe of consciousness*, I've been wondering where certain strange questions I sometimes ask myself come from. I read that nobody currently doubts that mental activity requires cerebral activity, but there is disagreement when it comes to defining the type of relationship that is established between the mind and the brain. And who hasn't asked himself this before, without reaching a decisive conclusion? It's a question of knowing whether it's simply cerebral activity that gives rise to the mind or whether, on the contrary, there is a distinct, immaterial entity that uses the brain as an instrument to manifest itself, causing mental activity. Does spirit exist? Is mental activity the manifestation of spirit or only of matter?

Outside it continued to snow. What did Robert Walser do when it snowed? I felt an irrepressible desire to go out into the street and step on the snow. I thought about the passage of time. I confirmed that man does not have the length of his body, but of his years. He must drag them with him when he moves, an increasingly onerous task that ends up defeating him. I went out into the street and stepped on the snow. 'I step on time / railway line / under the snow,' says a poem by Carlos Pardo. I wondered if I wasn't dead in my home. The home, the hearth, is a heavy chain that ties us and wishes to bind our feet until death. I walked a long way. Suddenly I was Walser and was on a by-road. And the snow carried on falling, as in a song by Adamo that reminded me of my tormented youth. I wanted to disappear back then as well.

7 MARCH
ON DISAPPEARING

Till when will we have to listen to commentaries by great writers saying that they write in order not to die completely? We already know what they're pretentiously talking to us about, what sort of immortality they're dealing with. Let us hear an example of such aspirations, let us listen to André Gide: 'The reasons that drive me to write are many and the most important are the most secret, I think. Perhaps most of all this: to put something out of death's reach' (*Journal*, 27 July 1922). It's a question, therefore, of writing in order not to die, of entrusting oneself to the survival of one's works, this may be what links the artist with his creation most strongly. The genius faces death, his work is death made vain or transfigured or, according to Proust's evasive words, made 'less bitter', 'worthier' and 'maybe less probable'.

But is it possible to keep trusting or believing in an immortality of one's own? I am more interested in the world of the writer Kafka, who did not wish to keep anything from death. What's more, he addressed the ability to die through the work he wrote, which in fact means that Kafka's work was already in itself an experience of death – Kafka was always a dead man in life – an experience that seemingly, if we hold to what Kafka suggests, we would have to know beforehand in order to reach the work, to reach death. It couldn't be more Kafkaesque – or more lucid.

I prefer Kafka's vision to that of Gide, our energies should be focused on the need to disappear in the work. If we look carefully at today's world, which is undergoing such transformation, we'll see that what's needed is not to remain in 'the lazy eternity of idols' (as Blanchot wrote), but to change, to disappear in order to cooperate in the transformation of the world: to act namelessly and not to be just an idle name. You're Girondo today, Walser tomorrow, and your real name is lost in the universe, you want to put paid to writers' mean dreams of survival, you want to join your readers on a single anonymous horizon where you could finally establish a relationship of liberty with death.

22 MARCH

Light and shade, pleasant and discordant noises at home, the cheerful song of the woman Rosa's hired to clean the house on Tuesdays and Fridays, the dull drone of the washing machine. I can hardly think and I end up taking refuge in the diary. I decide to relate Tuesday's trip to Cuenca, where I gave a lecture, I read *Theory of Budapest* and asked those present to take my dramatic words seriously, corresponding as they did to a real drama experienced lately. I then stayed to listen to Ramón Costa Baena's lecture. 'We novelists are an unscrupulous bunch,' he started by saying. And I jotted down these words of his: 'The novel is a hybrid genre and a large part of its charm arises from the alluvial nature of its materials. There is nothing that doesn't suit a novelist in action, when he's in the course of writing his novel.'

It's only three days since I returned from Cuenca, but I can hardly remember anything about the trip. I still have a scrap of paper with Costa Baena's description, which I jotted down I think because of the adjective 'alluvial' used alongside the noun 'nature'. I spent the whole of the return journey from Cuenca turning the adjective 'alluvial' over in my mind. I don't remember much else. An agreeable conversation in depth with the writer Guelbenzu, the hanging houses, a young girl – who reminded me of the young Montano – on a bridge over a stream holding a sparkler, the supposedly poetic but in fact horrific dusk. I remember little else.

What I do remember is that I spent the whole of the outward journey to Cuenca wondering whether or not I should go to Matz Peak at the beginning of June to read excerpts from this diary in the open air at midnight – the 'mountain spirit'. It is, no doubt, an extravagant invitation, which has obsessed me for some time now. I can't help it. I see myself there alone, in shorts, the only foreigner surrounded by German-language writers, not understanding a word anybody says, after a journey by aeroplane, train, coach and cable-car. I'm sure that, if I end up going to Matz Peak, everything will be so odd and novelesque that, on my return, I shall be able to write a fair few things about what happened to me up there. But I have one doubt. Is it worth undertaking such a long journey just to come back and relate the interminable series of strange experiences I'll have had? What if I stay at home and simply imagine them? Do I not trust in my own imagination? Must I travel so far in pursuit of real events when those I imagine on Matz Peak are bound to be superior? Or do I think that what I'll find on that peak is beyond my powers of imagination? I would love to be surprised by events, but what if I climb the peak and everything there is bland, outrageously normal, a handful of nutters in Tyrolese costume, reading their rubbish at midnight in front of a few tents and seeking the *mountain spirit* inside a circle of torches? What if it turns out that the dull drone of the washing machine I am carefully listening to now is actually much more odd, normal or stupid?

21 APRIL

I'm absolutely convinced that publishing in the hands of businessmen is just a passing episode.
CARLOS BARRAL

Every year the same at around this time. The number of illiterates in this country is on the increase, but this seems to be unimportant, there are more and more Book Days and it's up to me to explain why we have to read. Yesterday, on a radio station, I was invited to explain to listeners in two seconds why they should be encouraged to read. For them literally to be encouraged, I replied. I was going to add: and at the same time to achieve the spirit's salvation, Musil's ideal. I didn't say this, it struck me as excessive and also I'd have overstepped the two-second limit.

I am no longer so rigidly literature-sick. Or rather I begin not to understand why I must advocate reading. Let every illiterate in this country do what he wants, of course. Besides, I hate virtually the whole of humanity and I spend the day planting mental bombs against all those businessmen who publish books, those departmental managers, market leaders, marketing funambulists and economics graduates. I plant mental bombs against them and against their disciplined followers and the rest of the world in general. So I wonder why I should lend them a hand and recommend that they read books if I only wish them ill, if I only want their stupidity to grow and for them to crash once and for all as they travel on the train of ignorance that we all pay for, but that one day they will pay a high price for, falling into the bottomless pit of failure, taking themselves elsewhere, into a different industry. What's more, I loathe them so much that I'd be delighted if they were obliged to read, if a perfidious decree appeared from somewhere, a drastic order to become acquainted with books, and suddenly this country's cities turned into libraries of forced, chaotic, daft intellectual activity.

In this way the failure of these haughty illiterates' lives would be twofold. On the one hand there would be the already in itself resounding failure of all life, to which would be added that brought about by contact with literates – nobody doubts by now that to be a writer is to fail – not to mention with books, those astonishing 'extensions of memory and imagination' that we take to beaches and cause to fail not by reading them but by burying them in an unconscious great *book of sand*, very different from Borges'.

This would be my revenge for the calls to advocacy that always arrive at around this time and for the constant doubts that plague me and drive me wretchedly to say that no one can be advised to read, but also drive me to think that really, however much I don't like it, I should advocate reading, albeit only in a stylised way by saying, for example, that there's nothing to say, except that, without literature, life has no meaning. But, of course, I can only convince those who read of this. And the fact is many of those who read believe it's an obligation, and they are almost more dangerous than Pico's moles because they convey an obvious sensation of boredom, they seem not to have read a memorable statement by Montaigne: 'I do nothing without joy.'

With this statement, Montaigne wished to indicate that the concept of obligatory reading is a false one. If he came across a difficult passage in a book, Montaigne left it. The point is he saw in reading a form of happiness. Like Borges, who said that a book must not require effort. Borges agreed with Montaigne, though he loved to quote Emerson, who contradicted Montaigne and, in a great essay about books, asserted that a library is a kind of magic box. The best spirits of humanity are imprisoned in this box by an enchanter, and they're waiting for our word to come out of their silence. We have to open the book, then they awake.

That said – I wish to distance myself from any new temptation to advocacy – the company of literature is dangerous, so much so that I'm really not sure I should applaud people I value for reading a lot and getting so involved in books; you see, I wish them well, and anyone who has read Kafka, for example, is perfectly aware 'how much excessive anxiety for nothing' (to quote Pessoa) there is in literature.

As Magris says: 'Kafka was perfectly aware that literature distanced him from the territory of death and enabled him to understand life, but leaving him outside. Just as it enabled him to understand the greatness of his Jewish father, a model man, but did not exactly enable him to be like him.'

Precisely because literature enables us to understand life, it leaves us outside it. It's hard, but sometimes it's the best thing that can happen to us. Reading and writing search for life, but they can lose it precisely because they're entirely focused on life and on the search for it.

It may be the melancholy of the evening in which I am writing, but the truth is I'm talking about an inextricable knot of good and evil, of light and shade inherent in reading and literature. All this is hard, why fool ourselves? It's a hardness that, according to Gombrowicz, good literature has as the product of an instinct to sharpen spiritual life. There are times when I would recommend reading to my worst enemies.

Precisely because literature enables us to understand life, it tells us what can be, but also what could have been. There is nothing sometimes further away from reality than literature, which is constantly reminding us that life is like this and the world has been organised like that, but it could be otherwise. There is nothing more subversive than literature, which is concerned to return us to true life by exposing what real life and History smother. Magris knows this very well, he is deeply interested in what could have been, had History or human life taken another course. Anyone who's interested in this is interested in reading. This is not advocacy. After all, there are times – like now – when I wouldn't recommend reading even to Pico's moles, even to my worst enemies.

V
The Spirit's Salvation

'Sharp receptivity and spontaneity of thought,' said the mathematics teacher. 'It seems that, through attaching excessive importance to the subjective factor in all our experiences, his understanding has become confused and he is driven to use these obscure metaphors.'

Only the teacher of religion remained silent. From Törless' speech he had retained the word 'soul', mentioned so often, and he felt sympathy for the young man.

But all the same he had not managed to form a clear opinion of the sense in which Törless had used it.

ROBERT MUSIL, *The Confusions of Young Törless*

I reached the mountain refuge at the foot of Matz Peak on the afternoon of 7 June, after a lengthy journey that, following Miss Schneider's detailed instructions, I began by plane from Barcelona to Geneva and continued by train from Geneva to Basle, where I spent the first night of my trip in the Thann Hostel, reading the pages that Montaigne devotes to his passage – exactly that, for him *passing* was the chief characteristic of the human condition – through the city of Basle, where in his *Journal of Travels* he noted down that the clock in this city, not in the suburbs, however, was an hour fast: 'If it strikes ten, it's only nine o'clock; because, they say, this defect of the clock once saved the town from a threat that had arisen.'

I read Montaigne's Swiss pages and ended up wondering at what point in the history of this city the Basle clock started telling the right time again and I told myself that it must have been a fascinating moment for all the citizens, something like the adventure of going in search of the authentic life and finding it exactly, at a time that is right, in a high climate, which showed the location, beyond the infinite, not of this world's false void, but of the true void and nothingness or, who knows, which may show the salvation of the modern void, the salvation of the spirit in an age when reality has lost its meaning and literature is an ideal instrument for utopia, for building a spiritual life that finally tells the right time.

A salvation of the spirit – to be precise – linked to the salvation of the literary, a kind of salvation that I consider essential for me when it comes to being able to endure the wait – possibly in vain – for the day to come when one discovers beyond doubt the way to disappear from this world and really to do so for good.

The Journal of Montaigne's Travels to Italy, through Switzerland and Germany was the perfect companion from the very start for my long journey to the Alps. Montaigne's journal bears witness to the experiments or daring essays on subjectivity in the text their author worked on in such an innovative way, a traveller on horseback through sixteenth-century Europe, a traveller who, when asked about his motives for leaving Bordeaux, his native land, answered like this: 'To those who ask me the reason for my travels, I tend to respond: I am well aware what I am fleeing from, but not what I am searching for. In any case it is better to exchange a bad state for an uncertain one.'

Soul and travel are the concepts most obstinately and frequently investigated by the traveller Montaigne, who seems to be fleeing from the dark grave where the spirit of his time lies: 'The soul while travelling is constantly being exercised as it observes unknown and new things; and I know of no better school for the formation of life than consistently bringing before it the diversity of so many other lives.'

This sentence accompanied me as soon as I departed

from Barcelona. On the first night of my journey it can be said that I fell asleep thinking about it and about the Basle clock. The following day, I abandoned the Swiss city and began the second stage of my journey by coach, which would leave me at a cable-car, which in turn would leave me at the refuge at the foot of Matz. The meeting of writers was not on the peak of this mountain as I had absurdly supposed – there are not so many mountaineering writers – but in this mountain refuge, where those taking part gradually gathered during the day.

As I had already suspected in Barcelona, this meeting struck me as odd from the start, not because it was, but because the 'mountain spirit' and the literary geography it belonged to made me feel like an intruder or stranger in the midst of this atmosphere so far removed from my world. But I could find novelesque material here, especially if somebody helped me and I ceased to be incommunicado because of language. I only wished Miss Schneider would arrive – why was she taking so long? She had arranged the complicated itinerary for my trip to perfection and spoke Spanish moderately well, which gave me some hope that she could be of valuable assistance for me to find my bearings here at the foot of Matz Peak.

I am shy, I can't help it. To the person who welcomed me on behalf of the organisation, I must have seemed like a sad, inarticulate wretch. The fact is he sent me straight to reception, and in reception they sent me straight to an inhospitable room with a bed like in a monk's cell and a horrible Alpine painting. My shyness still had time to grow when I settled down in the bar of the refuge to read Montaigne's journal, or rather to pretend that I was reading it – protected behind the book, I actually proceeded to observe everything I saw there that was strange, unknown and new – and some of the writers began to ask me if I was French and to view me with insulting pity when, hiding my double odyssey's identity from them, I replied politely in Spanish.

I thought I noticed that, apart from my logical unease in this world that I did not know, this gathering nevertheless had certain peculiar nuances. I thought I noticed this when, on leaving the bar of the refuge and going out to see what kind of preparations were under way for the session of open-air readings at midnight, I bumped into various ruddy-cheeked writers devoted in body and soul to the consolidation of their national awareness, singing at the top of their voices part of an opera by Wagner, the *racconto* from *Lohengrin*.

The evening was in full decline and the Wagnerian scene, with a backdrop of red clouds fading on top of the neighbouring rocky peaks, struck me as both strange and of an indisputable aesthetic beauty. Taken aback by this unexpected combination of fatherland and dusk, I continued wandering, helped an electrician who was wearing a black headscarf – a broad and vociferous man, I helped him to install the microphones for tonight's open-air reading – and ended up returning to the bar of the refuge, with my French book under my arm.

'Montaigne and horse,' a German writer called Franz suddenly said to me in Spanish, no sooner had I entered the bar. He seemed very ingenuous, as if, unlike the others, he loved to presume to speak my language. I was restless and still stunned by the Wagnerian dusk and didn't know what to say to him, though there wasn't much I could say. Franz proceeded to tell me, in an impossible Spanish – which makes me think I may have misunderstood him – how the previous evening, on the way to the refuge, he had eaten with the colleagues travelling with him at a roadside restaurant, where they had been given some little Spanish birds called *writers*, served wrapped in vine leaves and roasted, but even so they bled when you cut them. For a moment I became very paranoid and wondered whether it wasn't all a trap, a joke in very bad taste, set from some part of the globe at my expense.

'Little Spanish birds, writers,' my colleague Franz kept saying, as if he wanted to frighten me. And he laughed. All I did was plead with the gods for Miss Schneider to come soon, for midnight to come, when the session of readings in the moonlight would allow me to retreat into a corner and listen to German words without feeling I was being watched all the time. But it seemed that neither Miss Schneider nor midnight would ever come.

Midnight came, it always does. Miss Schneider must also have arrived. If she did, it was after midnight; but I shall never know.

I dined with the dead. The good part about not understanding a thing is that one can understand that thing however one chooses. Also, being radically alone and incommunicado, one has plenty of time to watch, analyse, delve into the surroundings. I dined with an illustrious group of the dead. There must have been about thirty writers with their eyes sunk into a monumental potato salad, talking melancholically about the peaceful setting and the eternal harmony of the Alpine universe. I remembered a poem in which the men and women of a town called Spoon River, in short epitaphs that are autobiographies, that are poems, tell the story of their sorrowful lives from the graveyard where they lie buried. And I remembered the island of Pico, where there was not a soul in sight, but everything seemed ready for the wind at any time to bring voices speaking from sadness, grief and death.

I dined with writers who, had they not been dead, I would have thought were civil servants. I dined with the constant impression that I was really in Haut-les-Aigues, a corner of the Jura near the Swiss border, where Dr Alfred Attendu, in a story by Wilcock, directed his panoramic Re-education Sanatorium, meaning hospice for cretins or refuge for the mentally retarded. I looked at the writers, I listened to their voices, and all the time I thought about Dr Attendu, who overturned an age-old prejudice and affirmed that the idiot is simply the primitive human prototype, of which we are just the corrupt version, subject, therefore, to disorders, to passions and to unnatural vices that do not, however, affect the authentic, pure cretin.

I dined with cretins, lousy, dead writers cum civil servants. This race of writers, people who copy what has been done before and lack any literary (but not financial) ambition, is a plague even more pernicious than the plague of publishing managers working away enthusiastically against the literary. I spent the whole dinner in silence watching these writers, trying with my severe gaze to reproach them for their worthless literature. At various points I remembered that I was a heartless man with only literary emotions. And at various points I also struck quixotic poses. In an attempt to amuse myself and also to lash these morons who, at the start of the twenty-first century, were trying to finish literature off, from time to time I imagined that the whole of my body, because of the gigantic potato salad's peculiar side-effects, was changing inside and I was turning into, I was *embodying* the history of literature's complete memory. And they were so stupid that they didn't even realise.

There was nothing nice or exotic or original about this meeting. It was really just another literary conference of the many scattered throughout this world of corruption. It was a conference of twits, sectioned idiots, poets with swollen lips and piggy eyes who seemed to be digging holes to sit in. This dinner with dead writers was endless and extremely irritating. After dinner, all of them appeared to be supplied with sticks. It wasn't necessary to understand German to see that they were beating one another, as if it were a therapy imposed by the conference organiser, who, seeking to eliminate any trace of social aggressiveness from their mental void, seemed to have thought it best for them to whack each other with a stick. I realised that, since I had reached that refuge at the foot of Matz, only the vociferous electrician with the black headscarf had given reliable proof of being alive. The others were dead people who, among other things, were nothing out of this world, but at the same time they were *out of this world*, bitter enemies of the literary and direct allies of Pico's filth.

The electrician was friends with a mountain guide, who lived nearby and spoke Spanish because his wife was Cuban. This guide, who was from Basle and was called

Thomas, dropped by the refuge shortly after the dinner ended and, although he was a little difficult to follow, I was finally able to talk to somebody, while waiting for Miss Schneider to arrive. From the whole of our conversation, I could only make sense of the following: he liked Cuba more than the Swiss mountains, he sometimes turned into a 'very black Negro Cuban' and danced until dawn. Both the electrician and Thomas claimed – I later saw that they were lying – to have a passion for free events. Hence they planned to stay for the reading session. In July they were going to attend another literary gathering, which was also free, a festival taking place in Leukerbad; they went to everything in the Alps that was free.

The first session of open-air readings commenced at midnight. I was relieved that, as Thomas translated for me providentially in time, they didn't need me for the opening night session, nor was it entirely clear whether they would need me at any other time during the conference. I sat down with my book by Montaigne at one side of the stage, almost on the stage, at a distance from Thomas and the electrician, who were seated in an area of the stage that was more discreet and, above all, darker. I prepared to listen in German to all that fate had in store for me.

'*Boshaft wie goldene Rede beginnt diese Nacht*,' I heard the first dead writer recite. The sentence was in the programme I kept inside Montaigne's book, Thomas translated it for me during the interval: 'Malicious as golden speech this night begins.'

At the end of the long and quite monotonous reading session, divided into two soporific acts, I was just nodding off when suddenly someone whispered in my ear, 'Come what has not yet been'. It was Thomas, abruptly transformed into my alarm clock and impromptu translator of German prose in the open air. The sentence – 'Come what has not yet been' – pierced and roused my brain from sleep. I looked at Thomas, who smiled at me: an open smile, a solid set of white teeth, it was easy to imagine him with a dark face dancing until dawn. Then, as if he were telling me something personal, he added, no doubt by way of surprise password, 'You mustn't say you understand me.' He said this and left, he went to where the electrician was and there disappeared; I never saw him again, he merged with the area's imposing darkness, he may have vanished while dancing, I don't know what can have happened to him, and now I shall never know.

When, shortly afterwards, I approached this area of darkness to exchange passwords with other possible accomplices, also fighting against the enemies of the literary, a thick mist had settled right in the middle of that area of darkness and, as the footmen of Action Without Parallel were maliciously circulating, you couldn't see a thing. In fact everything now moved (because of the agents of Action Without Parallel, who suddenly revealed themselves as traitors to literature's cause, infiltrators of the walled conspiracy to destroy its work of resistance from the inside) in a radius of action whose centre was the action's own void. That said, not everything was so disappointing, since if, instead of talking to the members of Action, you talked to the walled conspirators, then you saw that the forces were divided: there were those of malicious Action with its void, but also those of the wall on the watch for enemy Action.

I recalled other times and took my leave in silence, there in the mist, of many worlds I hoped not to have to see again. I recalled other days, in which pale dreams in the hanging mist disappeared. I walked along in the darkness and mist; it started to rain. In the wind of the night, the road led nowhere, but it was good to walk in the fine rain that was falling. I recalled errant winds on other roads and other twilight rains on other days. Between false and genuine members of the resistance, as if I were walking to an ancient and literary rhythm, I, Robert Walser, began to stray across that dark area of thick, infinite mist, I began to walk alone and without direction on the by-road.

I remembered the horrible potato salad we had eaten. And by an association of images, perhaps searching in the domestic and ordinary for something to hold on to in the metaphysical fog I was beginning to move in, I recalled Rosa three days before, rubbing her eyes with the back of her hand and then taking a saucepan of boiled potatoes from the fridge and tossing them into the salad bowl. I had stopped on the threshold of the kitchen, watching her and the remains of the red umbrella to which I attribute creative virtues; I had stopped to observe the vibrant operation, watching how Rosa washed a stick of celery under the tap, cut it into little pieces and then threw it on top of the potatoes, while, with her old habit of doing everything quickly, she emptied a whole tin of olives into the salad bowl and some chopped onion and a cloud of cayenne pepper. It was only three days since I had witnessed Rosa prepare that dinner with her customary speed, but it seemed like an eternity. Because in these parts, on the by-road, commonplace tins of olives and ever ordinary chopped onion seemed to represent the soul of the conventional home, miles away by now, finally abandoned for good from the precise moment I had strayed into the thick mist of the area of darkness.

I might bump into Musil, I told myself. Everything was extremely senseless, but to seek Musil was even more so. He was hiding no doubt because he had discovered the real intentions of Action Without Parallel, a false resistance movement that had infiltrated the wall. Action's henchmen, as in a bad adventure story, were after him to eliminate him. That at least is what I thought I understood from the signs sent to me, from cracks in the wall, by the Chinese conspirators, on the alert against Action's movements. At one point I looked for someone to discuss this with, but the by-road was empty. With my book by Montaigne, I kept going, another night fell on the night that had fallen five hours before. Suddenly I saw a shadow move next to an empty house. I thought it might be – my mother had prophesied this in her diary – Hamlet asking after Rosario Girondo. I also told myself that it might be Emily Dickinson, white housecoat and sad dog. But it wasn't Hamlet, it wasn't Dickinson. It was a woman very like the young Montano, who said she was called Mzungu, just as the native Africans called the first white explorers. '"He who walks without direction" is what Mzungu means,' she explained. She was dressed in an old-fashioned way, with a thin lace net covering her dark hair, a gathered collar on a black velvet mantilla, her feet in buckled shoes. She was young, but her face changed at times and seemed to come from time immemorial. I walked with her while the night that had grown inside the first night lasted, I accompanied Mzungu's steps until dawn. At first light, I decided to carry on alone. She was short-sighted, she came up to say goodbye, in fact she came up to see if I had aged at all in the last hours. 'Goodbye,' she said to me, 'die sane and live mad.'

'Goodbye, Montano, goodbye,' I answered. I walked for hours until, turning off the by-road, I entered the silence of a forest without birds. Leaving behind the wood, I walked with Montaigne's book and Mzungu's memory along an infinite road that finally narrowed and turned into something like a winding staircase. And suddenly I saw Musil next to an abyss. White open-necked shirt, very black coat down to the feet and red broad-brimmed hat. He was staring thoughtfully at the ground. He seemed to be measuring the speeds, angles, magnetic forces of the fugitive masses of the abyss that opened before us. He raised his head and looked at me. Before us there was only void, Action Without Parallel and other enemies of the literary had us surrounded. 'It is the air of the time, the spirit is threatened,' I said to him. Musil looked towards the uncertain horizon. In the distance, far away, beyond everything, like a mirage of salvation rising from the void and the abyss, the sea was visible, with its shoals, swarms of white, triangular sails. 'Prague is untouchable,' he said, 'it's a magic circle, Prague has always been too much for them. And it always will be.'

The translator gratefully acknowledges the use of quotations from the following translations into English: Sebald, *The Rings of Saturn* and *Vertigo* by Michael Hulse; Goethe, *The Erlking* by Hyde Flippo; Walser, *Institute Benjamenta* and *The Walk* by Christopher Middleton; Michaux, *Ecuador* by Robin Magowan; Pavese, *This Business of Living* by A. E. Murch; Magris, *Danube* by Patrick Creagh; Kafka, *The Hunter Gracchus* by Ian Johnston; and three anonymous translations (found on the Internet) of Neruda, *Death Alone*, Nietzsche, *Ecce Homo* and Goethe's words to Eckermann.

The translator also wishes to thank the author, Euan Cameron and Miguel Martínez-Lage for their helpful comments.